THREE WEEKS IN SEPTEMBER

TED TAYLER

BOOKS

Vinci Books

vinci-books.com

Published by Vinci Books Ltd in 2026

1

Copyright © Ted Tayler 2018

The author has asserted their moral right to be identified as the author of this work in accordance with the Copyright, Designs and Patents Act 1988. This work is a work of fiction. Names, characters, places and incidents are the product of the author's imagination or are used fictitiously. Any resemblance to actual persons, living or dead, places and incidents is entirely coincidental.

All rights reserved. No part of this publication may be copied, reproduced, distributed, stored in any retrieval system, or transmitted in any form or by any means, including photocopying, recording, or other electronic or mechanical methods, nor used as a source for any form of machine learning including AI datasets, without the prior written permission of the publisher.

The publisher and the author have made every effort to obtain permissions for any third party material used in this book and to comply with copyright law. Any queries in this respect should be brought to the attention of the publisher and any omissions will be corrected in future editions.

A CIP catalogue record for this book is available from the British Library.

Paperback ISBN: 9781036700584

The EU GPSR authorised representative is Logos Europe, 9 rue Nicolas Poussion, 17000 La Rochelle, France
contact@logoseurope.eu

By Ted Tayler

The Phoenix

The Olympus Project
Gold, Silver and Bombs
Nothing Is Ever Forever
In the Lap of the Gods
The Price of Treachery
A New Dawn
Something Wicked Draws Near
Evil Always Finds A Way
Revenge Comes in Many Colours
Three Weeks in September
A Frequent Peal of Bells
Larcombe Manor

The Freeman Files

Fatal Decision
Last Orders
Pressure Point
Deadly Formula
Final Deal
Barking Mad
Creature Discomforts

Silent Terror

Night Train

All Things Bright

Buried Secrets

A Genuine Mistake

Strange Beginnings

Dead Reckoning

A Normal November

Into the Sunlight

Tame the Storm

One True Friend

Whispered Truths

A Morning Murder

Quick to Anger

Red Herring Season

Gathering Clouds

Still Standing

Chapter One

Monday, 1st September 2014

Sandy Moloney stared through the glazed front window of the Docklands Light Railway EMU. The Electrical Multiple Units have become a familiar sight above and below ground over the past two decades.

He glanced at the increasing cloud cover drifting across the sky. It aimed to obscure the sun. Nevertheless, rain showers would not be far away —a great way to celebrate the first day of his final working week.

The annual medical did for him. Retirement was possible between sixty and sixty-five, and several colleagues had already taken advantage of that. They badgered him to quit when he met them between trips abroad or after golfing days near London.

Sandy was sixty-four and divorced. Although he saw his daughter on high days and holidays, they weren't as close as thirty-five years ago when he bounced her on his knee.

Cora, his wife, took a fourteen-year-old Amy with her when she walked out.

Living in London wasn't everything people made it out to be, not if you lived alone. So, thoughts of retirement went on hold. Sandy knew of others in their seventies still putting in a shift on the railways. You could continue to drive a train or fulfil the role of a train attendant on the DLR if you kept passing the medical. With the prospect of four walls to stare at every day, Sandy determined to keep working as long as possible.

Then, he attended that medical. The doctor sighed as he looked at the paperwork before him. Sandy steeled himself for the news.

"How long have I got?" he asked.

"If you reduce the drinking, give up the cigarettes, take regular exercise and switch to a healthy diet, you might have another fifteen to twenty years, Mr Moloney."

"Oh," Sandy said, "I thought I was a goner when you sighed."

"Something showed up on your scans we can control with medication. We can delay the condition from radically influencing your everyday life for a while. Those things I suggested you do will be essential in supporting that treatment. However, I couldn't pass you fit to drive either a car or a train. Nor can I let you be responsible for the lives of hundreds of passengers on those driverless units you run on the DLR."

"It's not cancer then, doctor?"

"Do you remember the initial cognitive and psychomotor skills tests you took before you came for the scans?"

"Oh, those," said Sandy, "I remember. What of them?"

"Your results showed a marked difference from earlier

tests. That's why we carried out the scans; to discover what might have caused it. Deterioration in those skills is a natural result of ageing, but it can be an early indicator of dementia or Alzheimer's. The comments from your line manager suggest you live alone. Do you have family members living close by? Do you have an active social life?"

Sandy Moloney shrugged; he had little to offer in reply. The doctor nodded.

"Another factor affecting performance on these tests is depression. We'll get you on a more even keel, Mr Moloney, and check any changes as we progress. If the more serious conditions I mentioned manifest themselves, we'll manage those issues as and when they happen,"

Sandy had collected his prescription, driven home, and poured himself a large glass of red wine. Of course, he was depressed. Who wouldn't be? The wrong side of sixty, with no wife or partner. A daughter with no kids living out in the suburbs. He had a handful of friends across London in his social circle, with wives, children, and grandkids, but with each year, the company newsletters informed him of another death, and that handful of friends grew less and less.

What of his immediate future? The doctor recommended he give up his car and advised that his only safe choice was to take the retirement package. He could no longer captain passengers on the DLR.

One by one, the things he held precious had been taken from him. He dragged his eyes away from the last few bright moments of sunshine ahead and considered his fellow travellers. They looked a disparate bunch — nothing new there. London was a cosmopolitan city when he moved from Southampton as a young man. The bustling port on the south coast had suited him. There was terrific nightlife for a teenager, plenty of job opportunities, and living at home had never been a problem.

His grandparents arrived in Southampton from the southwest coast of Ireland towards the end of the nineteenth century. Many relatives emigrated to the United States, and when he reached twenty-one, Sandy Moloney considered searching for long-lost cousins in Boston and New York. The bright lights of London in the mid-Seventies won him over. The train that carried him from Southampton to Waterloo pitched him into a colourful, noisy mass of humanity that never hushed or stopped.

Working for London Transport, above and below ground on various jobs, kept Sandy next to the throbbing heart of the metropolis. It had been intoxicating, with everything and everyone always on the move. However, nothing stayed the same for long. The skyline altered with new buildings shooting skywards, jarring with the centuries-old structures the millions of tourists visited.

Sandy watched it as he worked on the overground and underground trains that crisscrossed the capital's network. He met Cora Flynn on a late-night tube as she returned home to Dagenham from a gig. Fashions in clothes and music altered too, and he cringed when he thought of their wedding photographs, now consigned to a suitcase at the bottom of a wardrobe.

The attraction between them had been immediate. Cora always said she knew the second she spotted Sandy walking through the compartment that he was Irish and the one for her. For Sandy, her wild, curly hair and dark brown eyes captivated him. The punk clothes, with slashed jeans, safety pins and chains, didn't deter him.

He grabbed the closest hanging strap and stood, swaying to the train's rhythm next to her. He knew his uniform and her outfit signalled an odd couple to the rest of those late-night travellers. But they melted away, so Cora and Sandy became the only two people in the world.

"Do you want to see my ticket?" she had asked.

"I want your phone number," he replied.

"Is this a new London Transport policy?"

"I prefer to think of it as an initiative. Do you think it will work?"

Their wedding at St Peter's Roman Catholic Church occurred nine months later. Sandy's uniform and Cora's slashed jeans were replaced by a modern suit and wedding dress for the occasion. The 70s fashions dated faster than any decade before or since. The following year, even the photos at the christening of their daughter, Amy, disappeared before the decade ended. Then, by 1990 both the women in his life left him.

The sights and sounds still flashed and crashed around Sandy as he threw himself into work to ease the pain. He nodded his assent whenever a colleague asked him to pick up an overtime shift. The money was little compensation. He had nobody on whom to spend it. Before he knew it, Sandy allowed twenty years to drift by, and when the doctor gave him the ultimatum, it suddenly made him realise that life had all but passed.

He had spent every day since arriving on that train from Southampton serving the public. He doubted any people travelling with him this late morning even cared. During his last week at work, he would move from Bank to Lewisham and back again. Colleagues told him there were regulars if you took the trouble to look at their faces. Sandy had to admit he stopped noticing. The different shapes and sizes, colours and creeds, men, women and children had become wallpaper.

Had he seen that elderly couple before, two rows back? Could he remember where they boarded? What of the students? What did they study? There were surely tourists; you could spot them, even without the cameras. He gazed at another elderly lady for a while. He remembered her getting on at Greenwich. She had been out of breath when she took her seat. The same as Sandy, she carried more weight than good for her.

It was no good; he couldn't recognise anyone. Nobody nodded or uttered a kind word. That was common when he began working in London many years ago. Millions travelled on the Tube, crushed together, hurtling from station to station in artificial light or, occasionally, total darkness. Even in the days before wi-fi, a conversation was out of the question. The deterioration speeded up the day Sony Walkman arrived. It was much easier to stick headphones in their ears and shut out the world.

The EMU slowed. They were pulling into Crossharbour on the Isle of Dogs; Sandy kept an eye on the passengers. People got ready to leave the train. Others shifted in their seats and watched people waiting on the platform. They were interested enough to look but not talk when they found a spare seat next to them. The doors closed. Another stop was successfully negotiated. Nobody tripped when making their way to the door or had to dash back for a forgotten item. More got on than left, so there were more straphangers.

Could he remember having seen any of the new arrivals? He saw nothing extraordinary about any of them, old or young. Several carried umbrellas or wore light rain jackets. Sandy checked the glazed window ahead. The sun had disappeared, and a smattering of showery rain now dappled the glass.

South Quay came next, and then Heron's Quay. Sandy walked towards the front of the cab. He wished he could get back in the driver's cab, but progress had almost eliminated that job. The captain operated the train manually in an emergency, but the occasion never arose since the DLR started.

Sandy and his driver colleagues weren't the only ones to find their posts being eliminated or transformed. The automated light metro system used minimal staffing on both train and major interchange stations. They staffed the underground stations on the DLR to comply with Fire and Safety requirements, but there was little to spare.

Young Moloney had arrived in London when the IRA wreaked havoc. He spent many nights underground wondering whether a bomb sat waiting around the next corner. Different brands of terror drifted in and out of London over the decades. Attacks on London Transport personnel had followed a steady upward trend. Everyone had to be vigilant. Many wanted to harm their fellow man for one cause or another. The Dockland bombings in 1996 had been the final atrocity from the Provisionals. Al Qaeda soon became a significant threat, and the events of July 2005 were shocking and brutal.

Sandy had been working nights that week. When Amy called, he was getting home and climbing into bed after an uneventful shift. She wanted to check he was safe. It took something dramatic to stir her interest in her father. The next call came in late December.

The minimal staffing levels concerned Sandy. How could you stop someone walking onto a station platform carrying a bomb if nobody was watching? A determined soul could wait until the coast was clear and then plant a device on the forum. Who would challenge them? Simple enough to buy a hi-viz jacket these days. What if they wandered up the tracks a hundred yards between trains and buried an IED? Who thought it worth checking they were supposed to be there?

They had arrived at South Quay.

Sandy scanned the platform for bombers or hi-viz jackets but saw none. Only suited and booted office-workers and business types from Canary Wharf. A group of middle-aged women, who Sandy imagined were ladies who lunch, followed the men onto the train. So many things have altered over the years.

The doors closed. The next stop was Heron's Quay.

The medication prescribed for him was working. It soon became routine to take it every day. The doctor said he needed to get more stable. He now suffered fewer bouts of depression. Sandy felt he had mellowed. He stayed alert the entire time the train stopped at the station. Although he hadn't admitted it to the doctor at their meetings, his concentration drifted over the past five years, especially on a warm afternoon.

It was time to move to the rear of the train. There were checks to carry out before they reached Canary Wharf, and finding a new vantage point for a change of scenery eased the boredom.

He took one last look at the front glazed window.

The rain had stopped. Sandy Moloney turned and headed up the aisle.

As he passed the elderly couple, something made sense that barely registered at first. There had been a dark shape across the track two hundred yards ahead. The EMU was travelling at 40mph. Sandy Moloney's ten seconds were up before he could react.

The IED detonated from a remote location in an apartment in Canary Wharf. The glazed front window of the EMU disintegrated. The sudden jolt caught every passenger unawares. Glasses flew off faces, and phones were knocked out of hands. Shouts and screams of alarm followed as the derailment nightmare unfolded. Everything shook as the train rapidly decelerated. People's belongings flew everywhere.

Sandy was hurled back into the standing passengers he passed. Seated passengers were tossed around like rag dolls as the cab twisted and turned. The elderly couple now lay under the seats opposite where they had been sitting. The lady's right leg suffered a break. Her husband had suffered a significant head wound.

The screams Sandy heard as he drifted in and out of consciousness came from the middle-aged ladies who got on at South Quay. The older woman, on her own and who joined at Greenwich, slumped in her seat. Apart from a massive swelling above her right eye, she looked calm. She was the last person Sandy saw.

As it ground to a halt, the stresses and strains on the three-car EMU played out against a cacophony of tortured metal and human suffering.

For a few seconds, there was silence.

The front car was a mangled wreck. The second and third cars had tilted precariously for endless seconds, then toppled onto their side, their bodywork remarkably intact. Those passengers, still mobile, attempted to escape through the rear of the third car. Heads appeared from the windows and doors of the rear cars. Help was arriving from members of the public who had been at the station. They summoned rescue services, but access was restricted. Those inside the EMU requiring urgent medical help lost valuable minutes from their golden hour.

The automated system controls were triggered, and traffic halted on the Lewisham-Bank DLR network. The bomb squad was alerted. The first explosion witnesses reported inside and outside Heron's Quay had to be confirmed. Then the search would begin for additional devices. The DLR would stop for a considerable time.

The terrorists in the apartment surveyed the scene from a safe distance — no words were necessary. The two men turned from the devastation they caused and removed every trace of their presence in the room. Thirty minutes later, they walked to the lift in the corridor, descended the twelve floors to the street, and went their separate ways. Busy pavements swallowed them in seconds.

Conversations they overheard as they passed by concerned their handiwork. The sense of panic they picked up in the voices was music to their ears. They both smiled on the inside; this was only the beginning.

Half a mile away, the streets next to Heron's Quay were filled with ambulances, police vehicles, and fire appliances. Police erected barriers and cleared the immediate area. The capital's media swarmed across every inch of ground, as near the action as possible. Overhead, helicopters circled. The police, security services, and Air Medical Services (HEMS) out of Whitechapel performed an unchoreographed dance routine.

Officers ran into every side street, shouting at every human being they spotted to move as far away from the blast site as possible. General traffic was at a standstill. Every parked car was scrutinised in case it posed a threat.

On the rail track, the bomb squad personnel edged their way forwards, checking for evidence that more explosions were imminent. Colleagues swept the platforms and approach roads, allowing ambulance crews to move forward.

Twenty-seven minutes after the explosion, the first paramedics reached the first car. The scene was one of overwhelming devastation.

Behind them, members of the public who had risked life and limb to scramble along the track helped the walking-wounded thread their way through emergency services personnel. Those fortunate enough to walk unaided were reaching the platform.

There were still passengers trapped inside the rear, two cars crying out for help. Everyone near the stricken EMU knew the poor devils in the first car had suffered the most. Those crying out as the paramedics dashed past were still breathing, their airways clear. They were not their priority, as harsh as that might sound.

The quiet ones demanded their urgent attention.

The paramedics entered the rear of the first car. Ahead of them, a shapeless mound of people. The blast and sudden deceleration of the train threw dozens of passengers helplessly forwards. People lay trapped by bodies and debris. Here and there, voices were shouting to get out. Elsewhere they made only moans and groans. The paramedics made rapid assessments as they drew closer. An older woman they passed was beyond help. A man pinned to his seat by a metal bar was unconscious but breathing. On the floor, trapped under the seats, lay an elderly couple. The woman had a badly broken leg and suffered a collapsed lung. A man, perhaps her husband, lay next to her. He wasn't breathing. It was going to be a long day.

Minute by minute, the situation moved from chaotic to controlled. The critical and seriously injured were extricated with help from the fire services where necessary and transferred to waiting ambulances. Local accident and emergency departments had already received dozens of casualties needing various degrees of treatment. Doctors were primed for worse injuries to arrive later, knowing that life-saving operations would be necessary and scheduled routine operations needed deferring again.

Hours passed. The only passengers who remained on the EMU were beyond help. Paramedics continued to work on their standard procedures after the bombing. The scene should be as undisturbed as possible. They must preserve the casualties' dressings, clothing, and belongings for forensic evidence. They had to keep pieces of shrapnel from the device inside the first car for examination.

The authorities had learned many lessons over the past twenty years. Every scrap they encountered could be the key to determining responsibility. Knowledge added to the vast data security services had amassed increased the odds of preventing the next attack.

They removed the bodies of the eighteen people who perished on the EMU to the nearest morgue. The first bodies arrived a few minutes before four o'clock. A final body arrived at half-past five. Six hours had elapsed since Sandy Moloney started what turned out to be his final journey. There was a certain irony that the EMU's captain was the last to leave.

News bulletins on TV and radio had carried reports of the original incident. As the drama unfolded throughout the afternoon, the scale of the attack became more evident. Derailments are not an uncommon event; often, they don't result in any injuries. It was a while before the explosion witnesses reported hearing was confirmed as an IED. Everyone soon forgot about the minor disruption to the network and the passengers involved. The tone of the bulletins grew more sombre as the afternoon progressed.

Across the capital, in many households, family members waited for news. The DLR carried one hundred million passenger journeys each year.

Many Londoners rode the EMUs daily to and from work, school, or college. The cars ferried people to business meetings, shopping trips, and social outings. But, until they heard from their loved ones, nobody could be sure they hadn't been on the Lewisham-Bank train that left the terminus before noon.

In Vincent Gardens, Belgravia, Geoffrey Fox awaited the return of his wife, Grace.

Geoffrey had been in their small rear garden after lunch. Grace travelled by bus and train to meet a school friend in Greenwich. This visit was a regular occurrence on a Monday. The mode of transport might have changed in recent months, but Grace kept in contact with as many old friends as possible. There were fewer and fewer each year. Time was short and precious.

He pottered in the flower borders and trimmed a few overhanging bushes. He was careful not to do too much damage. Then he planned to sit on the seat they often shared and study his efforts. The late morning showers had scudded through, and now a warm sun peeped through the clouds. Their sheltered spot was a sun-trap. Geoffrey rested his eyes and fell asleep.

Three o'clock had come and gone when he awoke. He rechecked his watch. Grace should have been home by now. He returned indoors and called upstairs in case she had just come indoors. There was no reply. He stood at the bottom of the stairs. Perhaps, he should call Daphne? To check whether they chatted longer than usual and whether Grace had caught a later train.

When he replaced the phone, Geoffrey was worried. Daphne had told him she dropped Grace at the DLR station in Greenwich at the same time as always. She begged Geoffrey to ring back with news.

It was rare for Athena's parents to watch TV during the day. Geoffrey couldn't stand the nonsense between the music on the radio, so he was happy to do without entertainment, apart from his Times newspaper. That kept him abreast of everything he needed to know. It often occupied several hours of his day as he went through one thoughtful article after another. Finally, he switched on the television.

Geoffrey Fox perched on the arm of a leather settee as he watched the rolling news report from Heron's Quay. Grace would have been on that train. She could be injured or even worse. It was time to call their daughter, Annabelle Grace Fox-Bailey. He hoped she was at Larcombe Manor with her husband, Phoenix. Whatever needed doing, those two would want to be involved. He returned to the hallway, picked up the phone, and dialled.

"Daddy?" asked Athena, surprised to hear from her father.

"I'm afraid your mother travelled on that train today, darling," said Geoffrey. "I haven't heard from her."

"Sorry, Daddy," said Athena, "we returned from the North of England in the last hour. Phoenix and I have been travelling for hours. What train? Where did this happen? Why did Mummy go on a train without you?"

"She visits Daphne, her old friend from Greenwich, most Mondays. They have coffee somewhere together, and then your mother comes home. Taxis in London cost the earth these days, and now we're eligible; we've picked up

Freedom Passes and Sixty Plus Oyster ID Cards. That provides free bus travel and concessions with the Senior Railcard on off-peak Oyster fares."

Athena was incredulous; that didn't sound like Daddy. He always travelled first-class everywhere. She couldn't have helped the Olympus Project without her share of the family fortune she inherited when reaching twenty-five.

"I don't know why you two are scrimping and saving, Daddy. Forget that for the time being. Tell me what's happened."

"Mummy takes the bus to Tower Gateway and then travels to Greenwich, with one change of line. The whole trip takes her fifty minutes. On her return trip, she was due to change at Westferry from the Lewisham-Bank line. When she reached Tower Gateway, it was only a fifteen-minute walk home. Walking has been part of her exercise regime these past weeks. However, the consultant still reckons she's overweight and putting too much strain on her heart."

"So, where did this accident happen?" Athena asked.

"The train derailed at Heron's Quay just before noon. It wasn't an accident, darling. On the news, they said there was a bomb; someone left an IED on the tracks. I'm watching the latest news now. Emergency service people are scrambling over the train and the tracks. It's a mess. It had to be a terrorist attack, but nobody has claimed responsibility yet. If Mummy was in the first car...."

"Phoenix and I will be there by six o'clock; if we can get hold of our helicopter pilot at such short notice. You stay by the phone. We'll find out where they are transferring the survivors. As soon as we know something, either Phoenix or I will call. I love you, Daddy. Try not to worry. Mummy will be fine."

Geoffrey replaced the phone and walked into the

lounge. On the screen, there were wide-angle shots of the three-carriage EMU. Paramedics hustled three stretchers along the track carrying casualties. Those poor beggars must at least be alive, though Geoffrey thought, or they would move much slower.

It was fast approaching four o'clock. The live feed ended, and in the studio, the newsreader updated the confirmed number of casualties.

"Seventy-three passengers are continuing to receive treatment at the A&E departments. A further one-hundred and three have been released with minor lacerations and bruising. Those that remain in the hospital include twenty-eight with serious, life-altering injuries. Eight of those twenty-eight are critical. At this time, the death toll is eighteen. Screens are being erected by the track to allow the removal of the bodies of the deceased. That operation will start in a few minutes."

The programme switched to one of the hospitals, where a senior doctor confirmed the number of fatalities and sent his condolences to the families. The leading causes of death were severe trauma associated with crush injuries. As for those on the critical list, the next twenty-four hours were vital. When pushed on whether the number of deaths might rise, he said it unlikely that the eight would make it through the night.

Geoffrey sank into a chair and waited for the call he hoped never came.

Chapter Two

Meanwhile, at Larcombe Manor, Athena and Phoenix confirmed their plans. Biggles was en route from Filton airfield. He would land on the grounds in ten minutes. They were to fly to Fairoaks, a small airfield southwest of London. Forty-five minutes after take-off, an Olympus driver would drop them in Vincent Gardens one hour later.

Athena rang her father.

"We'll be with you by six, Daddy. Any news?"

"Nothing yet, darling. All the survivors are out of the train. Only body bags to bring out now."

Even though she tried, Athena couldn't hold back the tears. She wanted to hold her father and take away the pain. Where was Phoenix? He had gone to the ice-house to find out what information Giles and Artemis had gathered. Athena could hear Biggles approaching.

Athena stood, drying her eyes by the window. Phoenix was standing on the lawn waving to her as Biggles came in to land. She waved back and headed for the nursery door. Maria, Elena and Hope were inside playing.

"We need to shoot off again," she told the nanny, "can you feed this one and put her to bed? I've no idea when we'll be home again."

Athena gave their daughter a quick cuddle and kissed her forehead.

"Night, night, poppet," she said and dashed away before the tears returned.

"Something's up," thought Hope.

Athena emerged from the main building onto the lawn and ran towards the helicopter. Phoenix was already seated. Biggles waited until she had fastened her belt, and then he was up and away, heading for Surrey.

"Any news?" asked Phoenix.

"Daddy was in a state," she replied. "He knows the casualties are now out of the train, no matter how major or minor their injuries. The bodies are leaving as we speak. He said there were eighteen fatalities. What did you learn?"

"Artemis had details of those recorded as having left the hospital after treatment. Your mother's name wasn't among them. She was still checking on the rest. Several will stay in overnight."

"Did Giles have any clues this was imminent? Who might have carried out the attack?"

"Nobody has claimed it so far," said Phoenix, "but it has certain hallmarks that point to Islamic State. Giles is monitoring the usual websites and forums. As I left, he had captured feed from CCTV cameras in Canary Wharf. He may find something. I asked him to investigate what trackside stretches are picked up by nearby cameras. Maybe we can identify who planted the device. Giles reckoned it had to be a remote detonation, which means hunting for the best vantage points and finding out who was in them when the bomb exploded. The problem is that vantage points are in the hundreds. That's why people pay big bucks to live or work there."

"You haven't asked the obvious question yet," said Athena.

"What? Why was Grace using the DLR?" asked Phoenix.

"Precisely," said Athena, "you need to have a serious talk with Daddy when this is over."

"Look, we've more urgent things to confront," said Phoenix, taking hold of Athena's hand. "Let's pray we find your mother sat up in a hospital bed, wondering what the fuss is."

"I have a bad feeling, Phoenix," sighed Athena. "Daddy will fall to pieces without her."

The flight with Biggles lasted the time he had told them at take-off. The private airfield was well-equipped, and the driver in the limousine was waiting for them to arrive. Within a minute of touching the tarmac, the car was gliding through the gateway from the airfield. They joined the flow of traffic travelling the three miles before joining the M25. Sixty minutes later, they arrived at Vincent Gardens,

Athena stood on the doorstep with Phoenix and rang the doorbell.

Geoffrey Fox answered, his face grey with worry. Phoenix thought he'd aged a decade since he saw him at the christening seven days ago.

"Come along in, you two," he said. "I've been by the phone, listening to the radio, but I've heard nothing. Surely, they'll send a police officer around, won't they? Or will they send an automated message to my phone?"

Athena led her father through to the lounge and got him seated.

"Tea or coffee?"

"Tea, please," replied Geoffrey.

"Right, I'll get drinks organised. While you and I keep one another company, Phoenix will make the phone calls."

Phoenix joined his wife in the kitchen.

"Get the relevant numbers from Giles," she said. "We can't call him in the ice-house and give Daddy an insight into what goes on at Larcombe. Find out what progress he's made on the CCTV leads. Then you can find which hospital Mummy went to; there's still time to visit this evening. If we're looking at the worst-case scenario, we need to face it tonight. We have important operations to see carried out over the next few days."

"Either way, you must stay here at least for tomorrow," said Phoenix. The kettle had boiled; Athena made the drinks and carried them to the lounge. Geoffrey sat with his head in his hands.

"God knows how I'll cope if she's gone," he said.

"We could have lost her on several occasions in the past four years, Daddy," said Athena, wrapping her arms around her father. "We'll get through it together if we must."

Phoenix was in the hallway calling Giles.

"I need the contact details for each of the A&E departments involved. If other numbers are necessary for morgues, or what have you, then can you provide those too, please?"

"Of course," said Giles, "are you ready?"

Phoenix wrote the numbers for each of the hospitals where they transported casualties.

"The emergency services commandeered only one morgue," said Giles and relayed the number.

"Thanks, Giles. Anything new?"

"Our eagle-eyed former police officer caught sight of a possible bombing suspect. Artemis saw a man on a side street parallel to the DLR, four hundred yards from the blast site. He carried a rucksack over his shoulder. He was a Muslim dressed in European-style clothing. The surrounding crowds were animated, alerted by the explosion thirty minutes earlier, but he passed by without a glance. I agree with Artemis; the guy looked too calm."

"I'll leave you to carry on the search," said Phoenix, "he may not have been working alone. If we can place this man, or any companions, near the exit to a high-rise building in the locality, then we can eliminate the time difference. The vantage point is what we're seeking. Find that, and no doubt they will have spent those minutes super-cleaning the flat or office they used; this wasn't a random attack by a lone bomber. On the contrary, it has all the signs of being highly organised. Ask Artemis to identify this man. I want to know who we're dealing with."

"Will do, Phoenix," said Giles. "I hope you hear good news about your mother-in-law. She's a lovely lady. Maria Elena and I enjoyed her company at the christening. Mrs Fox was so happy, and we could tell she doted on little Hope."

"Thanks, Giles," replied Phoenix. "I'll start by ringing the last number you gave me. Let's hope the others aren't redundant. Grace and Geoffrey are the only grandparents Hope will ever have, so they're doubly precious."

Phoenix dialled the number for the morgue.

"Darling, you're back," said Athena as he re-entered the lounge three minutes later.

"I'm sorry, Geoffrey…." Phoenix began.

Geoffrey clung to his daughter and burst into tears. Athena was sobbing on his shoulder. Phoenix knew how much she loved both her parents. She was heartbroken. The morgue had confirmed the terrible news that Grace Fox was among the eighteen fatalities.

Phoenix wanted to hold his wife, to comfort her. But she and her father sat together, consumed by their grief, and now was not the time. Phoenix had never experienced unconditional love, nor had he grieved when his parents died. He liked to think he was a different person now, over twenty years later, but he had never regretted his actions.

He sat across the room in silence until Athena looked up at him.

"What happened, Phoenix? Do we know how she died? Where is her body?" she asked.

Geoffrey composed himself somewhat and, still clinging to his daughter, listened as Phoenix told them what he had learned.

"Grace was on the right-hand side, two-thirds of the way up the front car. It's thought she hit her head on the seat in front when the train decelerated immediately following the blast. The autopsy will provide the final answers, but her head injury doesn't appear to have been severe enough to cause her death. Initial examinations suggest she may have suffered a cardiac arrest."

"Poor Mummy," said Athena. "If she had a heart attack in many other circumstances, she might have lived, despite the problems we know she had. But, it would take too long for anyone to get to her in a crash like that."

"We can only hope it was quick," said Phoenix.

"Where did they take her?" asked Geoffrey.

"I'll call the driver," said Phoenix, "and ask him to return here. We can go to see her. The autopsies will take place over the next few days; it might be too early to make funeral arrangements. I'll ask what timetable they think we're using. We can stay here tonight. I'll return to

Larcombe in the morning. Darling, you need to be with your father. Stay as long as you both need."

Athena nodded. She wanted to return home to her daughter, but Phoenix was right. She was needed here. Maria Elena would cope, and Phoenix could take the opportunity for father-and-daughter time. For her part, she had her heart set on getting her father through the ordeal and preparing him for the future. Athena didn't want to lose him for many years yet. He was only in his late sixties and enjoyed good health.

"The car's outside," said Phoenix.

"I'll grab a coat," said Geoffrey, and he hustled out into the hallway.

Athena took the tray of cups and saucers through to the kitchen. She glanced at the His and Hers calendar by the fridge. It held appointments for the hairdresser, the chiropodist, the dentist, and the doctor. The flowers in the bowl on the window sill were her mother's favourites.

As she followed the two men to the waiting car, she realised that although the little things her mother had done to make this house a home remained, nothing would ever be the same.

After they arrived at the morgue, they confirmed who they were. Then Geoffrey was taken through to make a formal identification of the body. Phoenix and Athena accompanied him. Grace looked serene, apart from the wicked-looking bruise on her forehead. It was as if she was merely sleeping.

Phoenix watched as Athena and her father wept. The glass between them and their loved ones made the situation even more painful. However, he understood they must observe protocol. The autopsy came first. When they returned to reception, two other couples were waiting.

Two more families were going through the same nightmare.

"Go ahead, darling," whispered Phoenix. "I'll ask when we might expect to collect your mother's belongings and get information from a staff member before I leave. Wait for me in the car."

He joined them five minutes later, and they drove to Vincent Gardens. Once inside the house, Phoenix ensured Geoffrey was comfortable in a chair. Athena took a seat beside her husband.

"Her belongings will be released within forty-eight hours. So it might be a week before we know an exact date for the body to go to whichever undertaker you choose. We're looking at two weeks from today before any funeral can take place."

Phoenix then left Geoffrey and Athena alone, discussing what until then had always been a taboo subject. Athena had never asked what funeral service her parents wanted. Along with many others, it was something she hoped she didn't need to worry over for ages. He went into the hallway and called Giles again.

"It was bad news, Giles. It seems Grace died of a heart attack. The shock of the explosion was too much for her already weakened heart. She didn't suffer any traumatic injuries, thank goodness. At least she was spared that."

"I'm so sorry, Phoenix," said Giles. "I'm sure my colleagues here at Larcombe wish me to send their condolences. What will you do now?"

"I'm returning tomorrow. There are things I need to do. Athena will stay here for the time being."

"Right, I'll warn Maria Elena to keep Hope occupied until you're free to care for her," said Giles. "Leave that with me. I'll ask Artemis to tell Rusty that you'll be back in time for the missions planned."

"Thanks, Giles," said Phoenix. "I'll catch up with you tomorrow to hear what you've discovered. Yes, Rusty and I are heading north again on Wednesday. Athena and I posed as day-trippers over the weekend, checking the lay of the land around Rotherham."

"I can give you the latest figures in the morning, Phoenix," said Giles, "but your initial thoughts were correct. The number of men charged with child sexual abuse offences is only a drop in the ocean compared to the true scale of what has gone unchecked for a decade."

"Rusty and I will head to Rotherham and Rochdale on Wednesday morning. We will meet with our colleagues from the nearest Olympus groups and carry out our reprisals. Unfortunately, we can't rely on the police to be quick enough off the mark to stop hundreds of potential suspects fleeing the region or even flying back to Pakistan."

Phoenix returned to the lounge, where he found Athena and her father looking through photographs he had taken at the christening. The last happy occasion they shared. Little did they know. Phoenix's mind drifted to events leading to direct action in the North.

Twenty years ago, care-home managers had investigated reports children in their care were being picked up by taxi drivers. Over a decade ago, names of alleged perpetrators, several from one family, were passed to the authorities. Four years ago, the first group conviction occurred when they convicted five British-Pakistani men of sexual offences against underage girls. They never arrested the ringleaders. Two years ago, the Times newspaper reported that sexual exploitation in the town was widespread, and the authorities had known about it for over a decade.

That same year the trial of a Rochdale child sex abuse ring took place. Nine men went to jail for several offences against up to fifty young girls over the previous three or four years. At long last, someone in government thought action was required. The report from the resulting independent inquiry was discussed in the morning meeting at Larcombe last Tuesday.

The report's conclusion showed that the council had a bullying, sexist culture of covering up information and silencing whistle-blowers and was not fit for purpose. The report's writer attributed the council's failure to address the abuse to factors revolving around race, class and gender. Phoenix had read the article and despaired of any real justice for the fourteen hundred victims.

The apologists would have a field day. There would be a good deal of hand-wringing for the TV cameras. A few officials would do the decent thing, resign and then walk away with an obscene gold-plated pension. Another inquiry would follow in time. The horrors would get swept under the carpet once the spotlight fell on another sector of society.

Sometimes the Olympus way was the only way.

"Do you want a hot chocolate, darling?"

It was Athena; she had interrupted his train of thought.

"I don't think so, thanks," he replied.

"Daddy will try to get a few hours' sleep," said Athena. "I won't be long behind him. What time are you leaving in the morning?"

"I asked the driver to collect me at seven, sorry. I have to get back."

"Well, you had better have a word with Daddy now while I find the cocoa. I doubt he'll be out of bed early in the morning."

Phoenix nodded. Athena headed to the kitchen; he sat closer to Geoffrey.

"What a day, Phoenix," the old man said with a deep sigh.

"We're all going to miss her, Geoffrey," said Phoenix, laying his hand on his father-in-law's arm. "Do you mind if I ask you a question?"

"Fire away," said Geoffrey.

"What sparked this change of routine? The taxi firms around Belgravia have made a roaring trade, with trips to restaurants, theatres, railway stations, and airports. Why was Grace using the bus and train combination to visit her Greenwich friend?"

"I don't want Annabelle to worry," said Geoffrey, "but our investments have taken a hit over the past few years. I understand we're not alone, and thousands of couples would love to be in our position. They offered us these concessions when we reached sixty, but we always refused them. Grace agreed with me that there were far more deserving cases across the capital. Then, on our last visit to the chap in Harley Street, the chap warned us Grace was risking her health by not being more active and not exercising to reduce her weight. So, I contacted the authorities and took every card and concession going. Then we planned how to get Grace to visit her friend and organise a trip to the theatre, etcetera. It saved a good deal of money. We walked further, which helped us get fitter, and using the brain to find devious ways to get the most out of the system exercised the brain cells. We thought it was a 'win-win' situation. Sadly, it didn't last as long as we planned."

"I get it now. Geoffrey. When you feel ready, carry on with what you are doing. Use your brain, stay fit and healthy, and who knows? You might see Hope learn to drive, reach a university, even get married."

"Might Hope have a brother or sister?" the old man asked.

"It's not out of the question," replied Phoenix.

"Annabelle's forty this year," said Geoffrey, "time's not on her side. Especially with the two of you so involved in this charity business."

"We'll see, it's very much in our plans, but unforeseen events may overtake us."

"The best-laid plans and all that? Today has been a stark reminder of that, Phoenix. I'm glad you're here with Annabelle. She's in safe hands. I'll not keep her fussing over me for any longer than necessary. You and little Hope need her more than me in the long run."

"I'm away first thing tomorrow," said Phoenix, shaking the old man by the hand. "I've got business to attend to up north, but I'll be back by the weekend. How long I stay will depend on what emerges in the next few days. Never fear. I'll attend Grace's funeral. I had grown very fond of her in the brief time we knew one another. I was never fortunate enough to have a loving mother."

"Charity business up north, is it?" asked Geoffrey, probing for the truth, as always.

"Missing person cases," replied Phoenix.

Athena had returned to the lounge and caught the end of the conversation. Her father hugged her and wished them both goodnight. After the door closed behind him, Athena asked what Geoffrey's response had been to the question of why they had been saving the pennies.

Phoenix gave her father's reasoning as best he could without disclosing the under-performance of her parents' investments. Geoffrey hadn't gone into any detail. The banking crisis and subsequent recession had been a testing time. Athena seemed satisfied enough with his explanation.

"What did you mean by missing person cases?" she asked.

"OK, I admit the men involved don't know they will be missing in a day or two, but it was the best I could come up with at short notice. Your Dad is always keen to trip me up, to trick me into revealing too much on what goes on at Olympus."

"We had better get to sleep," yawned Athena, "that driver will bang on the door before we know it."

"That wouldn't do in Vincent Gardens, would it?" said Phoenix as he followed Athena out of the lounge to the stairs. "The neighbours would have an attack of the vapours if he rolled up, and tooted his horn, to let me know he's arrived."

"You're incorrigible," said Athena.

"How much did you overhear?" Phoenix asked, "your Dad wondered about the chances of an addition to the family."

"Not tonight, sunshine," Athena replied.

They had reached the landing. The light under the door to Athena's parent's bedroom suggested Geoffrey was still awake. She raised a hand to knock. Phoenix shook his head.

"He won't thank you," he whispered.

Sleep didn't come to either of them for what seemed forever. Grace Fox had been taken from them far too soon. Geoffrey couldn't imagine life without her. Athena worried that her father felt so alone he would follow his beloved wife before long.

Phoenix was thinking of the suspect they had spotted. Was he part of a cell? What were their future targets? How long before he could take his revenge on the men who murdered his mother-in-law?

Sweet dreams.

Tuesday, 2nd September 2014

Phoenix was awake early. In truth, he had only cat-napped during the night. Athena was still asleep beside him. The light under Geoffrey's door had gone by one o'clock. Phoenix crept downstairs and made himself a coffee; it was six-thirty. He needed to shower and dress; he returned upstairs.

"Is that for me, darling? How thoughtful," purred Athena,

He handed over the coffee and headed for the shower. Perhaps he could get the driver to pull in to Heston Services on the M4. He might find a bacon roll for sale to go with his coffee. He was soon dressed and ready to leave. The car pulled up outside the house at one minute to seven.

"Ring me tonight, darling," said Athena. "I'll see how Daddy is this morning in a few minutes. Kiss Hope from Mummy. Tell her I'll be home soon."

Phoenix kissed his wife goodbye. Then, as the door closed behind her husband, Athena heard her father moving around upstairs.

She knew they faced difficult days ahead — no time like the present to start.

The morning meeting at Larcombe Manor began at nine o'clock. Minos took the chair, with the two senior agents away in London.

Giles and Artemis had already arrived. Rusty and

Alastor weren't far behind them. As he read through the agenda that Athena had left yesterday, he heard Henry Case plodding along the corridor outside. Good, they could get started on time.

When Henry had joined them, Giles spoke: -

"Phoenix was leaving London at seven this morning. To keep everyone abreast of what's happened in the past twenty-four hours, Athena's mother was one of the victims of yesterday's terrorist attack on the Dockland Light Railway network at Heron's Quay. Athena will remain in Belgravia with her father until further notice. Phoenix is heading back to carry out the scheduled missions in the north of England. Everything is going ahead as planned, Rusty."

"How horrible," said Alastor. "Eighteen deaths so far, and two more unlikely to recover, I heard on this morning's news."

"An outfit that calls itself Islamic State has claimed responsibility," muttered Henry, "and posted another video online."

"I haven't seen that yet, Henry," said Minos, "another beheading? These are sick individuals at the forefront of this latest terrorist organisation to hit the headlines."

"The act of beheading was a standard method of execution in pre-modern Islamic law," Henry continued. "Its use has been abandoned in most countries, only Saudi Arabia keeping the tradition alive. In recent times, non-state Jihadist organisations have used beheading to kill captives. Since the turn of this century, IS has circulated beheading videos as a form of terror and propaganda."

"Two weeks ago, they posted a video of a US journalist's execution in this manner," said Rusty. "That got the world's attention rapidly."

"Where did the victim come from this time?" asked Minos.

"He was an American-Israeli journalist kidnapped in Aleppo a year ago," said Henry.

"This group must expect reprisals," said Rusty. "It doesn't pay to mess with the Israelis, even if he left the homeland a generation ago."

"Talking of reprisals," said Giles, "are you up to speed with the arrangements for Wednesday, Rusty?"

"Phoenix relayed the details they gathered over the weekend before they left yesterday. I spent an hour in the orangery yesterday afternoon going over the timetable."

"While the cat's away?" grinned Artemis.

"You were on a shift in the ice-house, and it helped to clear my head and confirm the details. I get why Phoenix spends so much time there."

"Good to know a few of my good habits are rubbing off on you, at last," said Phoenix as he slipped into the meeting room.

"Welcome back, Phoenix," said Minos, "you made good time?"

"We could have been home faster if we hadn't stopped for breakfast," said Phoenix.

"Do you want to take over, Phoenix?" asked Minos, half out of his chair.

"No, you can stay there, Minos. I want to check in with Giles and Artemis, and then I'll spend the morning with Hope. She was without her parents at the weekend, and Athena won't be back for several days because of yesterday. Rusty and I are moving to Rochdale and Rotherham this time tomorrow.

Each senior agent had something to say regarding the DLR terror attack. Grace Fox's death was personal. She was a member of the extended Olympus family. Phoenix listened to their comments and words of sympathy.

"I'll pass your thoughts and condolences on to Athena when we talk this evening. We must redouble our efforts to determine who was responsible and take appropriate action. We have other priorities needing our attention. This week's mission is one, and the increasing threat of the Grid can never be under-estimated. Whatever in-fighting might occur, we must challenge the criminal network it represents. They have had things their way for too long. However, that's for another day; our first task is to put a name to yesterday's bombers."

"To let us give that matter our full attention, Phoenix," said Minos, "you could see Hope for thirty minutes. We'll finish up the rest of the scheduled agenda for today, and then I suggest we pick things up on the Heron's Quay attack at ten-thirty."

"That sounds a plan, Minos," said Phoenix.

"Your good habits are rubbing off on me, too, Phoenix."

"Touché," said Phoenix as he closed the door behind him. He didn't need to be asked twice.

Chapter Three

Maria Elena was in the playroom with Hope. As the door opened, the little girl looked up, recognised her father and scrambled across the carpet to greet him. Phoenix scooped her up in his arms, and Hope clung tight but kept looking behind him, searching for her mother's face.

"Sorry, poppet," said Phoenix. "Mummy's not coming home today. She's staying with Grandad."

"So sorry," said Maria Elena, "it was a terrible shock. Giles told me last night."

"That it was," Phoenix agreed, "but we have to move on. We'll take time to grieve when the funeral takes place. We can't put our lives on hold for a fortnight while we wait for the nonsense associated with a terror attack of this nature."

"Giles asked me to be available to look after Hope until her mother can return. Will you need me again today?"

"We're very grateful to you for dropping everything to look after our daughter, Maria Elena. I'm in a meeting for the rest of the morning. Tomorrow, I leave on a mission. If you could prepare lunch for Hope and me, then once I return to relieve you around one o'clock, we won't need you again until the morning. Is that okay?"

"That's fine," the nanny replied. "We'll be fine on our own for two or three days, won't we, Hope?"

"Sounds as if we will have to be," Hope thought, wondering what caused this disruption to her routine.

Phoenix returned to the meeting room. He discovered Alastor waiting outside in the corridor.

"We've finished the minor agenda items, Phoenix," he said. "Minos suggested we take a five-minute comfort break before we got into the heavy stuff."

"Right, as soon as everyone is back, we'll get cracking," said Phoenix.

Two minutes later, he didn't wait for Minos to open proceedings. He wanted answers from the surveillance teams in the ice-house,

"What news, Giles?"

"The man Artemis suspected was identified as Ahmed Mansouri, a twenty-eight-year-old Tunisian. He came to the UK in early August via Sangatte. He lived in a makeshift camp there for several weeks. Mansouri was a person of interest to the French authorities, but he slipped away from under their noses and crossed the Channel from Calais."

"Do we know where he went next?" asked Phoenix.

"He moved to Slough, to a flat he now shares with Omar Harrack, a twenty-four-year-old Moroccan student."

"Why were the French security services looking at him?" asked Phoenix.

"He spent two years in Syria before returning to Tunisia a year ago," Artemis continued. "They suspected him of being involved in a bank raid in Marseilles in November and trafficking firearms and explosives from North Africa between February and April this year."

"Despite the obvious implications of activity such as that, the French security services didn't think it worth arresting this guy?" asked Phoenix, shaking his head.

"I can only imagine they thought he could lead them to someone more important in the organisation," said Giles.

"As soon as he escaped across the Channel to a place of safety, they washed their hands of the problem," muttered Rusty. "Don't you love being in Europe? We're the dustbin for their criminals and terrorists."

"Be reasonable, Rusty," said Henry Case. "We've become a breeding ground too, so they probably think fair's fair."

"Any sign of Harrack on the CCTV feeds we captured?" asked Phoenix, keen to move things forward.

"That was easier once we uncovered a name for Mansouri," said Artemis. "I followed the evidence from when he arrived in Dover to an address in the centre of Slough. As soon as we uncovered a photograph of his flatmate Omar Harrack from social media, we spotted him quickly. Harrack was on the opposite side of the street, walking away from Mansouri. We used the time stamps on the CCTV as a reference point. Then we calculated the distance both men would have covered in five minutes at an unhurried pace within the busy streets in Canary Wharf."

"Those calculations did my head in at school," said Rusty. "So, you reckon they walked two or three hundred yards away from an exit point of a building that fitted their purpose?"

"Roughly," said Giles, "they had to stay under the radar. Their appearance, although westernised, might have triggered someone's attention. By remaining cool, calm and collected, they raised no suspicions."

"Where does that place them then? Have we identified the building they used?" asked Phoenix.

Giles produced photos of an apartment block, the lifts, and the interior of a top-floor flat.

"This flat was rented last week. Someone paid for a three-month short-term lease in cash. Our agents have just finished going through the place. They left nothing usable behind them. Our team found no fingerprints and no trace of any of the equipment they used. The place had been deep-cleaned. A professional job from start to finish."

"Where were they headed when they left this building?" asked Phoenix. "Can we pick them up in Canary Wharf after the initial images you mentioned? Did they meet up later? Did a third party collect them; were they going to London by road or train? Have they returned by whatever mode of transport to the flat in Slough? Please tell me they haven't got away?"

"We're still piecing together their movements, Phoenix," said Artemis. "We've made good progress, but we all understand the urgency in this case. While we've been at this meeting in the main house, other team members in the icehouse have followed up on the things you listed. Giles has added naming the device used to that list. We have an operator hacking into computers that may contain that information. We won't get close enough to the DLR track itself for days to carry out our fingertip search; when we can, it will be far too late. If we can locate files on the analysis of shrapnel and other debris collected by the authorities, it will provide us with valuable information. We are checking Harrack's background too. After he arrived eighteen months ago, he signed up for a two-year History of Art course at a local college but has hardly set foot inside. Discovering his whereabouts before he landed at Heathrow in 2013 is a matter of priority. If, as you suggest, this forms part of an orchestrated series of attacks the two men have planned, then forewarned is forearmed."

Phoenix nodded. He knew he was stressed about not being able to get the answers he craved at once. Artemis was right; they had moved things forward in eighteen hours. They knew their targets now. Time and additional data allowed them to discover if they were still on the move or had gone to ground. If they had holed up somewhere, the surveillance teams would pick them up and follow them once they resurfaced. It might be wise to eliminate them in their hideaway before they could do any more damage. He would think things over this afternoon and determine the most beneficial option for Olympus while he took Hope for a swim.

Minos took advantage of the pause and brought the meeting to a close. Giles and Artemis must return to the icehouse to continue gathering data on the terrorists. As the agents left the room, Rusty and Henry stopped to chat.

"Nasty business, these beheading videos, Rusty," said Henry, "once seen, never forgotten."

"Every organisation in history who wanted their message heard has adopted scare tactics. Those tactics begin when talking has got them nowhere. The assassinations of public figures and the bombing of innocent members of the public have become their favourite methods. Kidnapping women and children to use as human shields and filming the execution of prisoners is relatively new. The depths to which these fanatics can stoop never ceases to amaze."

"I pray we never respond in kind, Rusty," said Henry. "I

have felt guilty for months concerning my role. I've carried out interrogations that have flown close to the edge of what's legal. Although I never cross the line, many wouldn't accept any of what we do is right. Those criminals I've killed were guilty as charged. I've never doubted that, but there have been late nights when I've laid awake wondering whether their deaths were necessary."

"The love of a good woman can profoundly affect a man, Henry," said Rusty, laying a hand on his shoulder. "That's where this is coming from, isn't it?"

Henry Case nodded.

"Olympus never asks us to act without justification, Henry," said Rusty. "You have saved countless lives in the past four years. You are serving the greater good by ensuring the criminals and terrorists sent to the lowest level of the ice-house never return to the surface to commit further crimes. Never question that. I don't."

"Thank you, Rusty," said Henry. "It's good to talk these things over with someone who understands. My problem is that I'm not sure Sarah sees things the same way."

"I struggled with the same thoughts when I first met Artemis, Henry," said Rusty. "How could a serving police detective throw her lot in with a secret vigilante organisation? She returned to her parent's home in Durham and wrestled with her conscience in the month before she came to live and work at Larcombe. I've never doubted her commitment to the cause since she arrived here. I'm sure many others, still in uniform, would welcome a return to a stronger police force. Both in numbers and the approach to crime in all its forms. As Artemis has told me more than once, at least we get things done."

Henry returned to the ice-house. There were no inmates to interrogate or take direct action against today.

He needed to maintain security at Larcombe Manor, help train new agents, and retrain those brought home from overseas assignments. While that situation remained, he was a happy man. Sarah couldn't find much to complain about with that role. The spectre of her uncovering his other darker duties remained. Henry Case prayed he could sleep well tonight.

Rusty hoped he put Henry's mind at rest. He walked to the apartment he shared with Artemis and made himself lunch. At two o'clock, Rusty returned to the orangery to review the plans for the next few days. As he settled to his task, he saw Phoenix carrying Hope on his shoulders as he crossed the lawns towards the workers' cottages. Time spent in the heated pool would make a welcome change this afternoon, but he had to fill in for Phoenix today. His relaxation must wait.

His best friend had put his family first. That came as no big surprise after yesterday's events. Rusty's relationship with his father may have been fractious, but he dearly loved his mother. He knew Phoenix's family situation and knew how important Grace Fox became to him. Someone would pay for destroying that relationship.

Rusty opened the first file and looked again at their primary target. Nine men from Rochdale and Oldham were found guilty two years ago of offences, including rape and conspiracy to engage in sexual activity with a child. The vile group exploited girls as young as thirteen and received sentences between ten and twenty years.

The court heard how the men plied their victims with drinks and drugs before passing them around for sex. The abuse took place at two takeaway restaurants in the Heywood area of Rochdale. The judge said the men treated the girls as if they were worthless. Last December, five men were jailed after an investigation into the sexual abuse of a girl reopened following the exposure of police failings.

The sentences handed out reflected the public revulsion at the crimes involved. On completing their time served, virtually every man had been ordered to be deported to their home country. Phoenix and Athena learned at the weekend when they visited the North that several men had already asked for legal aid to fight attempts to repatriate them. After the direct action this week, a marker will be left on the file for further action to respond to the expected outcry from the public. The men didn't consider the human rights of the girls they abused. Olympus would ensure they didn't find a loophole provided by the European Court of Justice that forced the UK to continue to provide them with family life.

Olympus agents working in the northwest discovered a minimum of seven men still grooming young teenage girls and boys. As a result, these children repeatedly went missing from care. Nothing much had changed in the region; no one had learned their lesson. Phoenix and Rusty intended to stop this activity for good.

The Olympus team had highlighted three men's names. They lived in the small town of Heywood, sandwiched between the most deprived places in the northwest. Head out of Heywood in any direction and you either get to Bury, Rochdale or Oldham. When Rusty thought back to the other missions near Manchester, Heywood seemed to be a carbon copy.

Few young people who lived there had any aspirations. If you got the chance to get out, you would grab it, Rusty thought. But they seemed content to steal what wasn't bolted down, get blind drunk, and do drugs. Was that what encouraged these older guys to consider them worthless?

Did the youngest ones bring it on themselves to a degree? Either way, it was wrong, and they must suffer.

Agents watched the council care homes where the most vulnerable kids lived. That surveillance would continue until tomorrow when the direct action began.

Rusty put the Rochdale file to one side. Ninety minutes away from Rochdale lay the South Yorkshire town of Rotherham. The sheer scale of that case appalled him. How on earth could something so widespread continue for over twenty years without someone speaking out?

The inquiry report that emerged last week was in the file for reference, but Rusty knew the men in prison were in the minority. There were dozens, maybe hundreds, guilty of a whole range of offences. This week, the Olympus targets were the ringleaders and the most frequent offenders who avoided arrest and appropriate punishment. It was no time to be hanging back, waiting for the authorities to wake up, at last, to arrest and charge them.

The report Minos and Alastor had compiled for Phoenix on Rotherham made for uncomfortable reading. The area suffered high levels of deprivation. A quarter of the children were affected by income deprivation, and that number was increasing. The government's austerity programme, now in effect for three years, would only intensify regional poverty. There would be a reduction in the incomes of the poorest households of families with children. Similar financial hardships fell on the disabled or long-term sick. Those in the greatest need were always the most brutal hit.

Rusty was a simple man. He ran away to join the army as soon as he was old enough. Yet, with limited education, he understood that poverty restricted people's ability to participate in society. The teenage girls and boys who became victims of these grooming gangs in the past decades couldn't change their lifestyles. Others determined their destiny. No wonder they felt abandoned, unloved and unwanted. The affection they found at the hands of their abusers was criminal. As Rusty ingested the context against which it emerged, he realised it wasn't only that their abusers thought them worthless; society had convinced these children they were useless too. What a mess.

Rusty spent the next two hours checking the plans for the rest of the week. Everything was in place. As he worked, he saw Phoenix and Hope return from their time in the swimming pool. They looked so happy—father and daughter in their little world. Hope laughed as she tottered across the lawn. Several times she stumbled and pitched forward on her knees. Each time, Phoenix lifted her, but Hope wriggled against his chest, keen to get down and try again. She would never concede defeat.

The innocence of youth, thought Rusty. Artemis often said she wanted a child. They were in a settled relationship. Both knew danger always lay around the corner for an agent on a mission. Even so, it was something to complete them, make them a family. On the other side of the coin, Rochdale, Rotherham, and possibly every major city and town across the country. What sort of a world was it into which they were bringing a child? Rusty closed the files and reports he had studied.

He was ready. It was time to stem the tide. The reports' evidence pointed Rusty to a lesson from this country's ancient history. The apocryphal anecdote in which King Canute showed his courtiers that he had no control over the elements. He could not stop the incoming tide, showing the futility of trying to stop the progress of inevitable events. Rusty was naïve enough to believe that Olympus must act regardless of their odds. If they didn't, the evil continued. There was a point when you had to put a stake in the ground and say - no more.

Wednesday, 3rd September 2014

Phoenix lay awake by seven. He wandered along the corridor to Hope's bedroom. She was lying on her back, grabbing her feet and rocking from side to side. She grinned as soon as she saw her father enter the room.

"Time for us to get ready," he said, picking her up. "You smell as if we've got cleaning up to do."

Half an hour later, Hope was clean, dry, and in her outfit for the day. With luck.

Maria Elena could manage any changes of clothes. Phoenix would be on his way north, his bags packed. He chatted to Hope for the fifteen minutes they had to wait for the nanny to arrive for the overtime shift.

"I hope you will be a good girl for Maria Elena," he said. "Daddy's got to go to work with Uncle Rusty. Mummy will be home tomorrow."

Hope looked at her father's face as he spoke. He thought she was taking everything in.

"Mummy," she said.

"Yes, she called me last night from Grandad's house. She misses you. Grandad says he can manage without her. He's brave."

Hope listened intently. It confirmed what she thought. Something terrible had happened. Mummy and Daddy would make it right. She was a fast learner. At nine months old, she understood that that's what they did.

Maria Elena tapped on the door at eight.

"Good morning," she said. As always, bright and breezy, even at such an ungodly hour. Giles must be doing something right.

Phoenix gave his daughter one last hug and handed her to the nanny's care.

"I'll be home on Friday. Athena will return from London tomorrow. So if you can hold the fort until tomorrow lunchtime, that would be great."

"We'll be fine," replied Maria Elena.

When Phoenix arrived at the front door of the manor house with his bag, he found Rusty sitting in the van waiting, with the engine running.

"As long as the traffic isn't horrendous on the M5 and M6, we'll be in Rochdale by high noon," he said, swinging the van towards the driveway.

"High Noon; what a great film," said Phoenix. "A man who dedicated his life to upholding the law, putting aside the considerations of a loved one to face a gang of deadly killers. Remind you of anyone?"

Rusty smiled.

"Let's go head them off at the pass, pardner."

"The posse will pick us up when we switch from the M6 to the M62. I've suggested to Danny Tipper, the group leader, that we stop at the nearest place to get a good lunch. We can brief everyone then."

"Do you want to listen to the radio?" asked Rusty.

"To save arguments, I suggest we opt for radio silence," said Phoenix, closing his eyes.

"You didn't get much sleep last night, I take it?" asked Rusty.

"I slept like a log, as it happens. Athena rang to say Geoffrey insisted she returns to Larcombe tomorrow. If she's in charge at headquarters, things will stay on track. Geoffrey needs to confront what happened on Monday without her fussing around him. He'll come out okay on the other side in time — Geoffrey's made of stern stuff. Athena can make sure Giles and Artemis do the necessary regarding the bombers. If we need to act at once because they intend to strike elsewhere in the next forty-eight hours, we'll get the nearest teams to disrupt their plans. If they're lying low, they can keep them under observation until we're free to eliminate them. No, I'm running through the likely scenarios in my head for the next three days. I don't need the distraction of Judas Priest this morning."

"I'll leave you to it then," said Rusty, relieved that Phoenix's favourite brand of music wasn't assaulting his ears.

A little over three hours later, they had left the M6 after a mind-numbing trek from Rugby. Rusty spotted the Olympus vans in his wing mirrors as they arrived to line up in convoy behind him. The vans bore dark blue or black livery and tinted windscreens. They carried no insignia to expose their true nature.

"We've got company, Phoenix."

"Good," said his friend, stretching out the kinks in his frame after the long journey, "I'm starving."

The lead van following them overtook and indicated left at the next junction. The four vans pulled into the motorway services and parked as far away as possible. Once inside the restaurant, the smells from the kitchen made Rusty's stomach rumble.

"You too?" asked Phoenix.

"I was late getting out of bed. So I only grabbed a slice of toast and a coffee."

The two agents waited in line, ordered their food, and

sat at the back of the room, where they found several spare tables. The two agents from the other three vans joined the pair in due course.

"I'm Danny Tipper," said the youngest-looking guy among them.

"Youth Opportunity Scheme?" Rusty asked.

"I moisturise," replied Danny, familiar with comments about his youthful appearance.

Phoenix ignored the light-hearted banter. Instead, he checked the restaurant clientele and staff and searched for faces turning their way. Nobody took any undue interest in the group.

"We'll eat first, and then I'll issue your instructions," he said.

The four teams drove away from the car park at one o'clock, rejoined the M62 and travelled east. They reached Heywood thirty minutes later. Each van drove to its designated position and waited.

In Gorton Street, Mohammed Rafiq, a thirty-four-year-old mechanic, lay underneath a three-year-old Ford Kuga. He was a sexual predator who had been a significant member of the grooming gang operating in the town for years. One of his victims came forward two years ago. Angel was fourteen. She had been in care for most of her life and was first lured into his spider's web with drink and drugs.

Rafiq recognised the familiar signs of vulnerability. He knew how to press the right buttons. He offered to take the young girl to restaurants and treat her to the food she could only dream of at the home in which she lived. His friends in the grooming gang either owned or worked at the restaurants they visited. The predator homed in on his target, but as with the others involved, he was putting the young girl in the shop window.

Rafiq raped Angel within a month of meeting her outside a takeaway in Bridge Street. Over the following six months, he drove her to various locations in Rochdale and Bury. Angel lost count of the number of men who assaulted her. Initially, she thought she pleased Rafiq by being 'nice' to his friends. He treated her better than anyone before had ever done. However, as time passed, he became distant towards her, and Angel realised he was merely using her.

The young girl went to the police and shared details of every abuser she could identify. She pointed out where the attacks took place and provided DNA evidence. She waited and waited. Nothing happened. The police and the Crown Prosecution Service had decided not to proceed. Reports from the care home suggested Angel was unruly and prone to exaggeration. She regularly skipped school and was caught drinking cider and smoking at twelve in a local park. The authorities declared her an unreliable witness.

Phoenix and Rusty exited the van. Its rear doors faced the garage entrance; the forecourt was quiet. The only sound inside came from a radio on a workbench on the back wall. 'Happy' by Pharrell Williams was the tune playing. There was an office on the right-hand side with the door shut. Rusty stopped by the entrance. He could watch the street in both directions and keep an eye on whoever sat inside the office. A glance told him, for now, they had fallen asleep. He needn't disturb him.

Mohammed Rafiq continued to work on the car. Phoenix slipped inside the workshop and crept alongside. Rafiq sensed a presence. Unaware of the danger, he slid the wheeled creeper board forward, thinking it was his employer.

"What's up, Nasim?" he began.

Phoenix tipped the creeper board over, grabbed the mechanic around the neck and applied a choke-hold. Six seconds later, the blood flow to the brain stopped, and Rafiq slumped unconscious. He gagged the predator, secured him with zip ties, and spoke to Rusty: -

"Ready to move. Open the van's rear doors."

Rusty checked the office for the last time. The guy still hadn't moved. He walked across the forecourt. Traffic moved steadily on the street, but nobody was in urgent need of repair to their vehicle. The coast was clear. As soon as the rear doors opened, Phoenix bundled their target inside. Rusty closed the doors and joined Phoenix in the van. It was time to transfer to the rendezvous point they agreed with Danny Tipper.

Nasim Khan emerged from the office an hour later. He turned off the radio and called out to his mechanic. What was going on? Why would he wander off, leaving the work on the Kuga unfinished without saying a word? The customer expected to collect his car at five o'clock.

The garage owner rang Rafiq's mobile. It was in the pocket of his leather jacket hanging on a peg on the wall. Nasim rang around the likely places Rafiq might have gone. Nobody had seen him.

Nasim Khan didn't know it, but Mohammed Rafiq had become the first of *the missing*.

Chapter Four

While events at the garage played out in the pattern Phoenix had planned, Danny Tipper and his colleague left their first port of call. They had watched the restaurant on Bridge Street for twenty minutes before spotting activity. Then, a man emerged from the alleyway leading to the accommodation over the business. He flopped into the driver's seat of an old BMW and drove away.

Shabir Amin, the fifty-three-year-old restaurant owner, was a colleague of Mohammed Rafiq. Angel had often eaten in his restaurant. Many of Amin's customers were on intimate terms with Angel. The BMW left the small town of Heywood and drove towards Bury. Fifteen minutes later, unaware he was being followed, Amin pulled up outside a secondary school.

"School's not out for another thirty minutes," Danny muttered.

"I used to say I had a dental appointment if I wanted to skip out early," said the agent beside him.

Two minutes later, a uniformed girl slipped through the gateway and ran towards the BMW.

"Fifteen years old, would you say?" asked Danny.

"About that, but I find it hard to believe they're related."

"I vote we follow where this leads us," said Danny. "I know we've got enough on Amin to justify picking him up. But we might catch other members of the gang. Who knows?"

The BMW moved away from the kerb, and the Olympus agents followed at a safe distance.

"He's off to Radcliffe, I reckon," said Danny as they drove further south from the school.

"What connections did we have with the gang this far out?" asked his colleague.

"One of the other girls whose story they dismissed as fantasy got brought here," Danny replied. "She said she went to a house situated two streets behind the Muslim Centre. A few of her abusers trotted off to prayers after they had finished with her. When she finally went to the police, she told them she'd been stupid. She was a naïve teenager from a broken home. Her mother struggled to cope and was often depressed and suicidal. Finally, it dawned on the kid they had exploited her vulnerability and low self-esteem. She had grabbed any chance to escape her home circumstances."

"The grooming gangs use such convincing methods," the other agent agreed, "they work hard to build trust in their victims. Unfortunately, they breach that trust when they take the youngsters to their friends and relatives and offer them for sex for heroin. What I find strange is how that other girl's evidence got brushed aside along with many others over the years. In particular, stories that kids in care told various agencies. Social Services' prime job is to keep them from harm. So why didn't they intervene?"

"There was a culture of fear," said Danny. "They didn't want to damage the delicate relationship between the ethnic groups in the area. Most offenders highlighted were Pakistanis. They feared it might come across as racially motivated if they had raised concerns. So, for years they denied they had a significant problem."

"Ease back a little, boss, Amin's turning into the side street up ahead."

The BMW turned into the street, slowed and parked on the verge. The restaurant owner heaved his bulk out of the car, moved around the car's front, and opened the passenger door. Danny noticed he had to unlock the door to let the girl out.

Amin gripped the girl by the wrist and led her up the garden path to the semi-detached house. The door opened before they reached the front step. The couple disappeared inside.

Danny had driven slowly past the property, keeping a close watch on what happened. Finally, he parked fifty yards further along the street.

"Difficult to tell how many were inside," he said.

"Does it matter?" asked his mate.

Danny smiled.

"Not really, but I'll contact our nearest team to provide backup; they're at least fifteen minutes away. So we'll wait until they're en route and confident of their arrival time. Then we'll break in and deal with whatever we find."

Danny made the call and then contacted Phoenix to let him know the score. Phoenix passed on the good news that Rafiq was secured. They made their move when Danny heard his backup was under five minutes away.

The big red key carried by his colleague took the side door off its hinges. The agents darted through the kitchen and into the lounge. Amin slumped on the settee with his hand down his trousers. He was still levering himself out of the sofa when Danny hit him behind the ear with a cosh. Amin was out for the count.

Another man stood in the middle of the room, and the young girl knelt before him. The Olympus agent fired off the taser; the young girl screamed. The man lay twitching on the floor.

"Fetch the van," Danny ordered. His colleague ran from the house, reversed the van up the street, and swung into the driveway. As the backup team entered the road, Danny and his mate shoved Amin into the van. The other man soon joined him.

The young schoolgirl had been in tears since the Olympus agents crashed through the door into the lounge. Danny spoke to her gently. He told her she had nothing to fear from them. Danny asked where she lived and radioed the backup team driver to be ready to drop her off at the end of her road.

"These two are evil men," Danny warned her, "no matter what they promised you. My advice? Forget you were ever here, and we'll make sure they won't hurt you or anyone else again."

The girl nodded through her tears and ran sobbing to the waiting van. When she reached the door, she turned back.

"What about the money?" she asked.

It dawned on Danny that this wasn't the first rodeo for this youngster. She was happy to service this unknown guy in return for money for her drug habit. The tears might be genuine, but they hid a tragic story that wouldn't end for her this afternoon. It wasn't his job to get her the help she needed. His task was to take Amin and others off the streets so they couldn't poison the minds of any more children.

Danny followed the other van up the street. He called the other driver.

"What happened on George Street?"

"Nothing yet, boss. Our man is in the supermarket working, but his shift doesn't end until six. The other team will pick him up as soon as he leaves. His car is under the trees at the far end of the overflow car park. He couldn't have picked a quieter spot."

"Thanks. Make sure your passenger gets home safe. Don't listen to any crap she feeds you. Drop her close to home and then make for the rendezvous point. I'll see you there."

The other van turned off and set off towards Elton. Danny watched it go.

"Have you ever been there?" he asked his mate.

"Don't think I have," he replied.

"When the sun's shining, you can be fooled into thinking it's a good place to live."

When they reached the rendezvous point, they parked alongside Phoenix's van. They were inside the light industrial unit on the Rochdale trading estate, which Olympus had rented. Danny got out and walked to the passenger window.

"Another two bodies to add to *the missing*, Phoenix," he said.

"Two?" queried Phoenix.

"Shabir Amin pimped out a school kid to a bloke in Bury. After he left the restaurant, I followed him to see what he got up to on a weekday afternoon. Here's a photograph of the client to whom she was delivered. Perhaps your people can identify him? He's carrying no papers."

"Did he not want to tell you his name?" asked Rusty.

"To be honest, he wasn't in the mood to talk after a belt from the taser."

"Send the photograph to my phone, Danny," said Phoenix. "I'll get Giles to start the hunt for him. If he's illegal, nobody will miss him. We can't risk letting him tell the others in the gang that someone is cleaning the streets of vermin."

"Will do," said Danny, "coming through now."

"Got it," replied Phoenix, "and... it's on its way to the ice-house."

"What did you do with the girl?" asked Phoenix.

"A team stationed near the supermarket is taking her home. They won't be too long arriving. She's no innocent, I'm afraid. The poor beggar is a drug addict. She was more interested in the money she didn't receive than what happened to Amin and the other bloke."

The Olympus agents sat in silence for a minute. They could ensure that criminals paid for their crimes and bring closure to many victims. But, unfortunately, they couldn't cure society's ills.

"Did you say six o'clock the supermarket worker gets picked up?" asked Rusty, eager to break the sombre mood.

"Give or take," replied Danny. "They should be here by half-past six at the latest."

Rusty looked at his watch. That was over two hours away.

"Any chance of a coffee and a sandwich? We've got to wait for a while."

While they waited for the van to return from Elton, they transferred Rafiq to Danny's van. They made sure the three missing men were tucked up safe and sound and then locked the unit. The four agents sat in Phoenix's van.

"A bacon roll's better than a sandwich," said Rusty.

"Black pudding is a favourite up here," said Danny's mate.

"You can't beat a bacon roll," said Phoenix. Nobody wanted to argue with the boss.

"Here they come," said Danny Tipper. The dark blue van stopped next to them. He jumped out and told the driver to follow them. They drove to a roadside café on Rochdale road out of Bury. Ten minutes later, the six agents stared at steaming mugs of coffee and a tray filled with rolls.

"Take your pick, lads," said Danny, "bacon, sausage, cheese, or ham."

"Are you sure there's enough here?" Rusty asked, knowing there was enough for twelve hungry labourers.

"Tuck in," said Phoenix. "You never know when we'll get the chance to eat again."

When they returned to the trading estate, full to bursting, it was just after six

At the supermarket in George Street, Abdul Sajid, the forty-one-year-old frozen food shelf-stacker, had finished for the day. He walked towards his beaten-up old Nissan at the far end of the car park. It had no tax or insurance, so he hid it from prying eyes.

Sajid couldn't see his vehicle for a while. There was a black van with tinted windows parked next to it. It made it impossible to see anyone in it. It had been a long afternoon, and as he reached the driver's door of his car, he yawned and stretched. Once he got home, he would sleep for a few hours until he met his friends.

The van's side door slid open, and Abdul Sajid got dragged into the back. He tried to cry out, but the hand over his mouth and nose held a cloth that smelt odd. So odd. Perhaps he could have that sleep now, he thought. The van door slid shut, and the driver pulled away from the parking spot. A third target was secured.

The driver called his team leader.

"All is safely gathered in," Danny Tipper confirmed to Phoenix.

"When they turn up, you can put Sajid in with the rest," said Phoenix. "We'll move on to Rotherham, leaving you to do the necessary and dispose of the bodies."

"Understood, Phoenix," said Danny. "Any news from Larcombe yet on the new face?"

"The ice-house believes he's Hamid Khan, thirty-seven years old," said Phoenix. "He's been missing for two years, as far as immigration is concerned. He arrived here in 2012, and they stopped him at the port of Felixstowe. They caught him getting out of a container with seventeen other men. At first, Khan appealed against deportation because he had strong connections and family in the UK. Then, when that didn't wash, he claimed asylum. Khan reckoned his life was in danger if he returned to his homeland. While he waited for a decision on that appeal, he lived with a cousin in King's Lynn. Khan didn't turn up at the immigration centre for his fortnightly appointment. He must have found stronger family links in the north. The authorities have been hunting for him ever since."

"Well, they can stop searching now," said Rusty. "Remind me, what did this guy Sajid do that warranted us grabbing him?"

"He's been grooming girls for over five years," said Danny Tipper. "He passed his victims among the male members of his family and the wider community. Kids often wander into the supermarkets to keep warm, shoplift, and buy ice creams in the summer. That was when Sajid befriended them. Cherry Staines was sixteen when she was stabbed to death in 2011 and buried in a shallow grave by her eighteen-year-old boyfriend, Nadim Sajid. Cherry had given birth to a son at fourteen by an unknown, older married man. That man was Abdul Sajid, Nadim's uncle."

"The men's families were unaware of the relationships and the child's existence," Phoenix added. "Cherry Staines had elected to speak to Abdul and Nadim's relatives. Unfortunately, the following week the boyfriend murdered her. Police suspected his uncle helped his nephew dispose of the body. They questioned both men, but Nadim Khan skipped bail and escaped to the Irish Republic by ferry. From there, he disappeared to mainland Europe."

"Abdul Sadiq never faced trial," said Danny, "Cherry Staines had a low IQ and had been the target of localised grooming from the age of twelve. Officials who dealt with her from the age of eleven described her as out of control three months after her twelfth birthday."

"Another case of missed opportunities and sweeping the problem under the carpet then," said Rusty.

"If Cherry had been a high-achieving student from a rich family, those responsible for her death would have faced a relentless search," said Danny. "Instead, the whole sorry business was just a blip on the headlines up here. Nobody cared enough about the poor kid to keep hunting for the answers."

The conversation died once again. The agents sat inside for several minutes with their thoughts on the tragedy. Then, finally, Danny Tipper broke the silence.

"You can get off to Rotherham, Phoenix," he said, "we've got things covered here. Are you meeting your next contact, Gus Dickerson, tonight?"

"No, I told Gus we'd meet tomorrow at lunchtime," said Phoenix. "Rusty and I will stay overnight in the Olympus safe house in Sheffield. We've got more dodgy characters to trace in the region, and I don't expect to get every one of them in one day."

"Good hunting, Phoenix," said Danny.

"We've done the groundwork, Danny. So, there should be no worries."

Phoenix and Rusty left the trading estate and drove off to join the M62. Forty-five minutes later, they headed south towards Barnsley on the M1. Within the hour, they would arrive at the safe house. Phoenix planned a whole night's sleep before meeting the Sheffield team leader tomorrow.

Phase one of *the missing* operation was complete.

In East Anglia, Artem Klimenko, the Ukrainian gangster, relaxed after another day dealing with finding work for the migrant workers he controlled. His office was in Wisbech, a once-wealthy river port whose architecture suggested a relocated slice of Holland. The town's streets had traditional English shops among an expanding share owned by people from abroad.

Most of Wisbech's ten thousand migrant workers travelled from eastern Europe with dreams of earning a better living. Instead, many soon found themselves housed in squalid conditions, exploited by corrupt gangmasters. Often, they didn't know who they lived with or the name of the person who collected the rent. The signs weren't hard to spot—the unease when questioned, appearing confused or unwilling to reveal information. Failure to provide a passport or payslips, and refusal to and over employment details, are key indicators of exploitation.

These workers in and around this corner of Cambridgeshire were among the three hundred thousand incomers to East Anglia over the past two decades. Sometimes they pick broccoli, sometimes they wrap flowers to go on sale at petrol stations, and sometimes they pack fruit for supermarkets. The majority living in the Wisbech area came here from Lithuania.

Numerous food processing factories and acres of farmland around Wisbech made it a magnet for migrant agricultural workers. The massive influx of eastern European workers dramatically changed the profile of the small town. Its population now stood at around thirty thousand, of whom a third were incomers. This migrant workforce had been what drew Klimenko here four years ago. Now thirty-three years old, he had since facilitated the smuggling of hundreds of illegal immigrants to the UK.

The Ukrainian gangmaster was a ruthless thug with one hundred accomplices across East Anglia. His office In Wisbech purported to operate a recruitment agency supplying workers to the agricultural and food sectors. To many, it appeared legitimate. However, the reality was far more sinister.

If you dug deeper, clear evidence existed of the exploitation of migrants on a large scale. The process began in eastern Europe, where Klimenko charged six hundred pounds to bring a worker to the UK, promising a good life and rich rewards.

Migrants got dropped off at night outside the town and moved to an HMO — a house of multiple occupancies that was not only overcrowded but almost uninhabitable. The places bore the signs of being occupied by dozens of migrant workers. Mould on the walls, broken washing machines and scrapped furniture in the garden — a ramshackle network of electrical wiring winding through every building.

Upon arrival, the migrants were soon pushed into debt by Klimenko's agents to increase their control. They were immediately charged one month's rent in advance. Their passports were confiscated and often used to commit identity fraud. If they worked, then they got paid less than the minimum wage. Illegal deductions taken from their pay kept them reliant on the gangmaster.

In the houses Klimenko controlled, each tenant paid fifty pounds weekly rent. That sum enabled him to collect over two thousand pounds monthly from homes in deplorable condition. Those same properties cost him six hundred pounds monthly to rent from their owner. Workers moved between properties, adding to their sense of insecurity. He controlled his accomplices with an iron fist. They adopted the same policy when dealing with migrants.

In several of the HMOs he operated, a member of Klimenko's gang would occupy one room. They acted as the resident alpha male, collected the rent, and usually spoke better English than everyone else. They were the spokesperson if authority came knocking. Initially, the local police turned to them for translation services in neighbourhood disputes. In time, they realised they only heard what Klimenko's thug wanted them to hear.

Soon after Artem Klimenko arrived in the UK, Hugo Hanigan and the Grid learned of his criminal operations. The Ukrainian demonstrated the attributes the Grid fostered. His activity made a mountain of cash that needed laundering. It wasn't long before they invited Klimenko to join the network of organised criminal gangs that Hanigan headed.

The gangmaster was always outspoken. In early July,

when Hanigan called the Grid leaders to a clandestine meeting in Surrey, he had challenged the maniac banker on several matters. He had found an ally in Gregor McGrath, the Glasgow gangster. An experienced criminal who was both respected and feared. Since that meeting and its explosive conclusion, McGrath had needed his wits and talented lawyers to keep him from prison.

Shabbir Shah, the Cardiff criminal, had gone to ground over the past month. Either he had returned to his home country, or he, too, kept his distance from the authorities. Klimenko knew of the power struggle in boroughs across London. The Mighty Quinn died in a brutal attack only two weeks after he had met him for the first time at the hotel. Someone had put the squeeze on the Grid. That Surrey conference had raised many questions. Who had been responsible for the killings around the country over the past few months? Was it a simple matter of inter-gang rivalry, as Hanigan had said? If so, why was there no evidence of a threat to his operations? Clearly, someone envied the profits he amassed for the Grid's coffers.

Because he disliked Hanigan, Artem wasn't in the habit of contacting him. Instead, notifications arrived by email or text when the Grid's leaders needed a warning or a reminder. Maybe Hanigan informed them of a fresh burst of activity by agencies such as HMRC, Border Force, or the police; or nudged them to find methods to increase the flow of funds to the Glencairn Bank.

The messages were coded, of course, in case they fell into the wrong hands. Artem thought Hanigan often behaved childishly. It served the Ukrainian's purpose to use the Grid's bank to cleanse his ill-gotten gains, but if he could operate without it, he would gladly do so.

Hanigan hadn't contacted him for ten days, but Artem

Klimenko wasn't concerned. Instead, he was curious about the rumours that the Mighty Quinn's territory had merged with that controlled by Colleen O'Riordan. A woman, indeed. What was the world coming to; her late husband had been a proper villain. Artem would have loved to have met him.

The outer door opened; one of his men must have dropped by with a problem. Artem looked at his Rolex watch. It was almost seven o'clock. He wondered what niggling problem it could be this time. The sooner he dealt with it, the sooner he could drive out to his favourite restaurant. Artem dragged open the bottom drawer of his desk. He took out two glasses and a bottle of vodka; work was over for the day.

As he poured measures into the glasses, he looked at a stranger's face.

"The office is closed," he said, "we re-open at ten o'clock in the morning."

"Now, Klimenko, that's no way to greet a colleague."

"A colleague?" asked Artem, getting up from his chair. If he needed to throw this young upstart out, he wanted to be on his toes, poised and ready to spring into action.

His visitor sat on a chair by the office door. He seemed unmoved by Artem's agitation.

"You and I will go for a drive in the country in a few moments. My men are arranging transport, so why don't you relax while we wait?"

"Who are you?" demanded Artem. His eyes darted from the young man to his leather jacket hanging on the back of the interior door to his PA's office. He could get the gun from the inside pocket if he reached it.

"You'd never make it," the young man warned.

Klimenko lunged across the office towards the jacket.

He placed his left hand on the coat against the wooden door and tried to grab the pistol. He heard a swish as something passed his head. Klimenko screamed as the thin-bladed stiletto pinned his hand to the door.

"I did warn you," said Tyrone O'Riordan, covering the distance between them in a flash. He held a second blade across the throat of the stricken Ukrainian. "Our ride has just arrived."

The door opened, and two men entered.

Tyrone retrieved the stiletto from the back of the gangmaster's hand.

"Get him outside into the vehicle. He won't need a jacket. We're not going far. Find a towel or something. Try the washroom. I don't want him bleeding over the seats."

Artem Klimenko was frogmarched outside and bundled into the back of a people carrier. On either side of him sat the two giants. Tyrone O'Riordan sat in the passenger seat, nodded to the driver to get moving, and then half-turned to talk with their captive.

"In case you haven't worked out who I am yet, and how you got into this predicament, maybe I should enlighten you?"

"Whoever you are, you don't know who you're messing with," Klimenko snarled.

"I know exactly who you are and what you have done," said Tyrone. "The head of your organisation has tired of your constant criticism of how he controls the Grid."

"Hanigan is a madman," said Artem, "he thinks none of us should criticise how he handles matters. Yet dozens of our people have died because of his decisions. So those of us who speak up must get heard."

"I visited Surrey last month. I overheard you say though you lived in the Fens, you still had your finger on the pulse of what happened across the country. How foolish. Hugo Hanigan died over a week ago. The Grid is now under new management. You know nothing."

"Who are you?" Artem asked once more. "How could you have been at that meeting? You are not a senior Grid leader. You are just a boy."

"There are many ways to listen in to conversations, Klimenko. Who do you think disposed of Hanigan's security team that night? Who rid the world of Michael Terrence Quinn? You have had enough clues to my identity. My late father might have excused how you treat female migrant workers you smuggle into the country, but my mother is not forgiving. That's why we're replacing you."

"You are the O'Riordan woman's son," said Artem.

"That I am," Tyrone replied. "Tyrone O'Riordan, at your service. My mother has taken control of the network of organised crime gangs scattered across the country. I carry out specific duties for her, such as this one. The role my father had me trained for gave me the skills to run the Glencairn Bank on her behalf."

"Good luck convincing the other leaders that letting a woman take over is acceptable."

"That remark explains this little trip," tutted Tyrone. "My mother hates men who abuse women. We found evidence implicating you among Hanigan's papers after I killed him. He kept incriminating snippets on every crime lord in the network if he needed a lever to use in negotiations. So when Colleen O'Riordan learned you forced female workers into sham marriages and made them sell a kidney to settle imaginary debts, it sealed your fate."

The people carrier halted in the gateway to a large field. In the distance, Artem could hear a heavy farm vehicle.

"Time to meet the grim reaper, Klimenko," said Tyrone.

The men dragged Artem Klimenko from the people carrier. Even though his main interest in East Anglia was the money he could make, he understood the harvest was well underway.

The men soon returned to the vehicle. The roar of the combine harvester drowned the screams of the Ukrainian gangmaster as it covered the spot where he lay, pinned to the ground by his arms and legs. As the sound of the farm vehicle receded, silence reigned over this small corner of East Anglia.

Tyrone made the call to his mother.

"All is safely gathered in," he said.

"How did Klimenko take the news of Hugo's death and the new regime in charge of the Grid?" she asked.

"He was more cut up about it than I imagined," replied Tyrone.

Chapter Five

Thursday, 4th September 2014

Phoenix and Rusty waited for Gus Dickerson and his team to arrive in the Sheffield safe house. The two friends had checked what was lacking in the kitchen when they came last night. A visit to the supermarket before it closed had filled in the gaps. Unfortunately, there was no time for fine dining. They had work to do, so the nearest takeaway was the next stop to pick up their evening meal.

Later in the evening, Phoenix had read through the Rotherham report files for the umpteenth time while Rusty watched a DVD.

"What is that?" Phoenix had asked.

"Filth," Rusty had replied.

Phoenix had seemed unimpressed with what he thought was a comment rather than the title, but Rusty didn't enlighten him further. It made a change for a safe house to have a copy of a recent film release. It had been a long day.

He wanted to unwind—a story about a corrupt cop on more drugs than criminals was an excellent way to relax.

This morning they had woken up, showered and dressed, eaten a good breakfast prepared by Rusty, and it was still a few minutes before eight o'clock.

"I'll call Athena first to catch her before she leaves Geoffrey's house. Then, I'll see where Giles and Artemis reached, tracking the two bombers. Once I know that we'll go through our schedule today to ensure we've covered everything. What do you reckon we should do for lunch?"

"You're very domesticated this morning, Phoenix. That's a side of you. I don't see that often."

"Gus Dickerson arrives at noon. I think he has the nous not to turn up with a dozen vans, but we are hunting seven targets across South Yorkshire. It would be cosy if we have a dozen of us tucked up in this three-bedroomed semi-detached house."

"Tricky," said Rusty. "We don't have enough food in the freezer to feed that many. Visiting a local eatery or ordering large quantities of takeaways raises problems. The good citizens of Sheffield might question whether this house is hiding a secret. Why not ring Gus and tell them to bring sandwiches?"

Phoenix gave his friend a stare.

"I'm calling Athena," he replied, "you can contact Gus. Tell him to limit the number he brings to four at the most. One vehicle only. We'll finish at two o'clock. After that, they can grab a late lunch."

"What about us?" asked Rusty.

"We got up early. I'll make our lunch for half-past eleven. I'm not going to a meeting hungry."

Phoenix rang his wife. Athena picked up on the second ring.

"Morning, darling. How are things?" he asked.

"Daddy's putting on a brave face. I think he'll be okay until the weekend. Perhaps I can travel up on Saturday and stay over until Sunday. Tell me what happened in Rochdale. Did everything go to plan?"

"Need you ask?" replied Phoenix, "we're in Sheffield now. Later today, we will start on the next stage of the mission. I'll be home by tomorrow evening. I'll see you then, look, I've just had a thought. Why don't you tell Geoffrey to pack a bag and get him to travel with you this morning? We can take care of him better at Larcombe."

"Daddy's an obstinate old devil," said Athena. "He wants me to believe he's strong and independent. But, I'll try, it would put my mind at rest, and he will have Hope to take his mind off other matters."

"I don't suppose you've heard when your mother's body will be released?"

"No, it's far too early. I doubt if we'll hear until the middle of next week. Daddy and I made a start on the funeral arrangements last night. If I spirit him away to Larcombe, we can finalise things. Then, once the actual date is known, maybe we could both return here and stay over until after the funeral?"

"I can't see that being a problem," said Phoenix. "One issue we might have is ensuring he keeps his nose out of Olympus' business while he's staying with us. So when you get back today, have a quiet word with Giles. He might persuade Maria Elena to be extra-vigilant and shepherd him away from sensitive areas with offers of time with his granddaughter."

"Leave that with me, Phoenix. Good hunting. I'll see you when you get home tomorrow. Stay safe."

Phoenix ended the call and rang Giles Burke.

"Good morning, Phoenix," said the surveillance expert. "I trust everything is still on schedule?"

"Everything is going like clockwork, Giles. What news do you have for me on Harrack and Mansouri?"

"They followed a circuitous route that took them around an hour's walk to reach Royal Victoria station. Then they used a train and the Tube to return to the apartment in Slough. We tracked them via CCTV for as much as we could. They travelled separately throughout the journey. We spotted no mobile phone usage on any camera footage, nor did a third-party meeting occur. They might have made the outward journey using the same route."

"What about the IED?" asked Phoenix.

"Its construction has been identified. Our hacker captured files that enabled us to prepare a detailed analysis for you to look at tomorrow. Everything's there, the makeup and every shred of evidence the emergency teams gathered on site. He closed every back door he accessed. So the authorities won't know he's been inside their systems having a poke around."

"It's frightening, isn't it?" said Phoenix, "nothing is safe these days. What's the world coming to; I look forward to reading it tomorrow. What have Harrack and Mansouri been up to since they got home?"

"They've not emerged from the apartment since they made it back. We have agents on twenty-four-hour surveillance. If they step outside their door, we'll know. Have you decided on a course of action?"

"These two aren't working alone," said Phoenix. "Have we got eyes and ears inside the apartment yet?"

"I discussed this with Henry Case last night," said Giles. "His opinion was that if these are experienced operatives, getting access to install cameras and listening devices would be impossible without alerting them. We have a tap on the landline, but they're too fly to use it. So instead, they'll use burner phones to contact other cell members."

"I'll think about what I might do next," said Phoenix. "Rusty and I will be busy for the next thirty-six hours. I might need to catch up with you and Artemis tomorrow evening after this show ends."

"No worries, Phoenix," said Giles, "oh, Artemis said to send her love to Rusty. He hasn't called since he left yesterday. Nothing changes."

"Nothing happened that we hadn't planned for," shrugged Phoenix. "Why worry the girl?"

Giles continued with his shift in the ice-house. Phoenix checked with Rusty that Gus Dickerson travelled light; he relayed Giles's message.

"I'll be in hot water when we get home tomorrow," muttered Rusty.

"Forget that for now. Let's get stuck into these reports. Gus and the lads will be here before we know it."

The two agents focused on the seven men they added to *the missing* list. Their ages ranged between twenty and fifty-five. Those men in prison were the tip of the iceberg. Unfortunately, Olympus could only do so much. They didn't have the workforce to clean the streets of every criminal out there.

As he read page after page compiled by Minos and Alastor from data gathered by the media and their investigative agencies, Phoenix felt his heart grow heavy. Hundreds of cases were known to the authorities before the independent inquiry report they received last week. Hundreds of cases got reported as the weeks passed. Victims still felt let down by the police and the council. The grooming continued in every area of South Yorkshire, and survivors reported activity levels rising, not falling. The gangs were aware people might be watching them now, so they became clever at hiding their tracks. Often, if someone reported something they believed would warrant the authorities' attention, it was not given the priority it deserved. The social care services treated it as something of a nuisance. How many would slip through the net?

"These comments stink of a cover-up," muttered Phoenix.

"Exactly what I thought when I read through this on Tuesday afternoon in the orangery," Rusty agreed,

"You're learning," said Phoenix. "Erebus would be proud."

"You were his favourite. Erebus only allowed me in under sufferance."

Phoenix continued to read. Why wouldn't you want a support group? Not only around this area but across the country. At least the one they had tried to tackle the problem. But, for whatever reason, it disbanded, and the authorities have resisted attempts to replace it.

"The police use the right buzzwords about protecting children and tackling child exploitation, but it's just words," said Rusty, looking up from his file. "Why turn up mob-handed to a potential witness's home address to get a statement? It signals to everyone within several miles radius that a young girl had reported instances of abuse. Imagine walking to school the next day. That's bound to deter victims that haven't come forward so far from reporting what they suffered."

"While we spent last weekend up here, Athena and I consulted Zeus," said Phoenix. "The media has consistently mentioned Pakistani men preying on young white girls. But that isn't the full picture. Athena was concerned that

Olympus acted against those that attacked and exploited children within their community. Zeus supported her view and agreed that British Asian girls were unlikely to report their abuse due to a fear of dishonour, scorn and retribution."

"Which name am I looking for here?" asked Rusty.

"Salim Qureshi, the oldest of the seven men we are targeting. He's a fifty-five-year-old shop owner from Brinsworth. Qureshi befriended young girls who came into his shop on the way home from school. Some were the children of his brothers and his cousins. He blackmailed the girls into having sex with men in an apartment above the shop. They were forced at knife-point to perform sexual acts. Dozens of men visited the apartment in the evenings. Fifteen men had gang-raped one victim before she could leave; her attackers included a father and son. He was a boy she knew — a fellow student at her school. The abuse was recorded on mobile phones by several of the men. Qureshi threatened to send the evidence to the girl's family if she dared to go to the police."

"That's enough," said Rusty, "he's going to the top of the list. Can we pick up that swine, please?"

"You've read the file, Rusty. When Gus arrives, we share the targets between the teams. One target each, taken within a specific timeframe. We locate them today, watch them tomorrow morning, and then coordinate our direct action, so seven men go missing within seven minutes. Friday prayers are an important time for Muslims. Some men attend the mosque every day. Others never do, but the window in which we strike will be the same."

"What is the significance of the number seven?" asked Rusty. "I never read that in the files anywhere, did I?"

"No, but in Islam, Hell has seven gates and seven

levels," said Phoenix. "Sinners go to different levels depending on the severity of their sins. The seventh level feels appropriate for each of these predators. Zeus thought it would send a message that would resonate with the imams of the region's mosques. The authorities have sacrificed many young women on the altar of political correctness. We can't depend on them getting to the heart of the problem. Most of the Muslim population is peace-loving and honest. The best way to solve the problem may be to foster a change from within."

"Time has gone on, as you predicted," said Rusty, "we had better get lunch now. Our visitors will knock on the door before we know it."

"Visitors," exclaimed Phoenix, "damn it, I'd better call Giles before I do anything else. Open a can of beans and put it on the toast. We'll have to make do and mend."

"I didn't expect high cuisine," muttered Rusty. "But I hoped you would dish up something more exciting than beans on toast."

Rusty plodded off to the kitchen. Phoenix was already talking to Giles Burke.

"Any movement from inside the apartment, Giles?" he asked.

"No change since you rang three hours ago, Phoenix," replied Giles.

"Odd they stayed inside for three whole days. Have they had any visitors?"

"Let me check the logs sent through by our surveillance teams. A paramedic visited the floor the apartment was on yesterday, around noon. As I told you earlier, we haven't had agents inside the building, so we can't confirm who has called them. The log report states that an ambulance pulled up outside the building thirty minutes after the paramedic arrived. The two-person crew went up in the lift. Ten minutes later, a patient came out on a trolley, and the crew carried them inside the ambulance. A female accompanied the paramedics, presumably, a relative of the patient. She wore a burka, covering her head and body from top to toe.

"Nuts," said Phoenix, "they've gone. The bombers must have spotted our teams. Get into that apartment. We'll find they've cleaned out everything that might have provided clues."

"Sorry, Phoenix," said Giles, "there was no evidence of a female living in the apartment."

"There was no female. Mansouri made himself ill enough to warrant a hospital check-up, and Harrack is the right height and shape to pass himself off as a woman. The outfit wards off suspicion. It's a common sight on the streets of major towns and cities. If the so-called female wasn't talkative, the ambulance guys have attended enough awareness courses to accept the silence as normal."

"How would they have dealt with the situation when they reached the Accident and Emergency Hospital?" asked Giles.

"I'll leave you to find that out, Giles," said Phoenix. "I suggest you and Artemis start the search for Mansouri and Harrack. A starting point will be whichever hospital is the closest to that apartment building."

Phoenix ended the call.

"Lunch is ready," Rusty called out from the kitchen, "was that bad news from Larcombe?"

"Afraid so, our two bombers were too cute for the teams watching them. Giles still has to confirm it, but I reckon they've moved on to their next target."

The two agents tucked into their snacks.

Rusty was reminded of his teenage years when he always

fed himself because his mother was incapacitated. When his father got drunk, he knocked her about after coming home from a lunchtime session at the pub. When Rusty got home from school, his mother would be in bed, nursing her wounds. So Rusty got something on toast to avoid his father's anger and made himself scarce in the neighbourhood.

Phoenix thought of Hope enjoying a bowlful of beans with toast soldiers to dip into the juice. Ninety per cent of it ended on her chubby cheeks but watching her gave him and Athena great pleasure.

Rusty was washing up when the doorbell rang. Phoenix checked the peephole. Four burly men stood on the doorstep. Everything in their demeanour screamed ex-military. He opened the door.

"Come on in, Gus, and welcome. Follow me through to the lounge. Meet Rusty, by the way."

"Gus Dickerson, it's been a long time," said Rusty. He stood by the kitchen door with a tea towel and a fistful of knives and forks.

"You never mentioned you knew Gus," said Phoenix, taken by surprise.

"You never asked," said Rusty, turning away and returning to the kitchen.

The new arrivals found places to sit, and Phoenix handed out the schedules he had prepared for the next mission. The three agents who had accompanied Gus Dickerson didn't look concerned, but Phoenix sensed a tension in the room.

Rusty finished his kitchen duties and sat beside him.

"We thought it best we reduced the numbers for this meeting," said Phoenix.

"That's fair enough," Dickerson said after flicking

through his copy. "If you take us through the critical points in these schedules, we'll link up with the others later this afternoon and brief them. The concept appears sound judging by what I've read."

"You might want to do more than glance at the details," muttered Rusty, "careless mistakes cost lives."

Phoenix raised a hand as Dickerson leapt out of his chair.

"Enough," he said. "Remember where you are and who you represent. Olympus has no time for petty squabbles between its agents. Whatever the issue is, you need to park it, and we will go ahead with this mission as planned. We can't have anyone on the team who isn't giving things their total concentration."

Dickerson stepped back and sat down.

The tension in the room was palpable. Phoenix ignored it. He was focused and expected everyone else to follow his lead.

"You've had a few minutes to check the schedules," he said, "are there any questions?"

"We'll get moving, boss," said Dickerson. "The start time for discovering the whereabouts of these jokers is four o'clock. Each of the six vehicles will check in with you at their appointed observation spot. We'll keep in radio contact throughout. I'll order my guys to stop once their target is in bed for the night."

"We could have chosen many more targets," said Phoenix, "but these were among the ringleaders and worst offenders. Besides, the men selected are creatures of habit. Locating them should be straightforward, and tomorrow the pattern of activity they follow will mirror what I've outlined in the schedules. Somebody might go off-piste, but choosing the afternoon window to grab them reduces the likelihood they will be hard to snatch."

Dickerson and his men left the safe house.

"What do you want to do before we drive to our observation point?" asked Rusty.

"Do you need to ask? I want the full story on you and Gus Dickerson. You were both one step from being sent packing."

"Sorry, Phoenix," sighed Rusty, "it goes way back. We were both SAS sergeants. There's only a matter of months between us in age and length of service. I was a fiery beggar in those days. As you know, a difference of opinion with a senior officer led to the corps and me parting company. I had my arguments with plenty of others over the years."

"You don't suffer fools gladly," said Phoenix. "It's what I liked about you from the moment we met."

"At the end of 2004, the Iraq War was in full swing. Operation Phantom Fury was a joint American, Iraqi, and British offensive. Gus and I were involved. The fiercest point in the conflict centred on Fallujah. The Black Watch was to help American and Iraqi forces with the encirclement of Fallujah. Their First Battalion was eight hundred and fifty strong and itching to fight. D Squadron of the SAS prepared to take part in the operation as part of Task Force Black, but Blair was nervous about the possible scale of casualties. They prevented us from taking any part in the ground battle."

"I watched this unfold while I was in The Gambia," said Phoenix. "I wasn't that interested. I only thought of returning to the UK to avenge my daughter's death. But, the way I read the situation, Blair conned the British public into that controversial military action. Over the next decade, it cost hundreds of young men and women their lives."

"Politicians aren't among my favourite people," said Rusty. "To a man, we were pissed off when we learned that what we trained for, to fight the enemy, was being denied us. The SAS are often the first in and last to leave in a theatre of war."

"What was Task Force Black?" Phoenix asked.

"We worked jointly with Delta Force in Black Ops against Al Qaeda and other insurgents earlier in the year. There were a hundred and fifty of us. We cleared over three thousand insurgents off the streets, with several hundred killed. Six men died, and thirty injured in the Operation. During a six-month tour of duty, the SAS carried out one hundred and seventy-five combat missions. The Task Force utilised our capabilities in reconnaissance and surveillance to watch suspects and gather intelligence for the coalition intelligence services. They named our operational process 'find-fix-finish'. Not far removed from the tasks we're carrying out here in Rotherham. We 'find' the insurgent, 'fix' a time and place where we take them, and 'finish' with a raid to take the suspect out."

"Rotherham is nothing like Fallujah, Rusty," said Phoenix.

"There's still time," said Rusty.

"Before you withdrew, what happened to cause this ill feeling between you and Dickerson?"

"We were at the sharp end, as usual, edging our way forward, clearing buildings and roads for the troops to move into the outskirts of the town. The opposition had loads of time to prepare for the attack. Iraqi insurgents and foreign mujahideen built strong defences and tunnels, trenches, and spider holes. They hid a wide variety of IEDs in the fortifications and stacked propane bottles, drums of gasoline, and ammunition in the interiors of darkened homes. Everything was wired to a remote trigger to set off when troops entered the building. They booby-trapped buildings and vehicles and wired grenades to doors and windows."

"It must have been painstaking progress?"

"I had been with a Delta Force crew that morning, helping to de-activate IEDs. Those boys were heroes. They knew if they got spotted, the bomb would be triggered remotely. The roadway ahead cleared, and we fell back. Gus Dickerson was responsible for clearing the houses on the left of the street or what remained. Dickerson gave us a 'thumbs-up'. My team leader called a light-armoured reconnaissance vehicle forward, and half a dozen young Marines trotted along at the rear. The vehicle attracted the snipers on the high buildings up ahead and came under fire. Because we believed they could take shelter inside, they hugged the walls of the houses and darted into doorways. Two Marines stepped over the threshold of a shell-damaged house and triggered a device. They never stood a chance."

"You blamed Gus Dickerson?" Phoenix asked.

"You heard what he's like just now," said Rusty, "he's slap-dash. Gus scanned through your schedules and reckoned everything would be fine. He's not a great one for detail. When we returned to base, our superiors asked questions, but Gus had all the answers. He reckoned he wasn't in that house. Whoever should have dealt with what was inside, whether one of our men or a Delta Force guy, must have missed it. The Coalition forces already had strained relations between them. Our government wanted us out of the real fire-fight, and flak flew over the US forces' treatment of prisoners. We were on our way home before the matter got further scrutiny. Gus and I never served together on the same missions after that. Not by choice. It's just the way the cards fell. He came out when I did, although I don't think he had to hit anyone. I didn't know he'd joined Olympus until Danny Tipper mentioned his name."

"Forewarned is forearmed, Rusty," said Phoenix, "I know you, and I've trusted you with my life on several occasions. If Dickerson becomes a potential risk to the complete success of this mission by cutting corners or not following my schedule to the letter, he'll leave. You know what they say about one bad apple. We need to watch each of these agents closely to see they remain focused one hundred per cent."

"Don't bite my head off, Phoenix," said Rusty. "But, if there's a weakness in your plans, they rely on each of the seven teams operating individually in different areas of Rotherham and the surrounding districts. Although we'll be in radio contact at four o'clock this afternoon, there's no guarantee we'll see the others for twenty-four hours."

"All the more reason to keep the radio contact open and ask the right questions," said Phoenix. "I'll keep the agents on a tight leash. So don't you fret."

Phoenix's mobile rang as they prepared to leave the safe house to drive to their start point. The Judas Priest ring tone alerted him that this wasn't the only problem they had to solve.

"Giles? What have you got?" he asked.

"You were right, Phoenix. The flat was empty. Every surface was wiped clean; clothes were washed. They even left a load in the washing machine. They must have set it going before they left. A strong smell of bleach everywhere. No laptops, phones, or weaponry of any kind."

"And what did you discover at the A&E department?"

"The crew were traced. Trolleys were stacked in the

corridors as usual. The crew had to hang around for twenty minutes before unloading the patient. The wife was left with her husband while they went to fetch cups of coffee. They still had a wait before they could hand over to A&E staff. When they returned, the couple had fled."

"OK, start with the CCTV at the hospital. Can we pick them up leaving? Did the female take a change of clothing in the guise of overnight things for her so-called husband?"

"Artemis has found an image of two burka-clad women in the foyer at the right time. She's searching for them on the Underground, the main-line terminus platforms, and the London airports. Nothing positive so far."

"Two women we can't identify as Mansouri and Harrack because of the disguises, terrific."

"We'll keep searching," said Giles. "You need to concentrate on the mission at hand. Leave us to salvage something from this mess. I'll call you at the safe house at eight tomorrow morning. Oh, before you ring off, Athena and her father arrived back just after lunch. I gather he took some persuading. I thought you wanted to know."

"Thanks, Giles. Rusty and I are heading out now. I'll talk to Athena tonight if we return home in time. I look forward to hearing from you in the morning."

Ten minutes later, Rusty drove them to Masbrough, a suburb half a mile west of the town centre. Phoenix took in the late afternoon view. There was a mosque and a sizeable football ground that stood out. Nothing else marked the area out as exceptional.

"Which lucky ticket did we draw, Phoenix?" asked Rusty.

"Osman Hassan, a thirty-five-year-old van driver. He works for a family-run firm that delivers Asian foods and spices to restaurants across the North of England."

"What was his role in the affair?"

"Hassan was a frequent visitor to Qureshi's evening parties. Hassan cherry-picked the most vulnerable, hooked them on drugs, and took them in his van when he made deliveries. Girls travelled to Bradford, Liverpool, Manchester, and even as far south as Birmingham. Hassan dropped the girls at various residential addresses, where they stayed until he returned later to collect them. You can imagine what happened."

"Is he driving today?" asked Rusty.

"Hassan's returning from Leeds and Bradford today. He should turn into this road at a quarter to six. We'll park here and keep watch. If he leaves home, we follow. If he stays indoors and goes to bed after Question Time, we can drive back to the safe house and pick up fish and chips on the way."

"What if he doesn't drive straight home?" asked Rusty.

"Creatures of habit, Rusty, be patient. He'll be here."

At five forty-six, Osman Hassan drove past the Olympus van, parked his van half on, half off the grass verge and went inside his house; lights out at ten forty-five.

"Not a lover of 'Question Time' then," said Rusty, "can I have mushy peas with my fish and chips?"

Chapter Six

Friday, 5th September 2014

Phoenix rose early. If everything went to plan today, he would be home by nightfall. When he and Rusty returned here last night, he felt it too late to call Athena. He knew Hope was an early bird. His wife and daughter were likely to have shared quality time already this morning. No matter how early it was and whether Athena enjoyed it as much as he did in similar circumstances or not.

"Good morning," said Athena. Phoenix could hear the sleepiness in her voice; sleep deprivation was a torture technique Henry Case utilised. Hope could play that game better than any grown-up.

"We got home last night," said Phoenix, "sorry for not calling."

"I understand," said Athena, "we didn't go to bed late. Daddy found the journey tiring, and everyone showered him with sympathy once we arrived. It was genuine and well-intentioned, but it got too much for him. So I'm letting him lie in this morning. I hope a good night's sleep will do him a power of good."

"Good to hear Giles say you persuaded him to travel to Bath with you. We can occupy his mind far better at Larcombe. That must be preferable to leaving him alone with his thoughts in Belgravia."

"Small steps, every day," said Athena. "How have the missions gone?"

"Phase One passed off without a hitch. Danny Tipper removed the three targets, plus an illegal immigrant guilty of a serious sexual assault on a minor. The guy had been missing from immigration for some time. They can stop looking now; nobody will find either of them. Our three original targets will be on a Missing Person list for a long time."

"Good, and where are you with Phase Two?"

"Each of the seven targets has been located. The individual teams reported to Rusty late evening and into the early hours. The younger ones among their number went clubbing in Sheffield."

"Is everything in place for today?" Athena asked.

"Gus has his teams on surveillance already. Giles is calling me at eight. Once that conversation ends, Rusty and I move into position."

"I returned too late to attend the morning meeting yesterday," said Athena. "Giles and Artemis had returned underground. Minos updated me on the Slough situation. Mansouri and Harrack are experienced and crafty. We can't be sure whether we are hunting two men dressed as women, two men, or a couple."

"If I were them, I would stick with the burka disguise,"

said Phoenix, "they knew we were watching. They would assume whoever had photographs of them uncovered their true identities. The bombers can't split up as they did in Canary Wharf, so the disguises are the only logical way to move freely."

"You're saying they can't split up because a Muslim woman travelling alone is an unusual sight," said Athena. "It draws attention, and that's the last thing they want. That's a valid point."

"Can you do me a favour?" asked Phoenix. "Ask Minos or Alastor to dig into the service record of Gus Dickerson. Rusty and he have a history. It may have been ten years ago, but it's still raw as far as Rusty is concerned. I want to discover whether he has any misdemeanours flagged on his performance since joining Olympus."

"I'll see to that. Could Dickerson be a problem, do you think?"

"I can keep Rusty on a leash; that's no hardship. We shouldn't have cause to cross paths with the other teams until this is over. If one of the Amigos turns up something incriminating, get it to Giles. He can relay it to me. I'll be in touch with the surveillance teams in the ice-house throughout the mission in case a target goes missing, and we need assistance."

"Hurry home, darling. We're missing you, aren't we, Hope?"

Hope rested her head against her mother's breast, listening to the conversation.

"Dada?" she asked.

Athena held the phone to her ear.

"Hello, poppet," said Phoenix, "are you being a good girl?"

Hope grinned from ear to ear.

"See you both tonight," said Phoenix.

"Okay, be careful," said Athena. "Hope rolled over onto her tummy anyway; she didn't want to listen to what you had to say."

"She's picked that up from her mother," said Phoenix and ended the call. He didn't need to wait for the response.

Giles called at eight as agreed.

"Phoenix," he began, "we've hunted high and low for Mansouri and Harrack. Unfortunately, they are nowhere on any CCTV footage we can access in London."

"Giles," said Phoenix, "start a search for two women wearing burkas, travelling together. They need those disguises. Get Artemis to check airports and ferry terminals. First, we need to confirm they're still on British soil. Start the clock when they left the hospital foyer and calculate when they could have arrived in Bristol, Cardiff, and Birmingham if they travelled by train. Check major cities further afield if they don't turn up there. If they're abroad, they're someone else's problem for now. If they're still in the UK, another large city is their next target."

Giles set the wheels in motion seconds after he ended the call. It was clear they still lagged behind the terrorists. The first task was to find where the bombers got to on Wednesday night or Thursday morning. They may have several steps to identify where the terrorists were this morning. Would there be enough time to confirm their whereabouts before they carried out their next attack?

The time was eight-fifty a.m. in Masbrough.

"When does Osman Hassan start work?" asked Rusty.

He and Phoenix sat in the van two hundred yards away from the delivery van. It hadn't moved since last night.

"Friday's his day for a handful of local delivery runs,"

Phoenix replied, "he finishes at one o'clock today, which gives him a long weekend. More time to play."

Across town, the pattern of activity for the day formed. The other six Olympus teams returned to their targets and sat, waiting for movement or following them wherever they went. The clock moved on.

Nine o'clock had arrived in Whiston.

Aziz Chauhan was getting out of bed. He had been clubbing in Sheffield until the early hours. Aziz checked how much of his cash remained. The taxi fare had been massive, and the others left him to pick up the tab. He'd get it back in kind when it was their turn to pay, but that didn't help Aziz today. He groaned and crossed the landing to the bathroom. His parents were already at work. Aziz heard his mother shouting at him to get up earlier, but he couldn't be bothered.

The young thug stood under the shower, trying to rid himself of the effects of the drink and drugs from last night. Aziz wished he could move out and find a place of his own. Instead, the boss kept making fun of him, saying he was a mummy's boy.

"Twenty years old and still tied to your mother's apron strings," Tariq Malik would say. "What would she think of what you get up to in your car?"

The other gang members laughed at him; the car had been a present from his father when he reached eighteen. Dad bought him a small family saloon. A sensible car, according to his parents. None of the local girls his age would be seen dead in it.

Aziz liked younger, white girls. His parents didn't realise that. Aziz picked them up from school when it was cold or raining. Several twelve- and thirteen-year-old girls accepted the chance of a lift. He kept indecent images of them on his phone to persuade them not to say a word about what happened before he got them home.

When the neighbours saw Chauhan driving past, they saw a smartly dressed young man from a decent family. They thought it a shame that many young people were unemployed these days. Aziz may have been short of cash this morning, but he ran with the gangs since he reached fifteen. Working for the Malik crew allowed him to make good money.

After he had showered and dressed, he wandered downstairs to get breakfast. His expensive wristwatch showed the time to drive to the local cash machine on his way into town. It didn't pay to be late. Tariq Malik ordered a beating when one of his boys stepped out of line.

The Malik family controlled much of Rotherham's violent crime and drug dealing. Each of the lads it recruited used untraceable mobile phones. Aziz kept the cheap pay-as-you-go phone his parents paid for in plain sight. His family were surprised at how little he seemed to use it compared to other young people.

The gang phone remained silent in a secret pocket sewn into his designer jeans. The vibration informed him when he needed to make a drug deal. If he was at home when he got contacted, Aziz told his mother he was meeting a friend. She was happy to know Aziz had become so popular. If only he could find a lovely Asian girl to marry.

At nine-thirty, Aziz reversed his car off the driveway. The Olympus team designated to deal with him followed at a safe distance. Aziz Chauhan didn't suspect a thing. He withdrew a hundred pounds from the ATM at Yorkshire Bank and then drove to Deepdale. Another working day began. Aziz collected the first batch of heroin that needed delivery.

The passenger in the van parked on the opposite side of the road from the taxi office took photos of Aziz entering and leaving. Any drug transfer happened inside, away from prying eyes. The driver nudged his mate; he spotted the lookout on their side of the road. The lad on the bike watched for the police. The Olympus agents were alerted to wait until Aziz cleared the street before setting off in pursuit.

Aziz headed for the address he had received. He understood the process. Tariq Malik had loads of money to dispose of and ran several cash-based businesses. The taxi firm and a cash and carry company. The money got laundered through those outfits. Malik employed Aziz to distribute the produce to lower-tiered dealers in each district.

This tier had people who chopped it up, added stuff to make it less pure, and made it more profitable to sell in smaller street-level quantities. Street kids often laced heroin with block weed to get kids addicted to other substances. It guaranteed a steady future income.

Aziz's friends, Jamshed and Ejaz, who came out with him last night, had permission to operate in the nightclubs. The stuff they moved was pure blue coke fresh off the boat. The addicts in Deepdale who bought a bag in the pub over the weekend might as well put talcum powder up their noses. It had so many impurities added to it after it left Aziz's hands.

When the coast was clear, the van drove away from the kerb.

"There he is," said the passenger, "he's stopped at the lights up ahead."

"That was lucky," said the driver. "I wonder how many drop-offs Chauhan has got?"

They were in for a trip around the districts dotted around the town centre. It would be a long morning.

In Rawmarsh, it was ten o'clock. Yusuf Shirani had just dropped a fare outside the Post Office. The fifty-one-year-old father of five would operate his taxi until after midnight today. He took the occasional break for a cigarette, a nasty habit he started at school. Yusuf did try to stop. His wife kept telling him his health and well-being suffered, but he couldn't stop altogether. If the fares dried up after lunch, he could grab a bite. Yusuf hoped to drive via Parkgate and attend the Eastwood Mosque this afternoon. The taxi driver wasn't a devout Muslim, but he always tried to find time to go to prayers on Friday.

Gus Dickerson contacted the lead agent in the van tailing Shirani.

"Everything okay in Rawmarsh this morning, lads?" he asked. The first communication he'd made with either of the locally based vans today. Phoenix was listening. He noted the fact but passed no comment.

"No worries, boss," came the reply, "our man is standing by his open taxi door, blowing smoke rings at the minute."

"Don't get too bored, will you?" laughed Dickerson.

Phoenix interrupted.

"Remember, Shirani's a villain, same as the rest. That taxi ferried girls around Rotherham for the past five years. He's got girls at home the same age as those being raped and prostituted, and he still does it. The guy is an animal. Concentrate on the job at hand. He has to become another mysterious missing person this afternoon."

Nobody said a word in the other two vans. Phoenix hoped the message hit home. Nothing incriminating had come through on Dickerson from Larcombe yet. There was still time.

The clock ticked on. Phoenix and Rusty continued to keep Osman Hassan under surveillance; one van delivery didn't differ much from the next. Park the van as close to the restaurant as possible, regardless of how it affects the traffic flow. Ring the doorbell to attract someone inside's attention. Open the van's side door, consult the delivery sheet, and carry the required sacks and boxes to the door. Leave them stacked by the door, blocking half the pavement. Ring again if there's no immediate response. When the restaurant doors are open, help get it inside and signed for, so you can drive to the next destination.

Rusty checked the time. He sighed; it was only twenty past ten. They had hours of this yet.

The teams in Bramley enjoyed a slow start. The two guys with Aziz Chauhan last night in Sheffield were late risers. Ejaz Rizvi was a twenty-four-year-old marketing manager who drove a flashy sports car. Jamshed Sadat, who lived at the other end of the village, was twenty-eight and married with no children. He worked for Tesco as a buying manager. Rizvi's wife worked for Yorkshire Bank. They earned a combined salary, without the drug income, which she knew nothing of, totalling over sixty thousand.

The two families had arranged Sadat's marriage. The couple tolerated one another. His wife enjoyed the company of friends she met through work. She liked to spend money on beauty products, clothes, and shoes. Jamshed wanted to party. He left her at home four nights a week while working on the club scene in the local cities. Malik paid him and Rizvi well for their efforts.

Both Sadat and Rizvi had a violent streak. It wasn't uncommon for a few drugs to be slipped to a new client in a nightclub to clinch the deal for more regular business. Why not sample the merchandise? Then, when you need more, come and see me when I'm in the club next week. The trouble was, now and then, someone ran up an unsecured line of credit. That resulted in the lads putting the frighteners on the person involved.

One late-paying client heard they had smashed his mother's windows when she called him after he got home from work. Another received a phone call telling him his fifteen-year-old sister would be late home from school. It was up to him whether she remained intact or not when she arrived home. Word soon got around. Pay up, or Malik's crew will hurt your loved ones.

Rizvi and Sadat operated as a pair. As much as they liked terrorising young men, it was young women they loved to attack. As a result, female clubgoers suffered systematic physical and sexual violence at the hands of the two men.

"Who got assigned to Tariq Malik?" asked Rusty.

"Gus Dickerson," replied Phoenix.

"Call him," said Rusty. "Call them all to check they've got eyes on their targets. It's too quiet for my liking."

Phoenix checked the time; it was twenty to twelve.

"Exactly," said Rusty, "this morning has dragged. Why didn't we snatch them out of their beds at six this morning? Why is the window Zeus specified so special?"

"Zeus had his reasons," replied Phoenix, "and one would have been to reduce the number of people who saw them disappear. Many of these men have families. They live on streets filled with people. Olympus always attempts to carry out its missions without revealing its identity; you appreciate that."

Phoenix received a call from Giles Burke seconds later.

"Yes, Giles, what do you have for us?"

"Artemis dug deep into Dickerson's track record since joining Olympus. He's been walking a fine line. She found frequent examples of him late filing reports, losing contact while on undercover operations, and somehow snatching victory from the jaws of defeat. Artemis said his colleagues in Nottingham, where he worked before moving to Sheffield, described him as a 'chancer'."

"Thanks, Giles," said Phoenix and ended the call.

"Olympus teams? Phoenix here; report your current position and status."

One after the other, the teams relayed the information.

Qureshi was working in the shop. Sadat and Rizvi were still lazing at home, recovering from last night. Chauhan left Deepdale and now visited Parkgate. Shirani had picked up a fare and drove towards Wickersley.

Phoenix could see Hassan fifty yards away with a sack of okra on his shoulder. That left one team to report back.

"Gus, care to join us?" asked Phoenix.

Silence.

"Waste of space," muttered Rusty. "I bet he's sloped off for a late breakfast."

"Hello, Phoenix?"

It wasn't Gus Dickerson. Instead, Phoenix recognised the voice of his colleague.

"Report your position and status. Do you have Tariq Malik under observation?"

"We stopped for diesel and temporarily lost sight of him."

"I repeat, do you have Malik in sight?"

There was a pause, and then Dickerson spoke.

"Stop worrying. You're like an old woman. What did you say earlier? Is he a creature of habit? We'll find him at one of his haunts. Anyway, we've got loads of time."

Rusty tutted. Phoenix shook his head.

"Find him," he ordered.

It was almost noon.

"The rest of these crews better be on their guard," said Phoenix.

Rusty shrugged his shoulders.

"One bad apple…" he replied.

"We'll sort Dickerson out once this mission is over. I won't let him foul up things."

Osman Hassan had one more trip to make. It was one of his favourites — a family-owned restaurant in Barnsley. The owners were brothers, and the eldest lived in a large house on the outskirts of the town. He had seven children, five of them still at school. Osman dealt with the son, Faizal, on most deliveries. Faizal was in his mid-twenties and talkative; the two men got on well.

In July, the third eldest child left school. Hasina was sixteen and started to waitress in the restaurant straight away. Faizal laughed when he asked about her and told him she would never be an academic high-achiever. When Osman first set eyes on her, he had wondered if she was simple-minded. Hasina may not have been bright, but she was beautiful.

Osman Hassan hung around the restaurant, taking his time getting the sacks and boxes inside every Friday since. He snatched a few minutes with the young girl every chance he got. Faizal didn't cotton on that Osman was grooming her and his real intentions. Faizal was unaware of the Rotherham man's involvement in the trafficking of young girls for sex.

Phoenix and Rusty tailed Hassan's van as it motored on the M1. The time was now half-past twelve.

"This has to be our man's last drop-off," said Rusty. "A

fifteen-mile trip to Barnsley, and then return to Masbrough. He'll be home well before two o'clock."

"Our surveillance teams indicated that he stretches this visit out," said Phoenix. "I don't care why. It's not going to matter."

Hassan parked in the restaurant car park. A young man opened the side doors and waved.

"Hassan's popular here," said Rusty. "He didn't have to ring twice to get someone to answer."

A young girl appeared in the doorway to the storeroom. She watched as Hassan and the young man carried the deliveries from the van.

"That young girl can't take her eyes off him," said Rusty, "at least we know the reasons for the lengthy stops. She's a beauty too, even if she's half his age."

"Such a shame," said Phoenix. "A blossoming romance nipped in the bud."

They watched and waited as Hassan chatted to the girl each time he passed. In time, they had replenished the stocks. Finally, the young man disappeared inside the restaurant. Hassan and the girl were deep in conversation. He got his mobile phone out of his pocket and took a selfie of the two of them standing by the storeroom door. The girl giggled and closed the door. She waved at Hassan as he drove out of the car park.

"That's one photo that won't reach the grubby hands of Salim Qureshi and his partygoers," said Phoenix. "The poor girl doesn't realise how lucky she's been."

Hassan drove back to Rotherham and called into the firm's offices where he worked. He handed in his timesheet for the week and then set off home to Masbrough. He could spend a quiet afternoon relaxing before the busy weekend. It would be fun. The promise of a new face among the girls he partied with had moved a step closer today. Hasina would soon see many more of the towns and cities surrounding Barnsley.

Osman Hassan looked at the clock on the van's dashboard. It was seven minutes to two. The dark blue van that had overtaken him slowed. Why had the van indicated left? There was no left turn on this quiet road. Could it be a police vehicle? Hassan knew he hadn't been speeding and couldn't remember running a red light. The van pulled into a lay-by and stopped. Hassan stopped behind it and waited.

A man walked around from the passenger's side. Hassan lowered his window.

"What's up?" he asked, "why did you pull me over?"

The speed with which the man struck took Osman Hassan by surprise. Rusty rendered him unconscious and transferred him to the back of the Olympus van before another vehicle drove past. He returned to the delivery van to switch off the engine, lock it, and then ran back to join Phoenix.

"Not bad, now make sure he's secure," said Phoenix, "we should hear from the others shortly,"

Aziz Chauhan became one of *the missing* at one fifty-four. The team assigned to take him had followed him home to Whiston. As their background files told them, he was alone when they rang the front doorbell. His colleague entered the house through a bedroom window. When Aziz opened the front door, the agent shoved him hard in the chest. As he stumbled back, he fell into the arms of the agent who had just run downstairs.

A minute later, he was in their van and driving towards the Sheffield rendezvous point.

"Rizvi and Sadat were together when we took them," Phoenix heard from a team leader. "Sadat drove to his friend's house at forty-five. That was the first time we had seen him today. It must have been a great night last night. We waited outside until the appointed time and knocked on the door. They weren't pleased to see us, and there was a brief struggle."

"Any problems?" asked Phoenix. "The neighbours weren't alerted?"

"No, Phoenix," came the reply, "it was a very brief struggle. They're sleeping like babies now."

"Good, see you at the safe house," said Phoenix.

The following two calls came from the teams tailing the two oldest abusers, Qureshi and Shirani. They were the ones who had been in the grooming gang for between fifteen and twenty years.

"His language was vile, but he proved no match for two men," said Qureshi's agent.

"We picked our taxi driver up while he had a crafty cigarette in a no-smoking area," said the agent assigned to Shirani. "At first, he thought he was getting a fine for dropping litter. Now he's dazed and confused."

"Six down, one to go," said Phoenix, "and all registered between one fifty-three and two o'clock. Inside Zeus's seven-minute window."

"We will arrive at the safe house together around the same time," said Rusty. "Do you want to avoid that?"

"We're using the A630 Parkway, which takes us on a direct route," said Phoenix. "You know me well enough by now, don't you? The team that had the furthest to travel are following us. Others are taking longer diversions. So our arrivals at the safe house will be staggered, thirty minutes between each. Maybe more if the traffic is bad."

"We haven't heard from Dickerson yet," said Rusty.

"I'll call him," said Phoenix.

"Crew leader? Status report, please."

"Almost there, Phoenix." The reply came from the agent riding with Dickerson again. "Malik was visiting one of the B&B's the council used to house troubled families. The place has a dozen rooms filled with vulnerable people. Most are women with small children. Battered wives, that sort of thing. Malik seemed to know most of them."

"Did you pick Malik up in the agreed time frame?"

"Give or take a few minutes," said Dickerson, deciding to answer at last.

"Any problems?"

"Nothing we couldn't handle,"

Phoenix heard groans in the background.

"Is that Malik? Was he injured?"

"He didn't travel to the B&B alone, Phoenix," said the other agent. "We never found him until the last minute. We needed to grab him quick because his bodyguard carried a gun. I had to shoot him. Malik pulled a knife, and Gus needed to stop him from using it. Malik has a stomach wound, and he's bleeding like a pig. I'm not sure if he'll make it to the safe house."

"What a nightmare," muttered Rusty.

"Dickerson, you realise you've put the whole operation at risk? Every dark blue or black van with tinted windows will be stopped and searched by the police once they learn about the bodyguard."

"They won't find his body. It's in the back, alongside Malik," said Dickerson.

"Not much consolation," said Phoenix. "Someone at the B&B will have seen your van. So where are you now?"

The driver relayed their position. Phoenix spoke to the other five van drivers: -

"Whichever one of you is closest, sort out the nearest

place to meet quick, make a detour and collect the four of them. Then destroy the van. If the police find it burnt out a few miles from the shooting incident, that should stop them chasing us to Sheffield."

Phoenix and Rusty arrived at the safe house without incident. It was two forty-five; Rusty carried Osman Hassan inside.

The vans containing Chauhan, Qureshi, and Shirani arrived at ten-minute intervals. Each team off-loaded their target, and the agents were told to return home. Their work was over; they would get a call when Olympus next needed them on a mission.

It was four o'clock when the last van drew up outside the front door. Sadat and Rizvi had arrived. Gus Dickerson and his fellow agent brought them indoors.

"Where's Malik?" asked Phoenix.

"He died on the way over," said Dickerson. "I told the other team to dispose of the bodies. No point hanging on to them. The team will return to pick us up later."

"Do you think it acceptable to ask someone to do your dirty work for you?" asked Phoenix.

Dickerson didn't reply.

Rusty looked at the six prisoners sitting on the floor. Then, he spoke to Dickerson's colleague.

"When they return, you'll get these men into the van and do the necessary. Is that understood?"

"Understood," the agent replied.

Rusty drew his gun and pointed it at Dickerson's chest.

"Get me his gun," he told the other agent, "he's staying with us."

Dickerson gave Rusty a surly stare.

"Sit down," said Phoenix.

The Olympus van turned into the driveway of the safe

house at five minutes to five. The neighbours might think the people who lived there were getting a new carpet in every room. But instead, the six men were rolled up in old carpets, carried out and thrown into the back of the van.

"You can't beat planning," said Phoenix as the van drove away.

"You can't keep me here," said Gus Dickerson.

"We don't intend to," said Phoenix, "but you must listen to a story before leaving. Our orders were to keep our seven targets under constant supervision. They needed to be snatched, with no one being the wiser, in the seven minutes between one fifty-three and two o'clock. Your conduct throughout threatened a successful outcome. Everyone who joins Olympus learns that at the summit is someone with the code name Zeus. He has a wife and three children. His daughter was engaged to be married in 2007. On the afternoon of the fifth of September in Iraq, her fiancé was on a search and arrest operation. A colleague heard gunshots behind him and turned to see his friend on the ground. It was one fifty-three. There was a brief firefight with the sniper in a nearby building, but he escaped. His colleagues tended to Zeus's future son-in-law, but he had received a mortal injury. He gasped his last breath at two o'clock. The whole mission hinged on the fact it was seven years ago, to the day, to the minute."

"How was I supposed to know?" whined Dickerson.

"We don't need to know," said Rusty as he crossed the room to stand behind Dickerson's chair. "Our job is to follow orders to the letter. We don't cut corners or switch off our concentration. That's what gives us a chance of coming back alive."

"We're going back home now," said Phoenix, "and you'll be coming along for the ride."

Gus Dickerson didn't look up. Rusty brought the butt of the gun onto his head.

"We'll take him to Larcombe. Henry Case can deal with him in the ice-house. We owe it to those American Marines if nothing else. We might get away with his conduct today, but an agent who operates like Dickerson could expose the Olympus Project and jeopardise our entire existence."

Chapter Seven

The journey south proved uneventful; the traffic flows were heavier than usual. It was early on a Friday evening. There were stretches of roadworks, too, on the M5. Phoenix couldn't see they made much progress since he and Athena drove north last weekend. That seemed so long ago now. So much had happened in the past week. Athena lost her mother. He had lost a mother figure he had never experienced.

Phoenix was glad he let Rusty drive. They swung through the pillars of the gateway to Larcombe Manor at a quarter past nine.

"Hope will be asleep," said Rusty as he pulled up by the transport section garage.

"You forget someone," said Phoenix.

Gus Dickerson sat tied up in the back of the van. They hadn't heard a thing from him throughout the trip.

Rusty sighed.

"I'll call Henry," he said. "I presume he's on-site this

weekend? I don't recall him mentioning a weekend away with the Reverend."

"Henry will be on duty in the ice-house if not," said Phoenix.

"He's a tortured soul at present, Phoenix. That relationship with Sarah Gough has changed him."

"For the better, as far as I can tell," said Phoenix, "and Giles too. They're both far happier since they found a partner. Why would you say he seemed tortured?"

Rusty told his friend about the conversation he had with Henry before they left for the mission.

"I've been so engrossed in other matters I've neglected to consider how everyone else is coping," said Phoenix. "You know how it is. I try to separate our personal lives and what we do for Olympus. It's a struggle. I want my life with Athena and Hope to be as normal as possible. Grace's death came as a terrible shock to everyone. That was only last Monday, yet Athena and I had to put our feelings on hold to see that we achieved our goals. Geoffrey is with us this weekend. He's grieving and needs us to help him through the coming days. Athena and I need to push forward with the Olympus timetable."

"Time to delegate, Phoenix," said Rusty. "You can't carry the full weight on your shoulders forever. I'll step up, and so will Minos and Alastor. We can rely on Henry to look after the training programmes and ensure Hugh keeps the Irregulars initiative on track."

"Hugh Fraser, do you know, I don't remember talking to him since he arrived? I insisted on recruiting him; we spent one afternoon in the orangery working on the Irregulars programme. That's it. What message does that send?"

"Don't beat yourself up, Phoenix," said Rusty. "You've worked miracles in the time you've been at Larcombe. Take a break over the weekend. Let the rest of us carry the load for a while. Now, get moving. Go to your wife; she will wonder where you are."

Phoenix got out of the van and made for the main building. Rusty drove off toward the ice-house. In the back of the van, Gus Dickerson was still unconscious. Rusty called Henry Case. The security chief was in the stable block and not due underground until the morning. Five minutes later, he joined Rusty.

"Sorry to interrupt your evening, Henry," said Rusty, "but we had to bring you a visitor."

Henry's shoulders sagged. Rusty lifted the bulky weight of Gus Dickerson on his shoulder and carried him to the lift.

"Straight to the third floor, Henry," he said.

"Who is this man, and how long has he been unconscious?" asked the security chief.

"Dickerson is the senior man from the Sheffield team. He carried several black marks against him before this mission, and he put everyone one of us at risk earlier today. He can't work for Olympus any longer. Phoenix doesn't trust him to keep his mouth shut if we dismiss him from service. Our security is paramount, as I know you understand. We have no choice. As for how long he's been out, it must be six hours. I clubbed him with my gun."

The lift was now at Level Three. Henry followed Rusty and his burden along the corridor to the final door.

Rusty laid Gus Dickerson on the floor. Henry checked his vital signs.

"It appears my work is unnecessary," said Henry.

"Dickerson's dead?" asked Rusty.

"You must have hit him harder than intended."

"I knew Dickerson from before," Rusty admitted, "he was the same loose cannon in Iraq."

"You're telling me it was personal?"

"I shall have to inform Phoenix," said Rusty.

"Phoenix has enough to worry about," said Henry, placing a hand on Rusty's shoulder. "Dickerson was never leaving Hotel California alive. I'll get his body disposed of in the morning. You saved me from facing the prospect of killing another human being. We'll keep this between the two of us."

"I told Phoenix of your concerns twenty minutes ago. He'll discuss them with Athena and then tackle you about them. I wish I kept my mouth shut."

"I talked to Athena after our earlier conversation, Rusty. Don't apologise. She understood my predicament. If you recall, she brought Sarah and me together. Athena sanctioned the use of trainee agents wherever possible to avoid my involvement. To date, the occasion never arose, thank goodness."

"Thanks, Henry, you're a pal," said Rusty. They left Gus Dickerson's body in the room and took the lift back to the surface. As Henry passed Hugh Fraser's door, he noticed a light. He couldn't make out what was said. But, despite the late hour, the former soldier sounded deep in conversation.

Rusty made his way to the main house and climbed the stairs to the apartment he shared with Artemis. She lay in bed reading.

"You're back, at last," she said, "did everything turn out okay?"

"The odd minor hiccup, but we got there," he replied.

"Is something troubling you?" Artemis asked. She had known Rusty long enough to tell that when he went quiet, it was because something played on his mind.

Rusty joined her in bed.

"The missions were both successful," he said, "but we hit a problem with Dickerson, the guy you ran the background checks on. I served with him in Iraq ten years ago, and he caused two unnecessary deaths. It was almost a repeat performance today. At least we won't have to work together again. Are you at the end of a chapter? I need someone to hold me tonight."

Artemis closed her book.

Saturday, 6th September 2014

The morning sun promised a fresh, warm start to the weekend. Athena and Hope were in the bathroom when Phoenix awoke. He found the pair of them fast asleep when he got upstairs last night. When she rose this morning, after Hope first stirred, Athena would have seen that he was home. She recognised that a good night's sleep after a mission was preferable to a late-night debrief and perhaps broken sleep.

Phoenix walked through to the kitchen to make coffee. He looked at the calendar. Today, Heracles and Aphrodite were to marry. He had almost forgotten. They had agreed that Olympus heads would not be on the invitation list. The couple wanted a quiet, family affair, and Phoenix would have felt uncomfortable anyway.

Elizabeth McLaren, the Duchess of Lochalsh, lived in Glenfinnan Castle in northwest Scotland. Aphrodite's education and breeding set her apart from the likes of a West Country boy. There were many names ahead of her in the line of succession to the English throne. But Phoenix hadn't rubbed shoulders with her class of person in his youth.

Lawyers who handled the McLaren family fortune were glad to provide significant sums of money for the Olympus Project. A clean bill of health from the Charity Commissioners continued to validate the Project as a charitable diversion where she could occupy her time.

Sir James Grant-Nicholls was a different character altogether. Heracles hailed from Musselburgh in Scotland and carved out a successful industrial career. When the two Olympians announced their engagement in April, Zeus, Hera, and the others were happy for them. Elizabeth was a widow, and her only son, Rory, was estranged from her. It wasn't unheard of for the children of titled people in Britain to adopt a hippy lifestyle. It seemed typical for a son or daughter to kick over the traces and rebel against the riches they would inherit. Their parents carried that innate entitlement; the children often didn't.

Sir James flew his plane from Scotland to Olympus meetings in England and offered Elizabeth a lift. Things moved quickly from there. Nobody mentioned Fiona Grant-Nicholls. When Olympus had an attack from within by Demeter and her son Hermes, Athena ordered Minos and Alastor to run a thorough background check on each of the Olympians.

Phoenix had sat in on the meeting when they went through their findings with Athena. Thanatos had felt sidelined. He was already under suspicion as a traitor. Then, sometime between the end of September and April, the thirty-year relationship between Janes and Fiona came unglued. There were no children. There were no suspicions of infidelity on either side uncovered by the digging the Two Amigos carried out.

Phoenix found it odd. Today the wedding was due to take place at Glenfinnan Castle. Should he mention it to Athena? She had read the report that her senior aides produced. Surely, she hadn't forgotten?

Phoenix finished drinking his coffee and wandered through to the lounge. Athena sat cuddling Hope on a settee. Both turned to look at him; Hope beamed a welcome.

"Good morning, darling," said Athena. "Are you going to tell me about yesterday before or after you've showered and dressed? Daddy will be up soon. We don't want him thinking you lounge around in your pyjamas throughout the morning."

"How long before Maria Elena arrives?" asked Phoenix. "Perhaps you can join me in the shower. It might be the only time we have alone to chat today."

"Cheeky," replied Athena, "but you're out of luck. Giles asked for the weekend off. He's gone with Maria Elena to meet his parents. They've moved to a cottage on the North Devon coast. So we've got to look after our daughter all weekend."

Hope looked hard at her father's face to see whether that would be a problem.

"Great," said Phoenix, "Rusty said I should relax with my family this weekend."

Hope smiled with satisfaction.

"That sounds ominous," said Athena. "Does that mean yesterday didn't go to plan?"

"I'll tell you after I've finished getting ready. I don't want to discuss it in front of Hope."

"Hurry back then. I'm more intrigued than before."

When Phoenix returned to the lounge, Geoffrey Fox had

crossed the corridor and joined his daughter and granddaughter.

"Phoenix, it's good to see you," said his father-in-law.

"You too, Geoffrey. I wish it were under happier circumstances, but you know you're always welcome here at Larcombe Manor."

Geoffrey took little Hope and sat her on his knee. She took great interest in his tie.

"Grandad's careless isn't he," Geoffrey told her, "that's an egg. I ate a boiled egg and soldiers for breakfast. I would think of Grace every minute of the day, Phoenix if I wasn't here. You two and Hope are a godsend."

"Did you hear any news while I was away, Athena," asked Phoenix.

She shook her head.

"We don't expect to hear anything before Monday."

"I thought I heard you in the corridor outside my room last night, Phoenix," said Geoffrey. "You got home late. I get the impression the people you do business with don't keep normal office hours, am I right?"

"Nothing much gets past you, Geoffrey," smiled Phoenix.

"I may not be as fleet of foot as in my younger days, but the old brain still functions."

Athena and Phoenix shared a look. Keeping the true nature of Olympus from Geoffrey was hard enough when he lived in London and only made the occasional visit. It would be doubly difficult for him to live under the same roof as us for an extended period.

"What are your plans?" asked Geoffrey. "I can look after Hope if you want to spend the rest of the morning together."

"I would enjoy an hour in the pool," said Phoenix. "We used to do that a lot before Hope arrived."

"I seem to remember it was where you first noticed me," said Athena.

Phoenix noticed her long before that morning, but their initial encounters had been frosty. They were like two fighters, sparring before deciding when to attack. Erebus warned him to tread with care. Athena's experiences had hurt her before arriving at Larcombe.

Phoenix swam alone for an hour that morning. He tried to rid his thoughts of the litany of victims of the sexual predator Sir Geoffrey Penrose, the target of his next mission. He sat on the pool's edge with his feet dangling in the water when he heard someone else enter the building. It was Athena. She stepped out of her tracksuit bottoms and peeled off her sweatshirt top to reveal a one-piece grey swimsuit.

Athena's appearance stunned him so much he stared at her, mesmerised. That was the moment he fell under her spell. Then, back in the present, he smiled at Geoffrey.

"We'll take you up on the offer, Geoffrey. I'm sure you can keep Hope amused until lunchtime. Athena was wrong about that early morning dip in the pool. It wasn't the first time I noticed her, but it was a significant moment. It was when I knew I loved her and wanted us to spend the rest of our lives together."

"We'll expect you when we see you then," said Geoffrey, smiling for the first time since last Monday.

Phoenix and Athena left Geoffrey with their daughter and collected their swimming costumes from their bedroom. Then, they walked, arm in arm, across the lawns to the old workers' cottages and the recreation facilities.

"You're an old softie at heart, aren't you," said Athena, ruffling Phoenix's hair.

"Rusty told me I needed to switch off more, to delegate responsibility to others. I could compartmentalise matters so that our home life and Olympus remained separate. I've allowed too much of my time to be on the latter. He suggested I risked burn-out."

"Forget that for now. Let's swim, enjoy the exercise and the fact we're together. We'll catch up on last week and the other stuff tomorrow. If Artemis hits a problem in the icehouse, we'll direct her to Minos for guidance. Between now and nine o'clock on Monday morning, only a national emergency will give them cause to disturb us."

That sounds good, thought Phoenix, as they reached the indoor pool. Half a dozen trainee agents were powering up and down the lanes. Nobody took any notice of them when they emerged from the changing rooms. They slipped into the warm water and let the worries of the world wash away.

An hour later, the pair sat in the next-door cafeteria with hot drinks.

"We haven't done this in ages," said Athena. "Can you remember what we discussed on those occasions?"

"You told me about Grace and her heart operation, how Geoffrey planned to cope with her recovery. We chatted about Elizabeth, the person before she died. Then we discussed Elizabeth the yacht and whether we should sell her or keep her. We reminisced about our days with Erebus and how much we missed him. There were other times, but I can't bring any to mind."

"Each of those was a personal moment," said Athena, taking Phoenix's hand in hers, "not Olympus problems we faced and perhaps struggled over to find a solution. But, times such as those are important."

Phoenix nodded.

"Fiona Grant-Nicholls," he said, watching Athena's face for a reaction.

"I thought we promised to avoid Olympus matters," she replied.

"The wedding is today, Athena. You haven't mentioned it. The date's on the calendar in the kitchen, but that's it."

"Zeus asked me not to," she replied.

"Is that all you have to say?"

"I spoke to him after the Olympus meeting in April when they announced their engagement," she continued. "I couldn't admit that we checked out each of the Olympians, including him and his wife, Hera. I merely pointed out that James married in 1982, and nothing showed that the situation had changed. He asked me not to discuss it with you or others. Zeus wanted to investigate further for himself,"

"What did he find?" asked Phoenix.

"Fiona couldn't have children, and this weighed on her mind. James's wealth gave her everything she could ever want, but she couldn't enjoy it. He kept many stories out of the press concerning her jet-setting lifestyle, alcohol and cocaine abuse, and her relationships with men and women. By 2002, they lived apart, and James set up a healthy allowance on which she could live well. Nevertheless, Fiona continued to struggle with her demons. In 2003, she appeared in an Edinburgh court on charges of driving under the influence. Fiona's solicitor told the court that she struggled under a mountain of debt. In February of the following year, she visited James in Musselburgh. After nine o'clock on the evening of the twentieth, Fiona disappeared."

"What do you mean? Why did this never get reported?" asked Phoenix, "surely, James would have phoned the police if she went missing? They could have organised a search. Musselburgh's a big place, just up the road from Edinburgh."

"James never contacted the police. He didn't mention the matter to anyone. Her family are from Cambridge. They rarely saw Fiona after she and James married. For months, nobody from the family asked where she had gone. Then, on the evening of the twentieth, Fiona visited an off-licence in Musselburgh. She bought a large bottle of vodka. There have been no sightings since that night."

"When her relatives asked where she went, how did James respond?" asked Phoenix.

"James swore blind she didn't return to the house that night," said Athena, "he said they argued. Finally, Fiona stormed out after he refused to give her a handout. Instead, he said he told her the bank of James closed."

"I'm at a loss to understand how he kept this under wraps," said Phoenix. "Minos and Alastor dug up so much detail, yet this escaped them."

"Zeus discovered that James used his wealth and celebrity to take out injunctions in the High Court based on his right to privacy. Finally, after seven years, with Fiona not surfacing and a body never discovered, he could have Fiona legally declared dead. In March of this year, he returned to court to make that application ten years after her disappearance. The court hearing dissolved the marriage."

"So, James *is* free to marry Elizabeth today," said Phoenix, "but the question remains. What happened to Fiona Grant-Nicholls?"

"What are you suggesting?" asked Athena, "that James murdered her and disposed of the body? Fiona was a mess. It's more likely she would commit suicide, drink herself to death, or overdose."

"Then why has her body never been discovered?" asked Phoenix.

They had talked so long that their drinks were cold. Phoenix stood.

"Let's get back to the house and make lunch for Hope and Geoffrey. I suggest you talk to Zeus before the next meeting on the eighth of October. Unless we can uncover the truth, that party at the Dorchester in the evening might be awkward."

"That promised to be a great night," Athena sighed. "We planned to stay overnight with Mummy and Daddy. They were babysitting Hope. Those plans are dust now."

"We can still make that trip. Unless Geoffrey is tearing his hair out in exasperation when we get back, I reckon he'll cope with tucking her into bed and reading her a story for one night. Didn't he do that with you in that house when you were tiny?"

Athena could count those nights on the fingers of one hand. Her father flew backwards and forwards across the world with his businesses. As soon as she was old enough, she had been off to boarding school in Surrey. Her mother read those stories to her over and over.

Athena took Phoenix's hand when offered, and while they walked to the main house in silence, she fought the tears that threatened her. Phoenix paused when they reached the door that led to their apartment.

"That is a job suited to Orion," he said. "He starts here on the twenty-second, doesn't he? Find out what Zeus knows, and if a follow-up is needed, set the old police dog on the scent."

"I'll agree on the condition we don't discuss Olympus-related matters for the rest of the weekend," Athena replied.

"Fair enough," said Phoenix, "what does Geoffrey enjoy in his sandwiches? Ouch."

Athena's elbow caught him in the midriff as she breezed past him.

"Daddy will eat what he's given, the same as you and Hope," she teased.

For the new head of the Grid, the fact it was a Saturday morning made little difference. Colleen O'Riordan pored over documents and reports in her penthouse apartment in London. The luxurious trappings she could now afford softened the fact that she worked so many hours these days.

It was a far cry from the daily grind in Kilburn when she was at Tommy's beck and call. Colleen had come a long way in a short time. One reason for her success was that she never forgot her roots. Knowing how rotten that early life had been strengthened her resolve never to return.

After Tommy's murder, Colleen moved swiftly to take control of the criminal gang he led. Angry voices spoke out against her at first. However, they soon quietened after the cruel way she disposed of those foot soldiers that kept a percentage of the profits from their criminal activities for themselves. Those who suffered may have been young men from the lowest branches of the gang structure, but the message was clear. Every penny of profits must pass to the Grid.

As Colleen paused in her work for a moment, she reflected on how much had changed. Less than a month ago, they buried her brother Sean. Hugo Hanigan had sent his lackey to ensure he never returned alive from the Dominican Republic. Colleen could never understand how the madman came to that decision. She had known him since they were young children in Belfast. Sean had been reluctant to replace Tommy as a gang leader, but the police sniffed around to discover who helped Tommy O'Riordan escape from Belmarsh prison. An escape that only lasted hours; until he got shot by an unknown assassin.

In the police's eyes, Sean was a possible suspect, and his drinking made him a weak link in the organisation. Hugo had told him to lie low for a while. Then, on a whim, he ordered his killing. Her son, Tyrone, made him pay with his life. Who would have believed it? Tyrone, the well-educated, fast-living young man she thought was taking the mickey out in Marbella, the same as his younger sister.

Colleen sold their beach-view apartment from under them, forcing them to stand on their own two feet. She told them cutbacks were necessary after Tommy died. Tyrone and Rosie returned for their father's funeral. Instead of her son moaning at how she treated him, he surprised her by telling her of the talents he acquired in Marbella from his father's gangland friends.

Without recriminations, Rosie had returned to her life in the sun; she wasn't afraid of hard work. Colleen knew her little princess would cope. If things got tough, she would latch onto a rich bloke to help smooth the way. As for Tyrone, he stayed in London to enforce the changes Colleen wanted.

The car bomb that eliminated Hugo's security people had been Tyrone's first task for her. Next, he executed the Mighty Quinn, the head of the nearest gang. Colleen's empire grew, but she wasn't content to stop there. It had been the first move in gaining control of every Grid gang in the capital.

Sean's murder accelerated her move to the top of the pile. Tyrone had murdered Hugo Hanigan and disposed of the body. From her apartment window, she looked at the penthouse where Hanigan lived. Tyrone now occupied that suite. Moreover, her son controlled the Grid's finances. He ran the Glencairn Bank in the City of London.

Colleen had proclaimed herself head of the network of organised criminal gangs that formed the Grid. Once Tyrone called her to confirm Hanigan's death, she switched her attention from adding one borough at a time to her regime to eliminating opposition wherever it existed across the country.

It was lunchtime. Colleen rang her son.

"Can you join me for something to eat, Tyrone? There's something I want to show you,"

"I've just got up, Mum," said Tyrone, yawning. "Give me twenty minutes. Then, I'll pop in for a visit."

Colleen busied herself in the kitchen, preparing lunch. When Tyrone arrived, they sat on the balcony, enjoying the warm September sun as they ate together.

"While you went up to East Anglia tidying up another loose end, I visited your place," said Colleen.

"I would never have guessed," said Tyrone, "what did you want?"

"I thought it was time we went through everything Hugo left. You soon cracked his computer codes to get the files he held on scum such as Klimenko. But we never found the combination to the wall safe in his bedroom written anywhere."

"What did you do? You didn't blow it open. I would have noticed even if I don't run a duster around as often as I should."

Colleen smiled.

"You can afford to pay someone to do that. I asked one of the lads your Dad used from time to time to help me. He had the safe open within thirty minutes. The ten grand I handed him in cash means he can fly out to Gran Canaria for a month this morning, taking his girlfriend with him."

"Did you find something worth ten grand inside?" asked Tyrone.

"A velvet bag containing two million in uncut diamonds rested on top of two old school books. There were other papers I hadn't gone through yet. You can take your time over those. What I found in the old books interested me."

Colleen went inside the apartment and brought them back.

"They're the same as the ones I used at school," said Tyrone, "but these aren't full of homework. They're a diary of names, dates and things that happened."

"These go back to when your Dad and I were kids," said Colleen. "Back then, Hugo was still Ardal James Hannon, the odd boy who wanted to mix with the rest of us but always remained an outsider. Hugo kept a record of every event where he felt mistreated. Every boy who hit him on the playground. Every child who didn't invite him to their birthday party. If he learned a secret, something we didn't want our parents or our friends to know, he recorded it."

"The computer files showed that he continued doing that right up to his death," said Tyrone. "You always told me he was mad, but this takes it to another level. I revealed the secrets that Klimenko kept hidden when I spoke with him. He couldn't believe I had so much on him — the same with McGrath last weekend. Hanigan had decades of scraps of information on that guy, where the bodies were, and where the money lay. McGrath knew if any of that came out, he would be a dead man. So he almost welcomed me, putting him out of his misery."

"You've had a busy week, Tyrone," said Colleen. "We've

removed the leaders that could get enough of the Grid's gangs to mount an effective opposition. There's no stopping us now. The rest will follow like sheep whether a woman's in charge or not. The figures don't lie. They're far better off with the Grid."

Tyrone handed the books back to his mother.

"These are old school, Mum. We'll hold onto the computer files Hugo amassed on members of the gangs. Then, whenever we need leverage, we can utilise what he gathered. The Grid's aim is total control of the UK. The police are an irrelevance. They persecute motorists, investigate ancient history, and try to embrace every minority group out there to show how on-trend they are. The Government has become paralysed by fear. Mostly the fear that the public will uncover another scandal. Five years ago, it was expenses. Who knows what will be next? The security services are underfunded and overstretched. They issue warnings over the threat of terrorist attacks, and then they are way off the pace when one occurs. Look at Canary Wharf on Monday. Nowhere is safe."

"Which leaves the field open for the Grid to operate without interruptions," said Colleen, "don't you love free enterprise?"

Chapter Eight

Tyrone O'Riordan returned to the penthouse after lunch with his mother; he wanted to spend a Saturday night in town. Tyrone was no longer short of money. His mother paid him well for his extra-curricular activities, and his financial nous worked miracles at the Glencairn Bank. As a result, he anticipated a healthy bonus at the end of the year.

Hugo Hanigan prided himself on having the inside track on commodities trading, but Tyrone reckoned he had only scratched the surface of what was possible. With higher risk came higher rewards. Tyrone was too impatient to sit back and wait for a sure thing to appear.

While he wondered where he might eat tonight and which casino he should visit, Tyrone browsed through the computer files they had discussed earlier. The school books his mother showed him offered little interest. They were old news. She recognised his computer talents gave them an edge in the financial field. But there was a gold mine of information in Hugo's files on his allies and his enemies.

Tyrone decided to talk to her next week. They needed

another expert on the investigative side. He didn't have time to delve into the detail, not with his work at the bank, plus the occasional assassination.

The file in front of him was for Shabbir Shah, the Cardiff gangmaster. The rumour was he had gone to ground a month ago, but Tyrone knew better. He had disappeared for good. Tyrone watched for news that a body had washed up somewhere on the coast or over the channel on the English side. So far, Shah hadn't surfaced. The weights Tyrone attached must have remained intact.

Something Shah said when Tyrone questioned him played on his mind. The gangmaster had been at the hotel near Oxshott in Surrey when Tyrone listened to Hugo's last big speech. Later that night, he sat with Klimenko, Quinn, and McGrath, putting the world to rights. Tyrone bundled Shah into his car when he left a club late at night and took him to a quiet spot where they talked.

Before he went for his final swim, he told Tyrone of his suspicions over the frequent deaths of Grid members up and down the country. Hugo dismissed them as unimportant and related to petty inter-gang rivalries. The gangmaster was convinced otherwise.

Shabbir Shah was pleading for his life, of course. Perhaps he made this fantastic suggestion to persuade Tyrone to spare him. The more Tyrone listened, the more he wondered. It didn't save Shabbir Shah, but Tyrone wanted to have the theory investigated further. What convinced him was another random event in the north of England, only forty-eight hours ago.

Tariq Malik belonged to the Grid. He wasn't the head man in the criminal organisation covering South Yorkshire. There were one hundred gangs in the area, many of them street-gangs. The more organised outfits were involved in drugs and firearms. Their overlord was Frank Rooney, a man who always offered unswerving support for Hugo.

Rooney could see the benefits gained from establishing a sophisticated network of gangs. The local approach was wasteful. Frank favoured 'together; we are stronger'.

Tyrone learned that Malik got shot, and a bodyguard was killed at a B&B in Sheffield on Friday afternoon. Staff members saw a body on the ground and Malik staggering out of reception, severely wounded. Women and children who lived there reported hearing gunfire. Yet, no one called an ambulance, and the police didn't arrive at the B&B until the evening to make enquiries. But, again, there were no bodies, only blood.

Malik had disappeared. The police visited his home; nobody had seen or heard from him since mid-morning. Malik was involved in every type of petty crime. The cops suspected something illegal had gone on at the B&Bs he operated, but they didn't have enough evidence to act.

Despite the clues staring them in the face, they remained unaware of any connection between Tariq Malik and rumours of the ongoing presence of grooming gangs in the town. Tyrone considered the evidence. He didn't hold with the activities of these grooming gangs, but Rooney expected Colleen to be ready to offer to help. The question wasn't where Malik had gone. It should have been; who shot Malik, and why?

Tyrone applied Shabbir Shah's logic to the mystery. Malik was a Grid criminal who attracted the notice of a secret organisation because of one of his crimes. They tried to grab him, but a shoot-out left the bodyguard dead, and Malik was injured. The attackers removed both men.

He couldn't believe he had given this serious consideration. He needed to talk to Frank Rooney to find out if there were any other strange occurrences. That could wait until Monday. Tyrone was ready to hit the town.

Sunday, 7th September 2014

Waverley station in Edinburgh receives twenty-five million passengers every year. Princes Street, the premier shopping street, runs close to its north side.

Times had changed.

The grand Victorian mosaic tiling that graced the floor of the booking hall suffered vandalism under British Rail. The threat of a terror attack meant Waverley Bridge no longer allowed vehicular access. Only in June they had banned taxis from entering the concourse. Once a familiar sight, they now parked in ranks outside.

The covered escalators leading to Princes Street were a recent improvement, as was the widened Market Street entrance. Signs of restoration were everywhere — none of this interested two male passengers who arrived on foot via the Calton Road access.

Ahmed Mansouri and Omar Harrack travelled from London King's Cross on the East Coast Line yesterday.

They discarded their disguises on the long journey north. The burkas had served their purpose. They allowed them to cross the city unchallenged and avoid CCTV whenever possible. If anyone searched for them, they wished to make things as difficult as possible. On arrival in Edinburgh, they studied the station layout once more and then spent two hours shopping for the items they needed today.

The main station facilities stood in the middle of a large island platform surrounded by platforms on four sides.

Eighteen platforms provided connections to Scotland, and a range of train franchisees ran trains between Edinburgh and every major city in England. So if you wanted a target that crippled rail transport and sent a clear message from IS, then this was it.

There was a surprise element to this attack that required the two men to contact a third terrorist. Amina Badour was a nineteen-year-old university student who travelled to Syria to join the Islamic State in 2013.

Her parents were distraught. At no time did they suspect their attractive, intelligent daughter of having extreme political views. Amina had been the first member of the family to attend university. She studied psychology in Edinburgh and suddenly disappeared at the end of her first year.

Their daughter joined dozens of other British extremists on the long journey via Europe to Istanbul. Each of the boys and girls with whom Amina travelled got radicalised online. From Istanbul, they moved to the Syrian border and headed for the IS city of Raqqa.

Why they were susceptible to online grooming was hard to comprehend. Perhaps it was a sense of adventure, and they got swept up in the emotion raised by the zealot that recruited them.

Amina Badour was soon married to an IS freedom fighter. Her life in Syria was nothing like she imagined, but she admired her husband and what he believed. When he died in an airstrike, she decided to escape from Raqqa and return to the UK.

The journey home to Scotland took Amina several weeks, and while in Belgium, she met Ahmed Mansouri. He arranged for her to cross the channel to England three days after him. Amani Badour wanted to avenge the death of her husband.

Mansouri and Harrack separated once they reached the main island of platforms. The two men dressed in the typical European streetwear of jeans and a hooded jacket. As three o'clock in the afternoon approached, Mansouri and Harrack prepared to carry out the first stage of the attack. They left their large suitcases next to fellow travellers on Platforms 9 and 11.

The station's platforms were crowded with men, women, and children. Very few people gave a second look at the men as they hurried down the platform towards the exits. Their suitcases lay unnoticed for a vital minute. As passengers and rail staff wondered who the cases belonged to, Mansouri and Harrack were already safe from harm.

The first explosion on Platform 11 occurred at precisely three o'clock. The Virgin Trains East Coast train pulled out of the station to journey south to London King's Cross.

The second explosion on Platform 9 (East) occurred fifteen seconds later.

Thirty-two people died, and over two hundred others were injured, many of them critically, on Platform 11. Ball bearings and shrapnel tore through everything in the nail bomb's path.

Twenty-eight people died on Platform 9, and around seventy people were injured. Across Waverley station, people ran, screamed, and tried to escape. Two explosions so close together meant there could be others planted somewhere nearby. An elderly lady dropped dead from a heart attack on Platform 1. In a rush to get to the escalators, people suffered injuries as they tripped and fell. It was chaotic.

Every train capable of being moved out of the station was waved off without delay, regardless of the timetable.

Incoming trains halted at the nearest signalling point. The emergency services were three minutes away.

Every available ambulance and paramedic was diverted to Waverley and blue-lighted at high speed. The stricken platforms soon crawled with men and women whose only aim was to help others. Members of the public, off-duty nurses, and police officers did what they could to assist the injured.

When the bomb exploded, the Scotrail service from Glasgow was still travelling towards the city centre and pulled up at Platform 9 (West). The driver immediately stopped the train and helped to evacuate passengers. They spilt out onto the platform in the immediate aftermath of the blast. In minutes, the three-carriage train would move out of harm's way and join the others.

Nobody could have known the local service carried another deadly threat. Amina Badour remained calm as she walked down the platform and crossed onto the Eastern side. What she saw was nothing new. Rivers of blood. Body parts. People with terrible injuries. Glass and debris were everywhere. Amina witnessed this happening to her people in Syria. Welcome to my world.

Amina heard voices shouting to her above the sounds of the injured souls. They told her to go back. She kept walking; her right hand was inside her jacket pocket. It was her time. The emergency services personnel surrounding her were working on people on the ground. Amina detonated the explosives in the vest she wore under her hooded top.

Outside the station, Ahmed Mansouri and Omar Harrack were on Calton Road. At the sound of the third explosion, they nodded to one another; the plan worked to perfection.

Amina Badour delivered a sickening blow for the cause;

her martyrdom was secured. The fight would continue. Their next destination lay a five-hour drive south.

Terror attacks aim to cause disruption and widespread fear. Waverley had suffered that worse than any other attack on mainland Britain. Bombings such as this aimed to produce the maximum number of casualties. Emergency responders were a legitimate target as far as the bombers were concerned.

Early in a terrorist attack, the exact intent, scale, and hazards are unclear. Without an informed appreciation of the potential threats, an emergency responder cannot evaluate the risks to personal safety on arrival at an incident. They think first of the patient, despite the training that tells them to prioritise their safety above the scene and survivors.

At Waverley station on that Sunday afternoon, the cost of caring more for the lives of others than themselves was great

Six medical personnel died; four policemen, two rail staff, and a GP who was on holiday from Newcastle. Seven already injured passengers died.

Three injured people later died of their wounds in the hospital. Twenty-three others were injured.

The bombings were the deadliest act of terrorism in Scotland's history. Public outrage was massive. The media linked the Canary Wharf incident in minutes. As a result, the government in Scotland and at Westminster came under severe pressure to act without delay.

At Larcombe Manor, an urgent call from Artemis interrupted the quiet weekend planned by Phoenix and Athena. Until later tonight, she was standing in for Giles

Burke, who wasn't expected back from Devon with his girlfriend, Maria Elena.

Phoenix and Athena were in their apartment with Geoffrey Fox; Hope took an afternoon nap. The family ate together earlier. It would have been a happy occasion if Grace Fox had been with them. Her death in the London bombing last Monday had been a cruel blow. The mood was sombre.

Athena was trying to help her father through a bad patch this afternoon. Since the tragedy, Geoffrey seemed in control of his emotions. But, in the past hour, his grief returned to the surface, and she found herself more affected than she realised.

Phoenix had spotted the signs when they talked yesterday. Now, he could see that his wife struggled to cope. She had returned from London with her father to enable her to continue with Olympus' business. It was fine throwing herself into her work to mask the pain, but it must come out in the end.

It was the only way. He had learnt that from bitter experience. The weeks following his daughter Sharron's murder had been terrible for him and Karen to endure. It hardened his heart and created the stone-cold killer that sought justice wherever needed. Over the years, that outer shell had softened by his relationship with Athena and the birth of their child. When he picked up Hope for a cuddle, he realised he'd become a big softie. It wouldn't be long before he shed a tear if the process went much further.

Phoenix took the call. He listened to Artemis as she relayed the dreadful news from Scotland.

"Was it important, darling?" asked Athena.

"It can't wait, I'm afraid," he replied, "you stay with your father. I'll go to the ice-house and sort it out."

Phoenix left them alone in the apartment and headed to Rusty's. A knock on the door brought his friend outside in seconds.

"Artemis called me," he said, "are you going underground?"

"We can't risk Geoffrey hearing what we're doing," said Phoenix. "Let's get to the ice-house and see what we're facing."

Athena watched from the upstairs window as they crossed the lawn. It must be serious, she thought. She sensed Phoenix had been trying to shield her from the impact of the news. Geoffrey came and stood by her side.

"Where are those two going, I wonder?" he said.

"Work never stops," replied Athena, turning away from the window and leading her father back to his chair. "It's nothing to worry over; you sit here and rest. I'll fetch Hope from the nursery. She's too fond of a siesta. I blame Maria Elena for getting her into bad habits."

"You change the subject so well, my dear," said Geoffrey. "No doubt I'll be let into the secret one day."

Athena allowed herself a smile as she made for the nursery. She felt wretched, but her Dad must never discover the truth behind the Project's charitable veneer.

In the ice-house, Phoenix and Rusty viewed the full horror of the Waverley station attack. Artemis had CCTV footage from every camera before the first explosion at three. Unfortunately, several cameras went down in the blast, but those closer to the exits were still operating.

"It's almost impossible to comprehend how anyone could do this," said Artemis. "The devastation of the two bombs was terrible enough, but this follow-up attack was heinous."

Phoenix dragged his eyes from the carnage and the panicked activities of those on the platforms.

"We need to let the emergency services see to the aftermath," he said. "I want to check what we've got in the build-up. Anything that gives us a clue where to begin the hunt for the terrorists."

The three agents studied screen after screen. It wasn't long before they spotted familiar faces.

"There's Mansouri, and that's Harrack wandering along the platform," said Artemis. "Right, the bombs were in the suitcases. What we saw on the platform suggests they dispersed vast pieces of metal in every direction. They chose the two platforms among the busiest at that time of the day. As with the DLR bombing, the planning was meticulous."

"Do we have anything in the minutes after the first explosion?" asked Rusty.

"Not from Platform 11," said Artemis, "and the gap to the second blast on 9 was only fifteen seconds. These other cameras might give us a view of the platforms from a distance."

Artemis brought images from half a dozen cameras up on the screen. They were grainy and shaky; neither agent could see much. The timestamp showed just after three o'clock. Then, Phoenix pointed to a screen. A girl walked steadily along Platform 9, only yards away from the mayhem on the other side, as if nothing had happened.

"Who's that?" he asked.

"No idea," said Artemis, "but the train originated from Glasgow Queen Street and travelled directly to Waverley. The journey time was around fifty-five minutes."

"Where is she going?" he asked.

The screen images disappeared with a flash of light and smoke.

"She was the third bomber," said Rusty. "Someone not present at Canary Wharf. Can we get CCTV from Glasgow?"

"Give me a few minutes," said Artemis, "you two check the station's external screens for sightings of Mansouri and Harrack as they left. Then, I'll dig around Glasgow to see if I can spot her boarding that train. We need a better picture to work with."

They found what they wanted as the afternoon ticked on to early evening.

At six o'clock, they sat together, and Phoenix ran through the scenario they had put together.

"Mansouri and Harrack recruited an at present unknown female accomplice. We need to discover where and when that took place if we can. Then, we need to identify her. Mansouri and Harrack left the station and set off to mingle with hundreds of shoppers on Princes Street. The clothes they wore won't help us keep them under surveillance easily once we hack into the CCTV systems in the city."

"When Giles is back, we'll prioritise those two items, " Artemis said.

"Learning the identity of the suicide bomber won't prevent them from hitting the next target," said Rusty. "These two haven't finished yet. London and Edinburgh have suffered so far; where will they strike next?"

"Rusty's right," said Phoenix, "the girl's identity isn't important. We'll let the authorities name her and notify her parents in due course. My bet is she's a British citizen. Our job is to find the two bombers. I'll talk to Fraser. If he has any Irregulars ready to roll, those guys in the major cities must be our eyes and ears from tonight. They need to be on the ground at once. If one of them can pinpoint which city, it will save you and Giles hours of work."

"I'll report our progress at the morning meeting," said Artemis. "Giles will have to hit the ground running when he returns from his break. I'll carry on working here until the handover is complete.

"I guess I might not see you before the early hours?" sighed Rusty.

"We can't help that," said Artemis, leaving her chair for a moment to remind Rusty how much she loved him.

Phoenix didn't stay to watch the lovers embrace. Instead, he headed for the lift to return to the surface. First, he needed to visit Hugh Fraser in the stable block.

As he walked along the corridor to the new logistics man's quarters, he passed the rooms which had been so familiar to him four years ago. So much had changed. He arrived as Colin Bailey, the fugitive. A stone-cold assassin who was running from the police. A man declared missing, presumed dead after the struggle with his nemesis Phil Hounsell when he collared him at Pulteney Weir in Bath.

Erebus, the originator of the Olympus Project, organised his rescue and brought him to Larcombe Manor. He became Phoenix and lived next door to Rusty Scott, the ex-soldier who soon became a firm friend. The rooms he now passed had been refurbished of late to allow Hayden Vincent and Kelly Dexter to live as a couple.

Henry Case occupied the same spot as in those long-ago days. The former military intelligence officer presented a crusty exterior to the world back then. Phoenix found him direct, if not always very polite. He lived up to his nickname 'Head'. Yet, in recent months Phoenix had realised that the tough outer shell was there for a reason. Inside, Henry Case was a sensitive soul.

Phoenix paused as he looked at where his old room had been. That was where he and Athena became lovers. Erebus had spotted the signs from the outset. Sparks flew when they first met, and, in truth, they made an unlikely pairing. Annabelle Fox, the university-educated former MI5 operative whose wealthy parents lived in Belgravia, London; and a West Country misfit whose real identity must remain hidden from the world.

They were like chalk and cheese. Phoenix found it hard to believe four years had passed. Look at them now; married, with a nine-month-old daughter. Time flies when you're enjoying yourself.

He knocked on Hugh Fraser's door. The fifty-one-year-old ex-Scots Guards captain answered.

"Phoenix, this is a surprise. Come in."

"We need your help, Hugh," said Phoenix, "but first, I need to apologise for not coming to see you more often. When we worked on the Edinburgh mission, I knew that you were the right man for this job. I told Athena we needed to move fast to get you here."

"I was pleased to get the call," said Hugh, "I needed a month to get things in Scotland squared away to my satisfaction. The man who succeeded me had to carry on operations in the same vein. It took time to find the right character."

I'll bet, thought Phoenix, someone prepared to produce highly detailed, colour-coded reports for every agent under his supervision. Nothing was left to chance.

"Where was I when you arrived here?" asked Phoenix.

"I moved in on the eighteenth, so that will be three weeks tomorrow," replied Hugh. "You were at Larcombe initially, but your attention focused on the christening over the Bank Holiday weekend."

"After that, I moved here, there, and everywhere," Phoenix said. "I should have finalised the proposals we worked on together. This weekend was supposed to be a fresh start for me. However, I have recognised the need at last to delegate more. I started with good intentions. My father-in-law is staying over, and my wife is grieving for her mother. Although we've tried to relax and to have forty-eight hours away from Olympus matters, events in Scotland have demanded our attention."

"I watched the latest news bulletin before you arrived," said Hugh, "if I had still been working in Edinburgh, I could well have been in the area. I assume this visit relates to those bomb attacks, and you need my help? What can I do?"

"Remind me, where did we get to with identifying the candidates for our team of Irregulars?" asked Phoenix. "I was to rubber-stamp the people you cleared with Henry Case, so they could be relocated if necessary and found housing if I recall?"

Hugh Fraser was not a man who enjoyed sitting on his hands. He was a man of action. When Phoenix and Athena checked the plans for the missions in Rochdale and Rotherham, he had been itching to get moving.

A phone call from Ambrosia on Saturday evening had been unexpected but most welcome. Their relationship was in its early stages, but Hugh hadn't felt so positive for a while.

Hugh's marriage foundered on the rocks years earlier. Nevertheless, his wife enjoyed the army life, the job security, the foreign travel, and the social perks that came from being a senior officer's wife.

The reality of life after he joined Olympus came as a shock to the system. Olympus didn't have social occasions; there were no regimental dinners where she could dress in her finery. Hugh got stuck into his new role with relish while his wife drifted into a series of affairs. In the end, she moved out without an argument ever materialising. He hardly noticed she wasn't there.

When Ambrosia contacted him on the day he arrived, there had been a tingle down his spine. An ambitious woman, ten years his junior, told him she was keen to work closely with him on the Irregulars project. Ambrosia had been the one to introduce the idea to the Olympus organisation leadership in the first place. Hugh Fraser was intrigued and excited.

Ambrosia urged him to go ahead with the programme without waiting for Phoenix to give his final approval.

"Be proactive," she had told him.

"I took the liberty of confirming the recruitment of the ex-service personnel cleared by Henry," said Hugh. "There were eighteen men and women on the initial list we scrutinised in the orangery. The accommodation has been identified for prospective agents across the country by Minos and Alastor. I allocated an agent to twelve major English cities and scattered the remaining six around the capital. As we get clearance for additional recruits, we aim to add to the numbers in each city to provide effective teams wherever we need their skills."

Phoenix was surprised at this news.

"OK," he said, "I can't criticise initiative. It was my fault we hadn't decided. So, we could use at least twelve Irregulars for what I need. It's doubtful these bombers will return to London. We have to hunt them in the provinces."

"They have hit two targets on the railways so far," said

Hugh, "bombing the tracks near Canary Wharf, causing a derailment; now creating mayhem at a mainline station at Edinburgh Waverley. As we move south, we can position an Irregular at the station in Newcastle, Manchester, Liverpool, and the other main centres. It would be a start. Our next requirement is more boots on the ground to beef up the teams."

"I'll get Henry involved tomorrow at the morning meeting. If Minos and Alastor have sourced the potential accommodation, we must find the bodies to fill it. Athena won't have any difficulty getting the funds released."

"Will Athena be able to give her full concentration on Olympus matters while she's dealing with her father and helping to arrange her mother's funeral?" asked Hugh.

"With my help, she'll cope," said Phoenix, a little disturbed that others had noticed his wife buckling under pressure. He knew they would work together to get through this.

Phoenix left Hugh Fraser's room and returned to the main building. In the morning, he could increase the pressure on these bombers. The hunt must start now. Time slipped away like sand through your fingers.

The next attack might be only hours away.

Chapter Nine

After Phoenix left him, Hugh Fraser called Ambrosia.

"Phoenix was just here," he told her. "He knows I jumped the gun on commissioning the first set of Irregulars. However, the bombings in Edinburgh have brought forward plans for getting them into action."

"I told you not to worry," she replied, "it was the right decision. We can't wait for Phoenix and Athena to decide the best way forward. Losing her mother has left her on the verge of a breakdown. I have mentioned this to Hera. While Athena was preoccupied, I got closer to Zeus's wife. She will convey our concerns to her husband. Little drops of water every day will wear down the hardest stone. We will be in a much stronger position when they meet in London next month. You have done well, Hugh."

"Thank you, Ambrosia," said Hugh, "will you be visiting Larcombe Manor soon?"

Ambrosia smiled to herself. Hugh wished to see her; that was good news.

"I must check my diary to see if I can drive south for a

day. I should love to meet you in person. Can you be free to entertain me?"

"Without a doubt," said Hugh.

"In that case, I'll make the arrangements tomorrow," Ambrosia purred. "Goodnight, Hugh. Sweet dreams."

Hugh Fraser replaced the phone; exciting times lay ahead. He turned on the TV and switched to the news channel. The warm feeling of talking with Ambrosia soon left him. The death toll from Edinburgh Waverley was now at eighty-five and could rise higher. Many of the three hundred people injured in the blasts remained in hospital.

There would be no sweet dreams tonight for the families concerned or the emergency services as they hunted the culprits. Hugh hoped his new bunch of Irregulars could provide a vital clue. That would only reinforce the position he and his ally currently held. From there, it was onwards and upwards.

Monday, 8th September 2014

The morning meeting began at nine o'clock as usual. Phoenix had ensured Athena got her father up in time to help Maria Elena organise Hope's morning. The young nanny was tired after her weekend in Devon with Giles.

Sea air and long walks along sandy beaches had contributed. Meeting her boyfriend's family had been another ingredient. However, the major excitement came on Saturday night when Giles asked her to marry him. Maria Elena had longed to accept outright, but she told Giles that he must ask her father's permission first.

Giles called the Urbano family home in Estepona on Sunday morning.

Senor Urbano had given Giles his blessing. Giles and Maria Elena broke the news of their engagement to his parents in the pub restaurant as they sat for lunch. On the way home in the car later that evening, she had promised her fiancée the best night of his life.

As soon as they arrived in the stable block, Giles saw the message from Artemis. A night of passion was cancelled. He was bound for the ice-house.

The others were already there when Phoenix and Athena arrived at the meeting room. Henry and Giles were deep in conversation. Artemis and Rusty looked relaxed and at peace with the world. Minos and Alastor were as impassive as ever.

"I'm sure you appreciated the seriousness of the terror attack in Scotland yesterday," said Athena. "Many thanks to those who put in extra hours helping the cause. Now, straight to business. Giles, what's the latest on the bombers?"

"When Artemis handed over late last night, my priority was to find Mansouri and Harrack somewhere in Edinburgh. I waded through hours of CCTV data with little luck. I searched for the two of them travelling either alone or together, but apart from unconfirmed sightings, I drew a blank. They disappeared on Princes Street at around half-past three. I found no trace of them after that."

"So, we're no further forward?" said Athena.

"Well, I asked another guy to check the Glasgow Queen Street cameras while I trawled through Edinburgh. He found our suicide bomber getting onto the train. The image was full-frontal, clear as a bell. We identified her in minutes; she was in the newspapers in Scotland last year; Amina

Badour was an ISIS bride. She ran away from university to join up with other young people radicalised online. They entered Syria through Turkey. It appears she returned last month via Belgium."

"Was she on a watch list?" asked Henry Case.

"It's possible," said Giles, "but there's no record of her coming back to the UK by legitimate channels. However, Mansouri was in that region before joining Harrack. So my guess is they smuggled Badour across the channel simultaneously. Badour then travelled north and laid low until the Canary Wharf bombing brought her from hiding."

"Mansouri is the brains behind this operation," said Rusty, "he wanted something more dramatic than the DLR derailment. So the delay between the blasts was deliberate."

"The public would have been appalled by the deaths of innocent civilians," said Artemis. "Although they moan about the emergency services at times, when they get murdered while doing their utmost to save lives, that stirs emotions."

"That emotion is then directed towards the Government to act," said Henry, "not merely to hunt the terrorists. The bombings are not solely to generate widespread fear. ISIS wants worldwide recognition for its cause by attracting headlines in the media. The TV and the newspapers filled with little else for a week. Until they are found and eliminated, then further scope exists of extra publicity for the ISIS struggle."

"I talked with Hugh Fraser last night," said Phoenix, "we have a skeleton crew of Irregulars available to carry out surveillance at the most likely railway stations. It could give us precious minutes to prevent the next attack."

"I didn't realise you had sanctioned that move yet?" said Athena.

"Hugh made an executive decision," said Phoenix. "Rusty and I were in the north of England last week. Hugh thought it best to start the ball rolling. Think of it as me delegating at last."

"As long as he doesn't make a habit of it," said Athena. "Executive decisions are designed to be made by the executive committee around this table."

"Point taken," said Phoenix. "Minos, can you confirm that you and Alastor have identified places where we might house these Irregulars?"

Minos nodded.

"If you needed two hundred rooms from next Monday, somewhere in the UK, that wouldn't be an issue."

"Unless they were in the one place, Milton Keynes, for instance," added Alastor.

"Good. My next question then is to you, Henry," said Phoenix, "how can we speed up the release of more recruits into the system?"

"If we could get together after this meeting, I'll take you through the numbers. Between us, I believe we can fast-track twenty or thirty today."

"Brilliant, Henry," said Phoenix.

Athena shepherded the meeting through the remaining items on the agenda.

"Was there any other business?" she asked.

Giles Burke coughed nervously.

"Well, I have news. Maria Elena and I got engaged yesterday. We plan to marry next year in Estepona. Both of our families are delighted."

It made a pleasant change to have good news to bring the meeting to a close.

Phoenix and Henry left together to continue their discussions in the orangery.

Minos and Alastor returned to the administration section to resume the daily grind.

Giles Burke walked out with Rusty and Artemis. He hoped to persuade her to start her shift early, so he could finally get to bed. He had been awake since eight o'clock yesterday morning.

Athena returned to their apartment alone. Her father was sitting, reading the paper when she arrived. Maria Elena was in the kitchen preparing lunch. Hope crawled on the floor, inspecting the tiles and the cupboard doors.

"Hello, darling," said her father, "I heard from the funeral director this morning. We have a date and time. It will be at the West London Crematorium, Kensal Green. Next Monday morning, at eleven-thirty."

"We should ring around this afternoon to make sure as many friends and relatives know the details then," said Athena. "How far is that from home?"

"Half an hour, perhaps?" her father replied.

Athena went to him and hugged him.

"It will be a difficult day, but maybe once it's over, we can try to move forward."

"I was thinking, sat here this morning while Hope was playing on the floor in front of me. Our place in London is far too big for me to rattle around in on my own. I'm not sure I could ever get used to not having Grace there too. Maria Elena was telling me her news when we had coffee together. She said Giles's parents have a bungalow on the North Devon coast. I might investigate moving this way. Somewhere closer to Larcombe, out towards Weston-super-Mare, or Burnham-on-Sea."

"Don't rush into any decisions yet, Daddy," Athena said. "We would love to have you closer, but make sure it's the right thing for you to do. You have friends in London, and the house is full of happy memories."

"I suppose you're right, but the money would come in handy," her father said.

"Since when did you need to worry about money?" asked Athena.

Geoffrey Fox didn't elaborate. He had mentioned the failing investments to Phoenix, but he didn't want his daughter to know. Things weren't too tricky, not yet. So he decided to change the subject.

"Where's Phoenix, anyway? Why didn't he come back with you after your meeting?"

"He's chatting to Henry. They're getting ex-soldiers off the streets and back into the housing that the charity has organised."

"Oh, very commendable," said Geoffrey. "It's disgraceful that the system allows young men and women who fight for their country to fall through the cracks. They should be first in the queue. Don't get me started."

"Olympus does what it can," said Athena, having said as much as she dared.

"Phoenix is with Henry, you say? How are the two love-birds getting on? Will Sarah be able to make it next Monday, I wonder?"

"I'll ring her this afternoon," said Athena. "While we eat lunch, I want you to think of the people we need to call this afternoon.

Phoenix returned ten minutes later, and Maria Elena left them to devour the lunch she had prepared. She hoped Giles was in the stable block and had energy left after working through the night. Unfortunately, the loud snores that greeted her meant she would be disappointed.

In London, Tyrone O'Riordan was listening to his mother, like any good son.

Colleen was talking to Frank Rooney, the South Yorkshire gang lord. Rooney had been a staunch supporter of the Grid ever since Hugo Hanigan offered the services of the Glencairn Bank to any crime outfit that needed their ill-gotten gains laundered. He could recognise a good thing when he saw one.

The positives from a network of gangs that dominated the country's criminal activities hadn't diminished with the death of the Irish madman. That was the gist of the argument Colleen put to Frank Rooney. He was old school and wasn't overly pleased to learn what was best for him from a woman. But, as the conversation ebbed and flowed, Tyrone could tell that Frank Rooney realised Colleen O'Riordan was no ordinary woman.

"The king is dead, Frank," Colleen had said, "the queen is in charge now. Nothing has changed; the primary focus of the Grid remains the same."

"You can't expect to walk in and take control without people having questions," said Rooney, "what makes you think you have the right credentials?"

"You wouldn't have asked my late husband, Tommy, that question, Frank," replied Colleen. "We were married for over thirty years. He was already running with a street gang when I met him. Tommy treated me like many men did in those less enlightened days. I was a trophy to be shown off if we went out with his gangland friends. He wanted me in the kitchen and the bedroom when we were home. It wasn't advisable to speak out unless you wanted a fat lip, but I listened. Tommy talked when he'd had a drink. I listened every day for over thirty years, Frank. I learned what to do when he got it right; and what not to do when he screwed up. Since he died, I've found that putting that learning into practice was easier than Tommy made it sound."

"I've heard the stories," said Frank, "you've been tidying house. Anyone who opposed Hanigan and flat-out refused to accept you taking over paid with their lives."

"I've taken the necessary decisions and issued the orders. I employ people to clean house for me. They're efficient. If you want to keep the law from your door, you must keep a distance. Hugo kept detailed records of occasions when the Grid's leaders failed to remember not to get their hands dirty. He might have passed that information on to the authorities if he wished to remove a problem, or he could have used that knowledge to blackmail people such as yourself, Frank. Do you remember Tim Hancock? He was a minor irritation to the police until the thirtieth of August, back in nineteen ninety-one."

Tyrone smiled at the silence that gem had caused on the other end of the phone. He was glad Hanigan was dead, but the madman had collected valuable information.

"I came up the hard way," Frank blustered, "I didn't get it handed to me on a plate. You talked your way into taking over Tommy's old gang in Kilburn, but that's an Irish mob. You lot stick with your kind. Then, as soon as you have Hanigan killed, you calmly announce you're replacing him as the head of the whole organisation. It's only natural people have doubts."

"Careful, Frank," said Colleen, "you never know who's listening. They might think you're challenging my position. That would be foolhardy. Almost as foolhardy as shooting Tim Hancock in the head all those years ago because he did a few drug deals on housing estates you controlled."

"Yeah, well, times were hard back then. Tommy O'Riordan would have done the same, I bet. But, look, we might have got off on the wrong foot," said Frank Rooney, realising he could sign his death warrant if he went up against Colleen. "The Grid has been good for everyone financially. If it continues, we'd be stupid not to keep on the right side of whoever's in charge."

"Now you're learning, Frank," said Colleen. "Tommy chose me from all the girls who chased after him because of my good looks. He never gave a thought to whether I had a brain. You and the other leaders need to grasp that with me in control; we will only get stronger because I have brains and a ruthless streak. Hanigan ignored the cracks in the network. Hugo dismissed the deaths of Grid personnel as natural wastage or the result of petty disputes between rival gangs."

"I attended that secret meeting in Surrey," said Frank, "I heard what was said. Hanigan explained why he did what he did. There have always been rivalries, especially between local gangs. So it's no big surprise when someone gets rid of the opposition. No idea how Hanigan found out about that scrote Hancock, but he deserved what he got."

"I suspect you didn't hear everything, Frank," said Colleen. "Many leaders left to drive home before the explosion in the car park. I ordered that surprise, by the way. I had the room bugged. Hanigan's security men were too dumb to do a thorough check. Listen to this conversation."

Colleen let Frank Rooney hear the comments made by the late Shabbir Shah.

'I believe we are under attack from a secret government unit, a security force not known to exist by the public. They appear from nowhere and then vanish like smoke. They are too well-organised to be a small rival gang. The deaths of

Grid members were too widespread. No individual gang has that reach.'

"That was Shah, from Cardiff, wasn't it?" asked Rooney. "He's no longer with us, I heard."

"Shah was among a group of men, including Klimenko, McGrath, and Quinn, who sat together drinking and chatting after you had left."

"They're dead too," said Rooney.

"The decision to move forward without them was mine," said Colleen, "but Klimenko posed a valid question earlier that evening. The attack on the helicopter carrying that judge's family was a mistake. Surely you agree? Someone not attached to any gang associated with the Grid killed those attackers. Listen to this, and then tell me what you think."

Frank Rooney listened to the voice of Artem Klimenko.

"What of those men here who lost valuable personnel since that ill-fated decision? Were the same people responsible for the London deaths in Selhurst and Park Royal? What of Handsworth, Solihull, Manchester, and Portsmouth? Is this a series of one-off attacks on the Grid by rogue elements from the criminal fraternity, or is a separate highly organised group responsible?"

"Aye, it stinks." It was the Scotsman McGrath who had spoken next. "The next question hangs over what occurred at Rayleigh. Almost on your doorstep, Artem. Who killed Tommy O'Riordan, and the others?"

"That's bugged me since it happened," Colleen said. "I even wondered if it had been my brother, Sean. There were several reasons Hugo had to die. First, he had Sean killed, and I wondered whether it was him who had got rid of Tommy too."

"I never heard what Shah had to say," said Rooney. "It

might have helped if he'd shared those thoughts with the rest of us when Klimenko said what he did. Instead, Hanigan brushed it under the carpet as you said."

"What happened last week in Sheffield, Frank?" asked Colleen.

"At that B&B, do you mean?" replied Frank Rooney, "Tariq Malik was holding his gut. Witnesses reckoned he'd taken a bullet. Nobody has seen him since. Why, what are you saying? There's a connection between these incidents? Are you serious?"

"The men sat around the table with Shabbir Shah thought he was crazy," said Colleen, "but when you join the dots, you get a picture. So when we've finished talking, I want you to go back to your people and see if anyone else, apart from Malik, has gone missing. Anywhere in the north of England."

"OK, I'll put the word out. It's crazy, though. How could an outfit be big enough to do this without us having heard of it? We've got people on the inside of most levels of the authorities. Any new initiative the police come up with has been planned for before it hits the streets, so its impact is minimal. It doesn't make sense."

"Call me back when you've done your homework, Frank. There's a good boy. Leave me to think. I'll make sense of it; then we will do something. Think of it like Tim Hancock. A minor irritation needs to be eliminated so the Grid can control every criminal activity across the country. Nothing can stand in our way."

Frank Rooney ended the call. He would get onto those checks at once. Frank had learned a lot in the past hour; an essential thing was Colleen O'Riordan would be a formidable enemy. He had to make sure she counted him among her friends. He didn't want to think of what the alternative might bring.

"That went to plan," said Tyrone, "Frank knows where he stands now. He'll pass the message along the line to the others. With his help, you won't need to ask me to remove any more Grid leaders, and you'll gain the respect of the main spokespeople. That's key."

"Exactly," replied Colleen, "if we get Frank Rooney on our side, then the rest will follow like sheep."

"I made a note of a few numbers while you two were flirting with one another," said Tyrone. "Frank mentioned numbers when he ridiculed Shabbir Shah's suggestion of a hidden force in the UK. Does he have a point, though? The armed forces face cutbacks but still have one hundred and sixty thousand personnel. There are twenty-five per cent more than that attached to the police in one guise or another."

"Maybe, but you can discount many of those because that number includes community support officers, traffic cops and wardens, and desk jockeys. When was the last time you saw a proper copper on the beat?"

"I try to avoid them as much as I can, Mum," replied Tyrone.

Colleen thought over what her son had said regarding the numbers for a moment.

"I see where you're going with this, Tyrone. Suppose you take smaller organisations everyone has heard of, such as Border Force and MI5. They have only got around twelve thousand people between them. If this organisation were twelve thousand strong, it would register."

"Not if Shabbir Shah was right," said Tyrone. "They appear from nowhere and vanish like smoke. The only way they could do that is by being a small unit. A highly organised group with extraordinary levels of intelligence and highly developed surveillance skills. Where would these people have originated? How do we find them?"

"Remember what they say about Chuck Norris?" said Colleen, "You don't find him. He finds you. When I learn how strong they are in numbers and confident we can defeat them, we will draw them out of hiding. I'll find a way."

Wednesday, 10th September 2014

Ahmed Mansouri and Omar Harrack arrived from Liverpool Lime Street at Birmingham New Street station at one in the afternoon. After an hour mingling with the crowds of Sunday shoppers on Princes Street, they had returned alone to Waverley to catch a bus south.

The two terrorists had then travelled to Liverpool, where a taxi took them from the bus station to Walton, a residential area north of the city. They were welcomed to a terraced house near the centre by a fifty-eight-year-old ISIS sympathiser named Bakar al-Hamady. They drew up a timetable for the third attack on Tuesday.

On Wednesday morning, the Syrian-born al-Hamady drove them to Lime Street station. The West Midlands Trains service to New Street ran every thirty minutes. It came south via Crewe, the major junction on the West Coast Main Line. Unfortunately, the Syrian didn't accompany them. Their fellow terrorists were already lying in wait, scattered around the Midlands.

The third attack was to be the most audacious and devastating - so far.

Mansouri wasn't finished yet. The disruption caused by the bombings at Canary Wharf and Edinburgh had been substantial, but the effects would be relatively short-lived. The fundamental aim was to raise the level of disruption to crippling. He wanted rail services cancelled indefinitely. People must be stranded in their homes, unable to get to school or to work. He wanted them stuck in the major cities, unable to get home. His plan was for vital equipment for industry and medical supplies to be held in limbo while the authorities made the area safe before removing any goods in transit. Mansouri wanted the British public too terrified to travel by train.

The media was giving high visibility to reports on the Edinburgh attack. The front pages of the daily newspapers and the headlines of news bulletins continued to cover the effects of the bombings in full. Canary Wharf was fading from memory. However, the pressure must be maintained so that the next attack would not fade from memory quickly.

The old Victorian station was undergoing a long-overdue refurbishment. Half of the modern grand concourse was opened in April last year. In the remaining half, redevelopment was ongoing, and those areas were closed to the public. As Mansouri and Harrack strolled from platform to platform, they noted the pressure points. They would make their task easier.

Large numbers of passengers were funnelled through tighter channels while work progressed around them. Birmingham New Street is a central hub of the national railway system. New Street is the sixth busiest railway station in the UK and the busiest outside London, with forty million passenger entries and exits. It is also the busiest interchange station outside London, with over five million passengers changing trains at the station annually.

Mansouri and al-Hamady had been attracted to New Street when they discussed potential targets online earlier in the year. Trains from every corner of the UK visited New Street. Since the Industrial Revolution in the middle of the nineteenth century, Birmingham had also formed well-established transport links with dozens of towns and cities scattered around it. Those links included road, rail, and canal.

Smaller branch lines disappeared in the 60s, but the major ones remained intact. New Street was a central hub for local and suburban services. The mayhem caused by a series of well-orchestrated strikes would be catastrophic.

Mansouri and Harrack carried typical tourist cameras while covering every available inch of the station throughout that Wednesday afternoon. In addition, individual pictures of specific places of interest were taken on their burner phones and sent to al-Hamady in Walton.

For operational reasons, trains departing New Street get dispatched by Right Away (RA) indicators. These display a signal informing the train driver it is safe to start the train instead of using the traditional bell or hand signals — the New Street power signal box at the Wolverhampton end of the station controls all signalling.

Harrack captured the images of the RA system and of that signal box. He made a note to secure a second angle from Navigation Street as they left the station to walk to their hotel. The box was visible from there and was another critical element in the plan.

While Harrack was at one end of the station, Mansouri was gathering data at the other. All trains arriving and departing had to use one of the several tunnels. New Street North Tunnel heads westwards towards Wolverhampton and passes under the National Indoor Arena. This tunnel is seven hundred metres long and holds two tracks. The Syrian was keen to learn what effect a bomb blast in the North Tunnel would produce.

Although only two hundred and forty metres long, New Street South Tunnel heads eastbound and passes under the Bullring towards Tamworth. This tunnel opened in 1854, initially holding two tracks; it was widened in 1896 to keep four tracks, with two double-track parallel bores. The Bullring is the principal commercial area for the centre of the city.

It was minutes before six in the evening when the two terrorists met on Navigation Street. Harrack took the final photo, and without discussing what they had seen or heard, they walked half a mile to the budget hotel where they planned to stay.

There was plenty of time to complete the preparation stage. The Syrian was to provide an outline plan within forty-eight hours. After that, Mansouri and Harrack would return to New Street station to double-check every step. Then, the other cell members would receive their tasks over the weekend.

These men would never meet face-to-face with Mansouri and Harrack or their colleagues. Indeed, the London and Edinburgh bombers' identities would remain secret from the rest of the cell. Sleeper operatives know someone will call to issue instructions. They don't know when that call will come, nor do they need to know who placed the call. If the authorities had suspicions about an extremist in the Midlands and arrested him, the integrity of the cell would not be compromised.

Once the sequence of steps in this dance of death had been verified and al-Hamady gave the green light, buildings in the city centre would collapse like a set of dominos.

Chapter Ten

Thursday 11th September 2014

The agenda for morning meetings at Larcombe followed a familiar routine. The intelligence section was always the first to report. Because so much would have happened in the twenty hours since they last met. National emergencies were the only thing to cause Athena to call a second meeting.

Since Tuesday morning, Phoenix believed they had been playing catch-up. When they started proceedings two days ago, Athena called on the ice-house personnel to update their overnight hunting expedition for the bombers.

Giles told her there had been unconfirmed sightings of the pair in Leeds, Cardiff, and London from agents on the ground. He continued to receive news from those examining hours of CCTV images from the four railway stations they believed could be involved.

"I wish I could give you good news," he said, "but we've got nothing concrete."

"Did we make a mistake limiting the search? Might they still be in Scotland?" asked Henry Case.

"No, Henry, we agreed once they have targeted an area, Mansouri and Harrack will move on," said Athena.

"We should ignore where they've been," Rusty agreed, "they won't hit the same place twice, and don't forget, Edinburgh was different to London. They used a suicide bomber to achieve an additional publicity coup. My fear is this campaign will escalate. The next attack could involve half a dozen bombers or even more. They wouldn't carry out an attack of that scale on a smaller target in the provinces. It must mean something to the outside world. So, it must be Manchester, Liverpool, Birmingham, or Bristol. Places with less than half a million population won't cut it."

"Which alternative transport options from Edinburgh to those four cities have we considered?" Alastor asked.

At last, they stumbled on a possible clue. By early Tuesday afternoon, the ice-house team found the bombers arriving in Liverpool late on Sunday night. They knew for sure now that they had travelled south by bus. Unfortunately, CCTV didn't cover the taxi rank from where Mansouri and Harrack drove to Walton, so most of Tuesday night into Wednesday morning had been spent on a fruitless search across Liverpool, with an emphasis on its three railway stations.

With Liverpool appearing to be the target for the next bombing, they needed boots on the ground. There were no sightings of the bombers on Monday or Tuesday on any CCTV camera they accessed. The Larcombe team were unaware that the men were tucked away on the city's outskirts with Bakar al-Hamady. Nor could they have known they would soon be on the move again.

Phoenix had raised the subject of the Irregulars at the

Tuesday meeting. The news that extra pairs of eyes and ears would be available so soon gave everyone a boost. They agreed to station six people at Liverpool Lime Street and four at each selected major station. Minos confirmed the accommodation was in place. Hugh Fraser assured Phoenix the veterans were fit and raring to go.

The Irregulars had been watching and waiting in Liverpool since Wednesday at noon.

They reported nothing unusual to date. Sometimes, you need a lucky break.

As he waited for Athena to ask Giles for his report, Phoenix prayed that they heard something positive.

"What do you have for us, Giles?" asked Athena.

"At one time, Birmingham was the CCTV capital of Europe," said Giles, "but they've reduced the numbers in recent years. The upside is the quality of the image on the ones that survived is far better. Here we have our two men taking photos on Navigation Street, near the Bullring."

"At what time?" asked Athena.

"Last evening, at six o'clock," Giles replied.

"We can put the Irregulars at Liverpool and the rest on standby," said Rusty. "We need more people in and around Birmingham New Street."

"How did we miss them at Lime Street? Maybe they used the bus again?" said Henry Case.

"Trains run to Birmingham very often," said Artemis, "we didn't have people on the ground until noon. As for New Street, that team arrived mid-afternoon and was outside the station, watching for people coming or going. The terrorists could have arrived hours earlier. The fact that several hours later they popped up on a camera outside the station suggests they stayed inside for a purpose."

"Surveillance," said Rusty, "I would love to see what's on

that camera he's using on Navigation Street. What could they see from there, anyway?"

"A signal box," said Artemis.

Phoenix felt his mobile phone vibrate in his pocket.

"Sorry," he said, "I'd better take this,"

He left the room and returned two minutes later. Giles and Artemis explained the significance of the signal box.

"Right, that was Hugh Fraser," said Phoenix, "we need to get the Irregulars patched straight to you in the ice-house in the future, Giles. Hugh's heard this morning from one of his team. They thought they saw Harrack in a tunnel leading out of New Street yesterday evening, but they were too far away to see where he went."

Henry tutted.

"Let's not be too critical, Henry," said Athena, "this initiative is in its early stages. We would have preferred to give these people specific training and instructions on what to do given various circumstances. However, we were desperate to find these two bombers and threw the Irregulars in at the deep end. Hugh Fraser will whip them into shape in time."

"We know they're in Birmingham now," said Artemis, "and we can keep up the search for the next occasion they surface. The more bodies we have at New Street station, the better. Can we allocate Olympus agents to supplement the Irregulars?"

"I'll see to that," said Athena.

"I think Rusty should draw up the operating procedures for both sets," said Phoenix. "We need a decision to follow, intercept, or eliminate to be automatic, depending on certain criteria. Those actions mustn't be delayed for a referral to Larcombe for an answer. Any delay will cost lives."

"Will you be going to Birmingham yourself, Phoenix," asked Giles.

Phoenix looked at his wife. She was still fragile. Grace's funeral was on Monday.

"Rusty and I will go there if the situation demands," he replied.

"We have enough teams of agents in the Midlands to cope with matters," said Rusty, "I'll work on the rules of engagement straight after this meeting. They will be with the Irregulars and our team leaders by tonight."

"We haven't a clue when these devils plan to strike," said Alastor, "we may already be too late."

"If Canary Wharf and Waverley have taught us anything," said Phoenix, "it's that they've thought out every stage in detail. Try to put yourself in their position. How would you tackle a mission such as this? Why did they stay in Liverpool for two days? Why not come south to Birmingham straight away? Where did they stay for three nights?"

"We may be looking for a fellow extremist who just gave them shelter or waited to help them plan this next stage in the campaign," said Henry.

"That's another search to add to my list," said Artemis.

"We will have the surveillance ramped up to cover the access and exit points within hours," said Phoenix. "My next move would be to check that my plan would go without a hitch. When they re-surface next, it will be to do a final dry run. The actual strike will happen within twenty-four hours of that. First, we must follow them back to their hideout, uncover any additional contacts they have established that might join them in this attack, and then eliminate the threat.

"I think we've covered the important items for today,"

said Athena. "Let's call it quits for this morning and get on with the list of things we've agreed to do. Time is of the essence."

Phoenix caught up with Rusty as he left the room.

"I wish we could be more involved, Rusty," he said.

"Athena and Geoffrey need you closer to home," said his friend.

"It shouldn't take long to write those procedures," said Phoenix, "tell them to listen to one of my favourite Metallica tracks. You've heard it often enough when we've travelled together."

"Seek and destroy," said Rusty, "yes, that covers it."

While the morning meeting took place, a visitor arrived to see Hugh Fraser. Piya Adani, the successful businesswoman who joined the Olympians only months ago as Ambrosia swept through the gateway, rattled over the cattle grid, and motored up the drive.

The hay fever season was behind her, and she was on top of the world. She had phoned Hugh Fraser last night to confirm she was arriving today. He promised to inform the estate's security personnel. Athena had told her she was always welcome at Larcombe Manor. Even though the senior Olympian may have wondered why she was keen to visit their logistics expert. Ambrosia didn't worry over minor details.

Hugh Fraser stood outside the old stable block when she arrived. Athena had pointed it out to her on her previous visit in between handing her a fresh tissue. The horses had long since disappeared, and now the block contained several offices, medical facilities, and living accommodations for Larcombe's resident senior agents.

Hugh gave her a tentative wave, and Ambrosia studied him through the windscreen. He was tall, dark, and distinguished-looking. If not handsome, then he was a fine physical specimen. Life in the armed forces and now working for Olympus had kept him fit. She found herself blushing as she got out of her car.

"Welcome to Larcombe Manor, Ambrosia," said Hugh, extending his hand.

His voice was warm, and the handshake firm.

"It's lovely to meet you, at last," she replied, trying to stop her knees from shaking,

"Come this way."

Hugh turned on his heel and marched her along the corridor to his quarters. Ambrosia hurried to keep up with him.

"This is me," he said when they stepped inside, "compact, but a place for everything, as they say."

"How beautiful; so neat and tidy, Hugh. It doesn't look as if anyone lives here. It's more like a show home."

"Now you're teasing me, Ambrosia. When you decide on the Army for a career, you learn how to keep yourself, your kit, and your surroundings in good order. Otherwise, you suffer the consequences. I knew when I came here that I wouldn't get the comforts of home. But the opportunity to work with Phoenix was too good to refuse."

"Bring me up to date with what's happened," she said.

"You have driven a long way to visit me," said Hugh, "surely I can make us a tea or coffee before we rush into business?"

Ambrosia was eager to hear about the Irregulars. Her pet project had fired up the Olympians at the first meeting she attended in early July. It was to be the launchpad for her accelerated rise in the organisation. Yet, the man who stood in front of her fascinated her. Ambrosia gazed into Hugh's grey-blue eyes and congratulated herself for choosing three-inch heels this morning.

The only other man in her life had been her father. She loved and respected him, but the self-made Indian multi-millionaire had been vertically challenged just like her. As Hugh studied her face, Ambrosia was struck by how warm those eyes looked. She had always associated blue-grey with the cold until now.

"It's not often you take this long to make a decision, surely?" Hugh asked. Ambrosia couldn't take her eyes off his mouth as he smiled at her.

"A black coffee would be fine," she said.

"Make yourself comfortable," said Hugh as he busied himself in what passed for a kitchenette.

Ambrosia stared at the bed briefly and then at the wooden chairs by the desk. All that remained was the two-seater settee facing the wall-mounted TV. She perched on the edge of her seat, reluctant to allow herself to sink back into the inviting soft leather.

Hugh carried two cups of coffee over and joined her on the settee. He sat back, totally at ease. Ambrosia felt the warmth of his thigh against hers; it was disconcerting. Her father had done his utmost to find suitable young men to woo her. He was keen to see her make a good marriage. Unfortunately, none of them interested her enough to divert her attention from the business.

The years passed quicker than seemed possible, and now here she was, only weeks away from her fortieth birthday. Her father's death in 2003 had been sudden, and she had thrown herself into her work. The company went from strength to strength under her stewardship, but that left less and less time for a social life.

Perhaps, it was time to relax and let nature take its course. Parts of her body were sending messages to her brain that were new and intriguing. Ambrosia moved back in the settee; her feet barely touched the floor, and their bodies grew closer than ever.

"How is it?" Hugh asked his face only a foot away.

"Wonderful," breathed Ambrosia.

"It's only instant they don't supply exotic blends for us here in the stable block."

Ambrosia hadn't been thinking of the cup of coffee she held. Instead, she had been dreaming of how Hugh would make her feel if things moved from this settee to that bed she glanced at earlier.

"You wanted to know how things with the Irregulars had been going? My initial move was establishing a skeleton team in a dozen major cities. Phoenix was taken aback by my actions but considered them a positive initiative. Of course, the outrage at Waverley station in Edinburgh caused Olympus to bring forward the programme. They concentrated on four highly populated cities, allocating more Irregulars to each. We supplemented the first eighteen with men and women fast-tracked by Henry Case."

"That's excellent news, Hugh. Finally, we're getting more people in the right places on the ground. I wish every ex-service person who has fallen on hard times to be recruited wherever possible. The increased intelligence they will bring to Olympus will be invaluable."

"I agree," said Hugh, "but we mustn't lose sight of the events that gave us this opportunity and why the veterans are so readily available to us. There was a significant loss of life in Edinburgh, many others suffered life-altering injuries, and the damage to the old station will take weeks to repair. Our veterans are at risk when they quit the forces. They have experienced disturbing things which leave them with long-term psychological damage. Without support for their PTSD, many veterans lose everything. Cuts to the armed forces have made things worse as veterans struggle to adjust to civilian life. The Government and military need to do more. These veterans were willing to make sacrifices for us. The least we can do is ensure they get the care they deserve."

Ambrosia could tell Hugh was a compassionate soul. Her heart went out to him. She placed her hand on his.

"Consider me reprimanded," she said, "I'm too wrapped up in this Irregulars project of mine. The bombings in London and Edinburgh were tragic. The families involved will be devastated. Olympus must find those responsible and bring them to justice. We can bring that about with the help of those people you now have in position. That is of paramount importance. The fact it raises our profile within the organisation is a bonus."

"Where do we go from here?" asked Hugh, not moving his hand from his lap, where Ambrosia's small hand still lay.

She would touch the stirrings of an erection that had laid dormant for far too long if he did. He hadn't looked at another woman since his wife left. The petite Indian beauty that nestled against his shoulder had awoken the beast.

"We put our trust in the Irregulars programme to produce results that will advance our cause," said Ambrosia. "We may be a new force within Olympus, but we are starting to shake things up. The next few days will be crucial. But, right now, I want us to do what both of us have been aching for since I arrived."

Ambrosia placed her coffee cup gently on the table. Then, she turned her body towards Hugh and leaned forward.

"Be gentle with me, Hugh," she whispered.

At Birmingham New Street station, the team of four Irregulars had been in strategic positions since early morning. Rusty Scott was still working on the operating procedures and the Olympus agents transferring in later in the day. So total coverage of every access point would be several hours away.

Jason Pride, thirty-three years old, came from Horsham in West Sussex. He was a veteran of the wars in Afghanistan and Iraq. Jason had lived in his car for a month last winter after being made homeless. He was invalided out of the Army with Post Traumatic Stress Disorder at the end of 2009, tormented by the horrors he witnessed during his brief army career.

He remembered snuggling deep into his sleeping bag on the back seat on bitterly cold winter nights. In those moments when he wondered whether he would ever get warm again, he believed his country had abandoned him. He risked life and limb for his Queen and country, yet he faced a bleak future.

Jason was bitter. There were immigrants from four corners of Europe and worldwide who had entered the UK since he joined the Army. Every one of them seemed in front of him on the housing list. His level of frustration was at boiling point. He was officially made homeless on December the first of last year when he had to leave a flat he had occupied for four years. It was partly his own doing. He drank heavily and had fallen behind with the rent.

The struggles with his PTSD were not going away, and because he was homeless with no fixed address, it was much harder to get the medication he needed from a doctor. The symptoms came and went. Jason might be okay for weeks and then find it impossible to even get out of the house. He didn't have that problem when he lived in the car.

The opportunity offered him by Olympus had been a lifeline. He now had a roof over his head, a part-time job, and the possibility of a future. This morning, he was close to the Hill Street access, which took passengers to the heart of the new concourse. His colleague was inside, having purchased a ticket. Kevin Watson was in the prime location to access any platform he desired. Kevin didn't plan to go anywhere. He was waiting to catch sight of any suspects the others missed.

Kevin was older than Jason by twenty-two years. He got wounded at Bluff Cove during the Falklands War when his landing craft had taken a direct hit. The longer journey time involved in carrying troops direct to Bluff Cove and differing opinions on how the landing proceeded caused delays in unloading. That delay had disastrous consequences. His Landing Support Logistics ship was a sitting target for the two waves of Argentine attack aircraft, fully laden and without escorts and air defence. Fifty men died that day. Kevin was among many survivors winched from the burning ships by brave helicopter crews.

Kevin had served in the Welsh Regiment with distinction, and after recovering from his injuries, he returned to his family home in Wrexham, Clwyd. His service career was over. He drifted from job to job and relationship to relationship; nothing worked out as he had hoped. He could see the faces of the men killed at the far end of the landing craft. Men he trained with, served with, and ultimately fought alongside. He would wake up screaming, soaked in sweat. He was too scared to sleep and turned to drink to mask the pain. Kevin lost the last job he held as a delivery driver.

Within weeks he was homeless. Kevin still believed that as a soldier, he should be strong. To ask for help was a sign of weakness. It took months for him to acknowledge his mental health issues. He had hit rock bottom. Then, out of the blue, Olympus came calling. It was his first step on a new ladder. He wasn't stopping until he had left his old life far behind him.

Jason admitted to his fifty-five-year-old new colleague that he met veterans from the Falklands campaign through to the present day during his time on the streets. Many now slept in doorways and begged passers-by. Every homeless veteran he met had PTSD or needed help, as many had become addicted to drugs and alcohol.

"We're two of the lucky ones, mate," Kevin said, "I won't waste this chance."

Luke Griffin, from Solihull, West Midlands, was thirty-four years old. He joined up at seventeen and completed tours of Kosovo and Northern Ireland. Luke left the Army in 2008 and returned to his hometown, where he worked in a warehouse. But he could not rid himself of the painful memories and turned to drink.

His life spiralled out of control despite being diagnosed with PTSD in 2011. By December 2012, he was homeless and using heroin. The Army had been perfect for him. They trained people to fight and kill — everything they needed; they did for them. When Luke left the Army, they forgot about him. Luke used drugs to block out the memories.

He had been getting his life back on track in the last twelve months. Help was there if you knew where to look and weren't too proud to ask. Luke Griffin had been clean for ten months. He was at the Stephenson Street entrance today, ready to do his bit for the country again. Luke might not be wearing a uniform, but he now had the chance to avenge his former colleagues. The men who suffered in the desert heat around Basra after he left the Army. The men he searched for today were the same enemy. It was payback time.

On the opposite side of the station to Kevin Watson sat Monty Jacks. He entered the station from Hill Street. Birmingham New Street had level access for wheelchair users. All the platforms had lifts, and every entrance had automatic doors. So Monty had been able to move around with freedom. He wasn't sure whether he could chase a terrorist in this chair, but there was nothing wrong with his eyes and ears.

Monty was from a West Indian family in Manchester. He was forty-seven and divorced. His wife had left with their three children in 2010, unable to cope with his disability and the dark moods that changed the happy-go-lucky, music-loving man she married forever.

The SAS sergeant lost both legs below the knee when his vehicle drove over a roadside IED in Iraq in 2008. He had woken up two weeks later at Selly Oak Hospital, Birmingham. Unfortunately, his troubles didn't end when he left there. When he got back to Manchester, he found it hard to adjust. His family life fell apart, and he was on his own. The next eighteen months were a blur to Monty, looking back now as he watched and waited for a sighting of the bombers.

When life got too much at the beginning of 2012, Monty approached Help for Heroes and spent three months at Tedworth House. While he was in the recovery centre in the West Country, he met many people going through the same things. Problems he encountered on civvy street were ones they had faced and knew how to overcome.

The camaraderie he experienced at that home in Wiltshire saved him. Suicide had seemed the only escape when he sat at home. He recovered his self-esteem. When Monty left to make a new home in Redditch, it wasn't what he *couldn't* do now but what he *could* do.

Monty Jacks had been awarded incapacity benefit in 2008 but had it withdrawn under the new system brought in last year. He remembered the assessment process as being totally and utterly degrading. His progress since moving to Worcestershire was under extreme threat.

Many veterans were already on the breadline. All they wanted to do was work, but for many, it was impossible. The challenges they faced were different to others who were out of work. They needed more support. Since last year, thousands of veterans got pushed to the breadline after being judged fit for work. Severely wounded veterans from Iraq and Afghanistan were once entitled to incapacity benefits and were told they no longer qualified.

When Monty Jacks had heard from Olympus, he reckoned this could give him something to make life worth living. The government didn't care. He was lucky to have a roof over his head. At first, he thought he wouldn't qualify for the role they offered. Monty told the guy who rang that others on the streets needed their help more than he did.

For once, the fact he was disabled was a bonus. He would be the first Irregular to carry out surveillance on the streets in a wheelchair. That had brought the smile back to Monty's face. He agreed to answer the call whenever Olympus needed him.

The four Irregulars had no idea how close they were to the two bombers. Mansouri and Harrack had yet to leave their hotel room, only a few hundred yards away. They were in constant contact with al-Hamady and the others in the attack cell. Messages travelled back and forth as they relayed instructions. The bombers were staying put. For the next series of checks on the plan's effectiveness, they relied on the men who would travel from the suburbs on the day of the attack.

Larcombe was unaware of this, so the Irregulars looked for their faces in the crowds, but they would never spot Mansouri or Harrack among them. The Olympus teams sent to assist would be armed with the same redundant photographs when they turned up in the early afternoon. Rusty's operating procedures would be ready and passed along the line to the team leaders.

The procedures might be impeccable, but how could the surveillance teams identify potential terrorists and implement them? Phoenix had thought they were playing catch-up earlier in the week. Nothing had changed. Olympus needed a break.

Chapter Eleven

Friday, 12th September 2014

Athena had read the reports from the Olympus team and the Irregulars that Giles had forwarded to her last night. The ice-house staff still searched for the bombers anywhere in the country. In case they slipped through the net. She was awake early and out of bed before seven. There was so much to do and so little time.

Her father told her at dinner last evening that the house in Vincent Gardens, Belgravia, had been valued at four and a half million pounds. Geoffrey was putting it on the market right after the funeral.

"Daddy," Athena said, "I thought you should wait a while. But, I warned you against making a rash decision, especially now."

"The estate agent told me she believes we're at the top of the market now. In six months, a delay could have cost me half a million. So no, I've made my decision. When I lock the door behind us when we leave for the funeral, that's the last time I set foot in the place. I'll stay here until I find a suitable bungalow along the coast, if that's okay?"

"Of course, Daddy," said Athena, "what about Mummy's things? What will you do with the furniture and your clothes?"

"I'll hand a set of keys to the estate agent. She will show a series of oil-rich Arabs around, no doubt. She assured me there would be no problem finding storage for my bits and pieces once the sale was complete. I'll only need a fraction of what's in the house in my new little nest."

"It will be strange not going there anymore. It's the only home I've known," said Athena. "Oh well, if you're sure you're doing the right thing. We're set for Monday if that's the right thing to say regarding a funeral. Sarah Gough is travelling up to Kensal Green. She wanted to meet with you beforehand. Perhaps, I should ask her to come to the house? Then, we can travel across London together."

"Will Sarah say a few words about Grace?" asked her father.

"If that's what you prefer," said Athena, "I've already taken note of the pertinent details. If I email those to her, she can prepare something."

"That would be better," said Geoffrey Fox, "I don't think I could manage it."

Athena hugged her father as his shoulders sagged after that. Monday couldn't come around soon enough. It might bring a pinch of closure and enable them to move forward.

Athena's cup of coffee was cold now. She had been staring into space for several minutes. She could hear Hope talking to herself in her bedroom, and the sound of the shower suggested Phoenix was nearly ready to face another day.

Athena poured a fresh cup when he walked through to the kitchen. His hair was still wet, and he looked tired.

"Coffee, darling?"

There was a grunt in response that Athena took to be an answer in the affirmative. Her husband must have had a restless night. Of course, she wasn't the only one with plenty on their mind.

"The news from New Street's surveillance yesterday wasn't encouraging," she said.

"That's an understatement," replied Phoenix, "I don't know what to do next."

"The morning meeting might bring better news," said Athena, "when Giles updates us."

The couple finished breakfast, saw to their daughter, and then handed her over to her nanny, Maria Elena. As they left for the meeting room, Geoffrey Fox put his head around the door.

"No rest for the wicked, I see," he smiled, "can Hope come out to play?"

"Maria Elena will give Hope her breakfast first," said Athena, "but if this weather stays fine, the three of you can walk around the grounds. The fresh air will do you good."

Phoenix and Athena left the room. The sound of happy voices followed them up the corridor.

"Your father meant no rest *from* the wicked," said Phoenix, "if only sunshine and laughter solved all our problems."

The others had already gathered in the meeting room. After the usual preliminaries, Giles updated the terrorist situation.

"We've searched high and low for Mansouri and Harrack. They haven't appeared on a CCTV camera anywhere in Birmingham in the past thirty-six hours. In my opinion, they've gone to ground in the city. Everywhere they might have travelled to has been scrutinised too, and they haven't surfaced. Artemis is trying a new program to hack into every hotel and B&B in the city. There's no point looking for a booking by name. I've asked her to concentrate on two men booking into somewhere between six and seven o'clock on Wednesday evening. It's a long shot. They could easily have several safe houses in the city."

"It's a start, Giles," said Phoenix, "what intelligence do we have on terrorist cells in the Midlands? I know it's risky, but can't you hack into our security services? It would be useful if they gave us a long list of possible names and addresses."

"That's not as daft as it sounds, Phoenix," said Rusty. "If cells exist, they have probably identified them, interviewed them, and filed the information for future reference."

This remark hit a sore spot for Athena. Her fiancée died in the London bombings of July 2005. One bomber had been on a watch list, but they took no action. A decade later, Rusty suggested the security services were no quicker off the mark than before.

The weekend stretched before them. Athena allocated tasks and expressed hopes for better news. She closed the meeting at lunchtime and reminded the others Minos was in the chair for Monday's meeting as she and Phoenix went to London.

As Henry Case and Giles Burke passed the stable block on their way to the ice-house, they heard a telephone ring.

"I bet that's someone for Hugh," said Henry, "he gets more than his fair share, I reckon."

"Phone calls, do you mean?" asked Giles. "I saw a car

parked outside here yesterday for ages. I've no idea who it belonged to."

"Someone he knew well, I believe," smiled Henry, "if my ears didn't deceive me."

"The crafty devil," said Giles.

"We shouldn't cast the first stone, Giles. Everyone along that corridor has been guilty in recent months."

"Oh, I must tell Maria Elena to keep the noise down. I hadn't realised how thin the walls were."

Inside the stable block, Hugh listened to Ambrosia on the phone.

"Yesterday was wonderful," she said, "everything I hoped it would be. I don't need to confess that it wasn't my first time. My father was old-fashioned. He started looking for suitable husbands when I reached fifteen. Some were even older than him; it was horrible. I refused them, but he wouldn't force me into a marriage I didn't want thank goodness. He thought of me as a rebel and didn't want me to go away to University. Even after I returned to the family business, he was still keen for me to marry well. It was important for him to believe I was still intact. I never let him know I'd experimented with two or three fellow students. It was only lust, not love."

"Yesterday came as a surprise," said Hugh, "a very welcome surprise. I can't wait to see you again."

"We will see much more of one another in the future," said Ambrosia, "don't worry. Although, after yesterday, that might be difficult."

The sound of her cheeky laughter made Hugh smile.

"The Olympus teams will join our Irregulars at New Street in the morning," he told her. "They will follow the same instructions on what to do if they have a confirmed sighting."

"We must cross our fingers and hope the terrorists break cover," said Ambrosia, "enjoy the weekend, Hugh. I'll call you on Monday."

Saturday, 13th September 2014

Events three thousand miles away changed everyone's plans.

Athena called an emergency meeting on Saturday afternoon.

Minos read them the news of another atrocity: -

"David Haines was abducted eighteen months ago by an unidentified armed gang while working in a refugee camp near the Turkish border. They seized Haines along with an Italian aid worker. Their Syrian translator and driver escaped unharmed. The Foreign Office ordered his family not to speak to anybody about the abduction."

"Didn't Haines appear in the Sotloff execution video that threatened Haines would be the next victim?" asked Henry Case.

"After that execution video surfaced," said Alastor, "it was admitted that the aid worker was one target of a failed American rescue mission. The jihadist group moved the hostages before the American commandos arrived."

"They showed Haines with Jihadi John," continued Minos. "He was declared as the next possible victim. John warned those governments that entered this evil alliance of America against Islamic State to leave their people alone."

"A video of the lead-up and aftermath of Haines' beheading was released earlier today," said Alastor, "it showed a second British captive, who it appears would suffer the same fate."

The room fell silent.

"The frequency of these executions is increasing," said Henry. "Is it possible the bombings are following a similar pattern?"

"These recent bombings are growing in size, if not frequency," said Rusty. "This brings us back to what Giles mentioned yesterday. Mansouri and Harrack won't be working alone on New Street. So, where are the other cell members, and what have they been doing for the past two days?"

"We couldn't trace where Mansouri and Harrack spent Sunday night until Wednesday morning," said Phoenix. "What if they stayed with another cell member based in Liverpool?"

"That's your weekend sorted, Giles," said Henry. "You need to trace people with possible links to IS in the Midlands and Liverpool. Even the authorities admit we have around twenty thousand jihadists in the UK."

"Needle and haystack come to mind," sighed Giles, "but that's what we're good at."

While Giles Burke and Artemis continued the search for clues, the crowds of shoppers in the commercial centre of Birmingham enjoyed a hot September afternoon. The Olympus agents and their new colleagues kept vigil inside and outside the nearby New Street station.

Trains arrived at every platform with a frequency that made the head spin. West Midlands Trains ran services from Lichfield, Longbridge, Redditch and Wolverhampton that interested Mansouri and Harrack. They noted that almost every platform was longer than usual and permitted two trains to stop simultaneously. There was a constant traffic turnover, with trains pulling away with their new passengers headed for distant locations. Some were stationary as people alighted or boarded, and new trains inched into the station, slowing to a gradual halt.

The possibilities for chaos were endless.

After discussing the initial planning stage, al-Hamady explained why Birmingham was such a fertile area for recruiting the men they needed to make this attack unforgettable.

The city is home to Britain's largest Muslim community, estimated at three hundred thousand. It was home to the alleged Saudi financier of the 9/11 attacks, the birthplace of Britain's first suicide bomber and the centre of the country's first Al Qaeda terror plot. The distinctive regional accent is heard the loudest in Belmarsh prison, where they hold most terror suspects.

Mansouri and Harrack listened intently as al-Hamady told them: -

"The ongoing troubles in Kashmir made it easier for a young Muslim from Birmingham to fly out and join our training camps. As a result, they became indoctrinated into Islamic State ideology. Kashmiri separatist groups acted as stepping stones to groups such as Al Qaeda and now IS. Twenty years ago, Kashmiri militant leaders visited Birmingham, urging the community to help fight against India. These visitors left a mark on the city's young Muslims. The result has been that terrorist recruiters have found young men eager to listen to their message rather than the moderate imams in the city's mosques."

Four young men who read the extremist views these militants had spread among their families were travelling into New Street this afternoon.

The Longbridge service carried Badawi Akhtar, twenty-six years old and born in Walsall. He studied for a chemistry degree at Aston University between 2005 and 2008. The thirty-minute journey from the north of the city was a pleasant one. The people surrounding him in the carriage were eager to shop in the arcades and malls of the Bullring. That augured well for the day of the attack.

The Redditch train would bring Fidvi Rahman into New Street from the opposite direction. His forty-minute train did not stop en route. Rahman was twenty-five years old and born in Balsall Heath but now lived in Winson Green. He was unemployed now, but until 2013 had worked at a supermarket.

Yafir Uddin was twenty-nine years old and born in Winson Green. He worked at a call centre in Wolverhampton. He had driven to Lichfield this morning. The cathedral city, with its Georgian townhouses, was light years away from his inner-city, working-class background. The journey to Platform 12B took between thirty-five and forty minutes.

Uddin travelled to Syria in 2012. Eleven months ago, he was arrested on suspicion of violent disorder but released as the authorities found insufficient evidence to prosecute. Earlier this summer, counter-terrorism officers searched his home as part of coordinated raids concerning an ongoing Syria investigation.

Zahar Osman was twenty-six-years-old had been born in Bangladesh, and came to the UK in 2006. His family lived in Wolverhampton. Osman was studying for a law degree but spent much of his time online encouraging acts of terrorism. He walked to the station to ride into New Street. It was only a twenty-minute trip.

Along with many IS militants, Osman was a prolific social media user. His videos urging others to travel to the training camps in Pakistan had racked up tens of thousands of views on YouTube. After becoming radicalised, Osman went to Syria in October 2013. He was featured in an IS propaganda video last year.

By three-thirty in the afternoon, the four young Muslims stood on different platforms at New Street station. Surrounded by crowds of fellow travellers, they could not see one another. They made contact by mobile phone, not with each other, but with Ahmed Mansouri in the nearby hotel. The young men confirmed that everything included in al-Hamady's plans would go smoothly. The next time these four men travelled by train, it would be a final step towards paradise.

All four had been susceptible to the warped messages of hate the extremist groups preached. They didn't have a strong affinity to the UK or the same beliefs their parents and grandparents shared. The extremists offered a solid identity to bond to, a sense of belonging. Brainwashing is easier in cultures with a focus on the afterlife. For them, paradise is only a moment away, a golden future to be entered into by the world of death.

Muslim suicide bombers fulfil their act of sacrifice with a smile because they believe they will reap huge rewards for eternity. They would receive forgiveness for their sins, and a place in paradise awaited them. They will be crowned with glory and welcomed by seventy-two beautiful virgins. They will avoid the suffering of the grave and the horror of the Day of Judgment, while seventy family members will also have places reserved in paradise.

Akhtar, Rahman, Uddin, and Osman shared these firm beliefs. Yet, they smiled as they relayed the good news to Mansouri. The young men were ready to fulfil their destiny.

Mansouri called al-Hamady in Liverpool, and the Syrian gave his instructions. The attack was to take place next Saturday afternoon. He told Mansouri to tell the young men to return home. Everything they needed to carry on the trains next week would now be prepared and delivered to their home address on Saturday morning.

After receiving the message, three young men moved towards the exit. They headed for the escalators that deposited them in Thousand Trades Square. A short walk took them to Grand Central to get the Midland Metro to Wolverhampton. Only Akhtar remained inside the station. He waited for the next train back to Walsall.

Monty Jacks sat on Platform 7; he had been on duty since nine this morning. He had wheeled his wheelchair up and down various platforms in the interim. There had been no sightings of Mansouri or Harrack; he saw nothing suspicious. Many attractive ladies at the station were suitably under-dressed for the mini-heatwave.

Badawi Akhtar wandered down the platform. Monty studied the young Muslim. He was sure he recognised the distinctive sunglasses and an unkempt beard. Of course, he wasn't one he was watching for, but why hang around so long after he got off the train?

Monty moved his wheelchair further up the platform. He stopped and checked the message boards. That train had come from Longbridge, where the massive car plants used to be until ten years ago. The next train leaving from this end of Platform 7 was going to Walsall. Monty knew the quickest way to make the Longbridge-Walsall journey was to go straight there via Aston. One stop, and you arrived in Walsall in an hour.

This bloke was stupid, or he had another reason to come into the city. As far as Monty could tell, he hadn't met anyone and never chatted with a soul. However, he had seen him on his phone for a while; this guy was worth a closer look. So he took a snap headshot of the young man on his phone.

Monty Jacks called the Olympus team leader outside.

"I have a suspicious one here, on Platform 7A," he said, "here is his picture. Can you get him checked out?"

"OK, Monty, will do," came the reply.

Monty Jacks looked across to where the man had stood. He had disappeared.

It was a quarter to four; the Walsall train was due to leave. Monty spun his chair around. Had his suspect left for another platform? It wasn't easy to see with the crowds jostling around him. There were dozens of people on the opposite platform as well.

Monty parked his chair by an electronic advertising board and scanned the faces facing him. The track a yard in front of him began to rumble. A train was approaching. It sounded heavy, and although it wasn't travelling fast, it didn't appear to be slowing.

Monty sensed someone behind him. A hand grabbed his phone, and then a foot shoved him hard in the back. His wheelchair shot forward. Monty realised it was a freight train he had heard. He heard screams as his chair reached the platform's edge and tipped over. One of them may have been his own. The slow-moving freight train and fifty heavily laden trucks halted when an emergency signal raised the alarm, but Monty Jacks was dead.

Outside the station, the other Irregulars were unaware their new team had suffered its first fatality. The Olympus team leader had contacted Giles Burke in the ice-house and waited for an update. He tried to call Monty back to ask if this suspect had been alone. Unfortunately, the call went to voicemail.

He made another call: -

"Finn, you're closest to Platform 7. Can you get over there, please? Three guys in Muslim gear went past me just now. They were last seen heading for the Bullring. Monty sent me a photo of a young Muslim in similar clothing a few minutes ago. The two events may not be connected, but one face that passed me rang a bell."

"Will do, boss," replied Finn, "I'm nearly there. I've just got to climb these stairs, and I'm on Seven. Everything's happening up here, boss. There's been an accident, by the looks of it. I can't get close enough to see what was involved. The Transport Police and Network Rail staff are moving passengers away. I can't see any paramedics yet. Hang on; someone has just reached the top of the stairs. Someone is on the railway track, boss. It doesn't look good. Oh, shit."

"What's up, Finn? What can you see?"

"A railway worker fifteen yards further up the platform has just dragged part of a wheelchair onto the platform, boss."

"Thanks, Finn. I'll call Larcombe and tell them the news. Maybe they can get those other three on CCTV too. I'm positive they will identify at least one of them."

"The lone Muslim must have seen Monty take the photo, boss. He was right to be suspicious. If we find a link to the other three, could this be the break we've been hunting for?"

"We live in hope, Finn."

Badawi Akhtar had left Platform 7 at once. He couldn't return to Walsall by train. He needed to find an alternate route home. Badawi could get a bus from Corporation Street that got him there in forty minutes. But first, he needed to call his handler. He wasn't looking forward to admitting he had killed a man.

"You fool," Mansouri yelled, "you have put the whole operation at risk. Who was this man? Was he a policeman, or did you believe he was from the security services?"

"He was a coloured man. Disabled and in a wheelchair. I'm sure he took a picture of me. So, I grabbed the phone and pushed him under a train."

"You have deleted the image?" asked Mansouri.

"I have destroyed the phone," said Akhtar. He was too scared to admit that he had seen the 'sent' message before he did so.

"Go home. Await instructions. You may be in luck," muttered Mansouri.

Sunday, 14th September 2014

"What a terrible business," said Rusty as he and Artemis watched the news report on TV as they sat down to breakfast.

"We missed this last night," said Artemis. They had enjoyed a rare evening away from Larcombe Manor, watching a show at the Forum in Bath followed by a late drink.

"Phoenix and Athena will have heard this news from Giles," said Rusty. "We'll be getting the call to a meeting soon."

"Athena will want to order an immediate response," said Artemis.

"If this was Mansouri or Harrack, how did they get this close to our Irregular without the others spotting them?"

Rusty's phone rang.

"Here we go," he said. Artemis pushed back her plate

and made for the shower. Sunday was not to be a day of rest.

Fifteen minutes later, the team sat around the table in the meeting room.

"Giles, can you bring us up to speed, please?" asked Athena.

"Monty Jacks' death was reported as a tragic accident last evening when the news broke. Since then, the police have interviewed his ex-wife. On the latest bulletin, the reporter at News Street said the police now considered suicide a possible reason for what happened. The reporter said Jacks had struggled to come to terms with his disability and had recently turned to Help for Heroes because of depression."

"We know that's unfounded," said Athena. "It may have been true in the past, and he sought help. But everything we learned about him indicated he was ready to return to action."

"I agree," said Minos, "Jacks was eager to show he could still contribute. He told us he was the happiest he'd been in years. It was not suicide, nor was it an accident. I believe it was murder."

"I have the clincher here," said Giles, "here's the last photo he took on his phone. He sent it to his team leader, who forwarded it for identification yesterday afternoon. The timestamp indicates he took it less than four minutes before he died. That phone wasn't discovered on the platform, tracks, or on what remained of Jacks."

"Have we identified this suspect yet?" asked Henry Case.

"It's not a face that's come up before. He's never been in trouble with the law. The security services haven't had their eye on him. We're still hunting on social media, university connections, and everywhere he might have been. He looks to be in his mid-twenties."

"The same old story," muttered Phoenix.

"Not entirely, Phoenix," said Giles. "Our team leader at New Street asked me to check the route to the Bullring for three other men. This first photo triggered a memory from several minutes earlier. They had left the station together. We had more luck there. It took longer to find the CCTV images than it did to identify two of the men. They've been high-profile for the security services for over a year."

Giles passed copies of the profiles of two of the suspects for the others to read: -

"Yafir Uddin is twenty-nine and lives in Winson Green. He visited Syria two years ago, and the security services have had him under scrutiny ever since. He's active on social media. His Twitter post yesterday welcomed the beheading and swore death to all infidels. He's not been shy about pinning his colours to the mast. If he was on New Street station yesterday, it wasn't an innocent afternoon shopping."

"At last, we're getting somewhere," said Athena.

"Which brings us to this charming character," said Giles. "Zahar Osman, originally from Bangladesh. Twenty-six and living in Wolverhampton. He's even more voluble online, and his YouTube videos nasties get plenty of views."

"And the third man?" asked Minos.

"Similar to the one likely to have been responsible for Monty's death," said Giles, "not a known radical. We'll find the links between them in time and name them."

"What's our next step?" asked Alastor.

"We put surveillance teams on the two we've identified," said Athena, "then extend that surveillance to the others when we locate them. It's obvious from their presence at

New Street and the reaction by one of their number to Monty Jacks seeing him there that they are up to no good. If we can link them to Mansouri and Harrack, this could be the cell planning the next attack."

"A dry run before the big day. Whenever that is," said Phoenix.

"We have a lead, at last," said Athena. "When these men reappear and make for New Street, we take direct action. First, we must avenge Monty Jacks' death. Then, if we can prevent these four from reaching their target, we will reduce the impact Mansouri and Harrack hope to achieve. Our next task must be to discover where those two have been hiding since Sunday."

"We've got people working on that, Athena," said Artemis, "the search area is narrowing by the minute. If they're in Birmingham, we'll find them."

"Will it be in time?" sighed Minos.

As the Larcombe team performed their duties in the icehouse, Phoenix and Athena attempted to relax. Tomorrow was the day of Grace Fox's funeral. They had decided to drive up to spend the last night in the house in Vincent Gardens, Belgravia. A car would collect them in the morning to travel across London to the West London cemetery. The Reverend Sarah Gough would join them an hour before the car was due.

In Birmingham, Mansouri and Harrack were in conversation with Bakar al-Hamady. News that the death of the disabled veteran was a possible suicide had come as a pleasant surprise. Akhtar was off the hook for now. Last night, Mansouri was seconds away from ordering his killing. Nothing must obstruct their bombing programme.

"We go ahead with the plan as arranged," said al-Hamady, "but there must be no more slip-ups. If there's any hint the security services are onto us, you must move to a place of safety. The other four are expendable."

Mansouri knew which mosque offered them security for as long as was necessary. It would be an impregnable place of sanctuary, right under the noses of the authorities.

The address had been given to them by al-Hamady when they studied plans in Liverpool at the beginning of the week. They could both be inside it within fifteen minutes of leaving this hotel.

The Olympus team leader at New Street had received his instructions from Giles Burke. The three Irregulars were to stay in place if Mansouri and Harrack surfaced. He had called Hugh Fraser at Larcombe last night to pass on his condolences about Monty Jacks. The logistics officer had been distraught about losing a man on the first mission the Irregulars had undertaken. Fraser had urged him to find the culprit and make him pay.

"Where are we off to, boss?" Finn asked his team leader as they drove out of the city at noon.

"You are going to Winson Green to keep watch on Yafir Uddin. Tate is off to Wolverhampton to look after Zahar Osman. It makes sense that the other guy lives on the Metro route between Birmingham and Wolverhampton. I guess the four men travelled into the city by train yesterday, and three of them used the tram to get home."

"There must be significance to where they travelled from yesterday, boss. So why not come in by tram too?"

"Giles Burke told me the CCTV cameras inside the station captured them on different platforms to the one Monty Jacks patrolled. So it might be possible to work out where the trains originated. I don't think it's the important element, though. I reckon it's the track they arrived on and the tunnels they negotiated. Imagine what damage a blast in a confined space could cause."

Agents Finn and Tate moved to a spot near the home addresses of Uddin and Osman; they would keep watch for the rest of the afternoon. Relief agents would arrive between six and six-thirty tonight. The team leader returned to Birmingham; time to check on how the Irregulars were coping with the loss of Monty Jacks.

The afternoon was warm and sunny in both Winson Green and Wolverhampton.

Finn saw plenty of activity on the streets surrounding the house but nothing from inside. The inner-city area was a melting pot of a host of nationalities. There was a strong presence of Afro-Caribbean and Asian families, some of which had been here for over fifty years. The prison familiar to many outside the city was half a mile up the road.

The agent was on a side street with a good view of the front of the house. If they had bodies to spare, Finn would have preferred someone staked out at the rear of the property. The row of terraced houses had alleyways that led to the back, but there could have been an escape route across the adjoining gardens. He became uneasy. He was the watcher. Why did he sense someone was watching him?

He checked his watch. It was a quarter to six. The changeover was only a few minutes away; he could get home and relax. He didn't envy his replacement hanging around here in the dark.

A car pulled up outside Uddin's house. A man got out; it wasn't Uddin. He walked to the front door and knocked. Finn kept a close watch. Was his man indoors? Had he been there throughout the afternoon watching TV? Or had he been wasting his time watching an empty house?

Finn didn't hear anyone approach. He only heard the swish of a blade.

A voice called out from the side street. The man at the house returned to his car and drove to where he stood.

"Throw him in the boot," Uddin said.

"I'll get the carpet bloody," said Rahman.

"So, burn the car. You won't need it for much longer."

Ten minutes later, the relief agent parked the car where the team leader had told him he'd left Finn. He couldn't see him. That was good; Finn was supposed to be out of sight while on surveillance duty. He walked along the side street. He walked past Uddin's house on the opposite side of the road. A playing field was fifty yards up the road, surrounded by metal railings.

A dozen local kids had been playing football. It was time for dinner. The agent watched as they made their way towards the gate. They laughed and joked until they got near the gate. Then the whole pack was screaming and running in every direction. The agent crossed over to see what had spooked them.

Finn's head was stuck on the top of one of the metal railings.

Chapter Twelve

Monday, 15th September 2014

Dawn had broken in Vincent Gardens. Athena awoke to the sound of her father moving around in his room. Today would be difficult for him. Funerals were never a happy occasion. There always seemed more to attend than weddings and christenings the older she got.

Phoenix stirred beside her.

"What time is it?" he groaned.

"Early," she replied, "but I'm getting up to check Daddy's alright."

Phoenix turned over to grab another thirty minutes. Then he remembered the news that came through last night just as they arrived in London. Another agent was murdered. He got out of bed and got washed and dressed in ten minutes.

The team leader took the rest of his crew to Winson Green last night to search for the body. They found it stuffed into a large skip behind a Chinese takeaway. Tate had returned from Wolverhampton to aid in the search, leaving his relief on watch. Neither had a thing to report so far. Osman didn't emerge throughout the day, but he had been busy.

While Geoffrey Fox and Athena tucked into breakfast, Phoenix sat in the lounge with a coffee mug and laptop. He needed to keep abreast of events. Phoenix was glad he hadn't eaten. When he called at eight, Giles told him Osman uploaded the execution to his YouTube Channel late last night.

Finn may have been killed outright with the first slash of the heavy ceremonial sword, but the images from inside Uddin's house showed what had happened next. The gruesome sight had received over thirteen thousand views. They saw Uddin and a second man, possibly Rahman, who they now knew lived close by in the video. Rahman stood to one side, smiling as Uddin completed the beheading.

Osman had added a biting commentary. Phoenix couldn't stomach it any longer.

Although the final act of today was not over, the time for grieving had to end. Olympus must seek revenge. Every member of that cell would pay with their lives.

Phoenix issued the order to Rusty Scott.

When he returned to the kitchen, Athena was washing the breakfast things.

"Did you want something to eat, darling?"

"I'll have another coffee in a while. Sarah will be here before long. How's your father coping?"

"I think he's cried all his tears in the past fortnight," said Athena. "Can you believe everything that's happened in that time? Last night was yet another tragic setback for Olympus."

"We knew before we tackled the Grid head-on that

losses were inevitable. The terror cells have been inactive for a few months on mainland Britain, but we are bound to suffer hits when they raise their heads. The murders of Jacks and Finn were more shocking because of the way they met their deaths and because these men knew we were watching them. However, our training has been good enough to date for our people to carry out covert operations without being exposed to danger."

"Someone watching for the watchers, do you mean?" asked Athena.

"Mansouri and Harrack have proved themselves to be tricky customers. They may well have arranged a security screen around these cell members. Protecting their assets if you wish. Until they blew themselves to kingdom come on whatever day they had planned."

"Is it possible someone other than Mansouri and Harrack arranged the security screen? Is there a Mr Big in the network of cells?"

"We never determined where they stayed in Liverpool from Sunday night to Wednesday morning, did we?" said Phoenix. "That's worth pursuing. I'll ask Artemis to check if any likely suspects have turned up on a watch list or persons of interest."

"Artemis will be busy enough without you adding to the list," said Athena.

"Yeah, well, Rusty's busy today and tomorrow. So she'll have time to spare."

A taxi drew up outside at ten o'clock. The Reverend Sarah Gough had arrived.

Athena welcomed her at the front door and took her to her father in the lounge. Geoffrey was dressed in a dark charcoal suit with a black tie on his blue shirt. He stood when the vicar entered the room, and she hugged him.

"Good morning, Mr Fox," she said.

"You can call me Geoffrey these days, Sarah," he laughed.

"Force of habit," she said, "when I've known someone since I was a teenager."

"Talking of habits," said Geoffrey, "I didn't expect to see you in a hooded jacket and jeans. All part of being a modern vicar, I suppose?"

Sarah had travelled up on the train in her day clothes.

"Oh, don't worry. I've got the traditional garb to change into before we leave. Shall we sit and discuss what you wish me to say about your wife?"

Athena left them to it and checked Phoenix was getting changed. She found him in the kitchen with a slice of toast and a mug of coffee.

"Daddy and Sarah are chatting. The car will be here at a quarter to eleven."

"Did Sarah mention Henry to you?" asked Phoenix.

"No, she didn't. Now you mention it. Everything's OK, as far as I'm aware."

The well-oiled machine run by the funeral director and the Kensal Green crematorium clicked smoothly into action at ten forty-five. The car arrived, and the four mourners from Vincent Gardens were soon seated inside. The black limousine cruised slowly through the streets of the city. As the driver swung the car between the gates to the cemetery, the hearse bearing Grace Fox's body moved ahead of them up the driveway at a modest five miles per hour.

Forty-five minutes later, the service had ended. Sarah Gough was magnificent. The congregation of family, friends, and former business associates laughed and cried in equal measure at her eulogy. Geoffrey looked content.

Athena stood by his side as the long line of mourners filed out.

Phoenix watched from a few yards away; he phoned Giles. Rusty would be in Birmingham by two o'clock. Phoenix warned Giles of the possibility that the potential suicide bombers had sentries; to prevent them from coming to harm. Giles would pass the information on to Rusty.

The line of mourners grew shorter now. They would soon drive to the hotel where Geoffrey had arranged the wake. As two o'clock approached, Phoenix stood in the crowded bar with a drink in his hand. He thought of Rusty and the mission he was missing. His responsibility was here, but he would have loved to have been in Birmingham avenging the deaths of their colleagues.

Athena was speaking with friends of her parents Phoenix had never heard of let alone met. These people were several rungs up the social ladder, so he thought it unlikely they would ever meet again after today.

Geoffrey was talking to Sarah Gough, who still wore her church vestments. Phoenix left them to it. He was hungry, and the food the pub had provided was enough to feed twice as many people as had attended. Still, he could make a start.

"How are you and Henry getting on, my dear," Phoenix heard Geoffrey ask as he crossed the room. He hoped his father-in-law didn't put his foot in it.

"Very well," Sarah replied. "We get together as often as possible. We saw you both at the christening, of course."

"In happier times," said Geoffrey, sighing, "we had no idea we only had one week left together."

"Henry and I haven't seen one another since that Bank Holiday," Sarah admitted. "We've talked on the phone, and I've written to him, but he's always busy."

"Athena keeps them busy," said Geoffrey, "but you two make a good couple, despite his work."

"In what way?" asked Sarah puzzled.

"Well, Head of Security is a label that could cover many tasks. Ever since I've known Phoenix, I've tried to discover the exact nature of what it is he does when he disappears for days on end. Rusty intrigues me too. Henry's more a man of action than a charity worker, don't you think?"

"Are you saying Athena is involved in something other than charity work?" asked Sarah. "Something more aligned with her work after she left Random House and joined the security services?"

"Perhaps, I've said too much," said Geoffrey, looking at the empty glass in his hand. "I'm not used to drinking alcohol at lunchtime these days."

Sarah left Geoffrey standing alone in the middle of the bar. Phoenix saw her heading for his wife. Something was about to hit the fan. He put the plate piled high with savouries and sandwiches on the table and went to help prevent this from becoming a disaster.

Rusty met the Olympus team leader at a safe house in Solihull. It turned out to be a five-bedroomed house with a large garden at the front and the rear.

"This is cosy compared to the usual places I get to stay," he said.

"There are many of us to accommodate," said the other senior agent, "we've diverted the Irregulars here, plus half of my team. First, we'll carry out our attacks, and then the rest of my crew will be alerted if our actions bring Mansouri and Harrack out of hiding."

"The noose is tightening," said Rusty, "Giles told me

before I left Larcombe that there were less than six hotels left to check. So we'll know their whereabouts by tonight."

"I can promise them a restless night," said the team leader.

The house filled up with bodies over the next hour. Rusty took the team through the details of the direct action and confirmed there were to be no prisoners.

At dusk, they moved into position. The first van drove to Wolverhampton. Twenty minutes later, the remaining two vans were making for Winson Green and Walsall. At nine-thirty in the evening, they swept the area around the terrorists' properties for evidence of surveillance. Several hidden cameras were disabled, but there was no sign of any people on watch.

The all-clear message meant that the four teams of two agents could strike.

Rusty paired with Kevin Wilson. The Olympus team leader with Tate.

Akhtar, Rahman, Uddin, and Osman would never go to paradise. The four men died in a swift burst of bullets from guns fitted with silencers within thirty seconds of the teams entering the house. The teams transferred the bodies to the vans and drove to Solihull.

"We will get rid of them in the morning," said the team leader, "Cannock Chase is nice this time of year. It's better than they deserve."

Rusty fetched glasses and two bottles of red wine. He poured the drinks and passed them to his colleagues.

"To Monty Jacks and Finn," he said.

The Olympus men raised their glasses and echoed his toast.

Rusty sent a message to Phoenix and the ice-house at Larcombe Manor.

'Mission completed.'

"What does Henry Case do for the Olympus Project, Annabelle?" asked Sarah.

Those attending the wake who stood closest moved away or pretended not to notice and eavesdropped. Sarah's raised voice could be heard right across the bar. Phoenix arrived just in time to persuade the two women to take the discussion into the quieter room next door. Both he and Athena could tell Sarah was agitated.

"What do you mean, Sarah?" asked Athena.

"Geoffrey tells me you keep him in the dark too. There's something more sinister at Larcombe Manor, and Henry Case is involved in it up to his neck."

"Look," said Phoenix, attempting to calm her, "Geoffrey has had these crazy notions ever since we first got together. Henry is our Security Head. The Olympus Project stands for certain basic principles. He thinks when Rusty and I go off on trips away from Larcombe Manor, we're involved in some form of skulduggery. We're merely spreading the message, reinforcing those basic principles."

"You may fool him with that, but I know Henry too well. He is a military man through and through. I'm not a naïve young woman, Phoenix; Annabelle and I have known one another since University. I'm aware of the career path she took after we left Cambridge. I met Henry when I visited Larcombe to discuss your wedding. We hit it off, and when I returned home, I did some digging. There has never been anyone interested in me, not in that way, since I entered the Church. It seemed as if men believed I was off-limits once they met me in my vestments. My research told me Henry attended public school. He went to Oxford to study History but left after a year to join the Army. His service record covered his early training and his transfer to military intelligence, but details were somewhat vague about his role towards the turn of the century. He joined Olympus at the outset. My concern is that his job in those latter years in the Army included interrogating suspected terrorists. If Geoffrey is right, that interrogation could have continued to the present day."

Athena looked at Phoenix. Was it time to tell the truth? Could they bluff their way through this? As they had on many occasions before with people like the Charity Commission. There had been many scrapes that had almost whipped away the charity cover to expose the Project's real purpose.

"Has Henry ever given you even the slightest hint he is involved in anything as unpleasant as you suggest?" asked Phoenix.

"Well, he wouldn't, would he?" said Sarah.

"Maybe, you don't know him as well as you think," said Phoenix. "Henry has been struggling with his conscience for months. He has also discussed matters with Rusty Scott and us, so he tells me."

"So, things happen at Larcombe Manor that are far from charitable?"

"Henry performed a role in the Army that necessitated the interrogation of suspects and prisoners. He swears he never crossed the line. Olympus has never asked him to do anything illegal, either. Recently, his relationship with you has become so important that he has considered resigning from his post. We persuaded him to stay because he is so important to us in the broader view of intelligence and security. He has handed the interrogation duties on to junior personnel."

"I wish he could have told me everything from the beginning," said Sarah, "or when we became close back in the summer. It's a lot to take in. I'm unsure how I feel about it, and don't think you're off the hook, Phoenix. You didn't answer my question. What do you do that needs people like Henry to interrogate people?"

"We need you to go home, Sarah," said Athena, "talk with Henry and decide where you go from there. You love one another. As for Larcombe and the work we do, it will depend on the outcome of those talks. If you and Henry can move forward together, we can help you understand the work we have done over the past six years with Olympus. If not, we hope you will keep your concerns to yourself."

"What of your father? He'll be moving closer to you soon, so he tells me. Will he be left in ignorance too?"

"If possible," said Athena with a smile.

A mobile phone rang in the hotel room where Mansouri and Harrack rested. It was now three in the afternoon Mansouri saw a call from Bakar al-Hamady on one of the burner phones on the bedside table. He picked it up and listened: -

"Abort the planned attack. Get to the mosque at once."

"What happened?" asked Mansouri.

"The cameras around our helpers' homes went blank an hour ago. I sent a friend in Wolverhampton to check on Zahar Osman. He found that someone had broken into Zahar's house, and he was gone. There was blood spray on the wall above the settee in the living room. We must assume the people watching us came from British security services, and they killed our helpers. I've left Walton, and I'm at the airport now. My flight to Paris is in ninety minutes. If I escape unharmed, I'll call you at the mosque on this number. Ditch every other phone you have, save the plans to a thumb drive, but destroy every physical and digital record. Is that clear? It is only a delay. If Allah spares us, I shall return to help you strike a crippling blow to the heart of this country. Go quickly, brother."

"Who was that?" asked Harrack.

"Our saviour," said Mansouri.

The two terrorists travelled light. They had left the hotel and were inside their sanctuary by twenty-past three. The smoke alarm in their room alerted the hotel staff and the fire service fast enough to save the place from lasting damage. A metal waste bin suffered the most. Documents, maps, and SIM cards it had contained were a molten mess. A rubbish skip at the rear of the hotel now held two laptops repeatedly smashed with the butt of a gun.

In the ice-house at three o'clock, Giles and Artemis analysed the data they had gathered in the past twelve hours. Added to the news that the threat to New Street station had diminished, it was interesting reading.

"It took forever, but we found the four young men and neutralised them," said Giles. "Now we have two hotels within a mile of the station where men booked into a room within the time frame we anticipate on Sunday night."

"Rusty has sent teams to both hotels," said Artemis, "we'll hear from them within the next thirty minutes. It will be a great day if we can catch Mansouri and Harrack in the next half hour."

"Our search around Liverpool threw up seven possible names," said Giles. "Seven might sound a lot. A city of that size is sure to contain radicals, no matter which religion or political leader they follow. If we can narrow that number, we might find the supreme head of the cell."

As the two intelligence agents worked on the list, the call came through from Rusty.

"We've confirmed the hotel. The fire engines were outside when we arrived. The birds have flown. I guess we missed them by ten minutes. Can you search CCTV cameras around Grand Central, please? We might catch up with them yet."

Giles switched his attention to Birmingham. Artemis stuck to the task of locating Mr Big.

Artemis found Bakar al-Hamady's name in several searches. Al-Hamady was fifty-eight years old and from Syria. He was an ISIS sympathiser. He had travelled to Pakistan, North Africa and Russia, and back to Damascus. MI5, Border Control and Merseyside Police referenced him as a person of interest.

Artemis noted the address the police had for him in Walton, Liverpool. Perhaps that was where Mansouri and Harrack had been for three days. Could this be Mr Big?

"I may have located our man in the North," said Artemis when Giles looked up from his computer screen.

"Good, but I fear another dead end with the other two. I found Mansouri and Harrack one hundred yards from the hotel, then again on the next street. After that, they disappeared again. They're not to be found anywhere within a mile radius."

"Could they have been picked up?" asked Artemis.

"It's possible, but why not get picked up at the hotel?" said Giles.

"Where might they have gone? What buildings are there on the neighbouring streets?"

"There's a mosque close by," said Giles, "with a hard-line reputation. Is it possible they went there?"

"The imams could offer protection until the police turned up with a warrant. Then, provided they had reasonable grounds to suspect criminals were inside, the police wouldn't have any trouble removing them."

"Olympus can't burst in guns blazing, though, can we? It would draw too much attention."

"We may have to be patient and wait," said Artemis, "what do I do about al-Hamady? He lives in Walton, by the way."

"Get a local team to visit him. Bring him in for questioning. Henry can find out what he knows."

Artemis made the call. They would find the house empty. The planner took off for Paris as they approached Walton. He had removed every item of interest before he ran.

At the mosque, Mansouri and Harrack were already scheming.

"A week more and the centre of the city would have been in ruins," cursed Harrack, "how did the authorities get onto us? We were so careful."

"We must pray and be patient," said Mansouri.

Tuesday, 16th September 2014

Yesterday had gone, and Tuesday heralded a period of calm at Larcombe Manor. The past two weeks had been hectic.

Phoenix and Athena brought Geoffrey Fox home with them in the morning. He would stay until he had sold his

Belgravia home and discovered his bungalow with a sea view to start his new life without his beloved Grace.

Rusty Scott drove from Birmingham. Four out of six wasn't bad. He had found a hard-line mosque that was a possible location for the bombers. Continuous surveillance would be in place until they reappeared.

Hugh Fraser was in the stable block checking on the date for the funeral of Monty Jacks. His estranged family insisted he wanted his ashes scattered in Manchester. Whatever the result, Hugh knew he needed to attend. It set a precedent. He hoped it would be a long time before another Irregular met an untimely end.

His hand hovered over the phone. Should he call Ambrosia first? A trip to Manchester early next week might bring the possibility of time in her arms later in the day. He knew she would be keen to discuss the next mission for the Irregulars.

Along the corridor, Henry Case flicked through the pile of reports he had to get through. There were more potential Irregulars to vet. Another batch of agents was soon due to start its refreshment programme. Longdon and Thomas had suggested minor adjustments to the schedule, many of which looked eminently sensible considering what clowns the two of them could be. The phone rang. It was the Reverend Sarah Gough.

"Sarah, lovely to hear from you," he said.

"Oh, Henry," Sarah began. Henry could tell she was on the verge of tears.

"There's something I need to tell you," said Henry.

"Why didn't you tell me at the very beginning when we sheltered from the rain at Burrington Combe?" she asked. "If what you do is legal, I can cope, although it's uncomfortable to think about. You used to call me 'padre' back then. They serve alongside the fighting men; some even carry weapons into battle."

"I was foolish enough to think I could keep you from ever finding out."

"Geoffrey Fox told me yesterday he had his suspicions. I tackled his daughter and her husband, and they gave me a sanitised version of the truth."

"I've grown to love you so much, Sarah, that the thought of this bringing our relationship to an end has been causing me sleepless nights. I would quit Larcombe and leave everything behind to be with you. So there, I've said it. I've been longing to tell you for weeks."

"Oh, Henry, they told me yesterday you have been in torment over this and how it might affect our relationship. You must know I love you deeply. I prayed for guidance last night after I returned home. I had to be sure it was right for me to accept you have duties to perform with which I might disagree. But I still want to share my life with you."

"Did you find the answer?" asked Henry.

"Not from my prayers. I googled Albert Pierrepoint, the hangman, and found he was married for forty-nine years. I thought if his wife Annie could reconcile what his day job was, so could I."

If only you knew, thought Henry. He was far short of the four hundred Pierrepoint had executed, but he and Sarah would never wander through the pet cemetery on a sunny afternoon stroll.

"When will I see you again, Henry?" asked Sarah, "I can understand now why you've been keeping your distance. I know the truth now, so you needn't be concerned."

"I'll drive to see you this weekend," said Henry, "and bugger the parishioners. I'm sleeping at the vicarage. If anyone complains, tell them you'll be reading the banns very soon."

"Are you asking me to marry you, Henry?" asked Sarah; the tears were now forgotten.

"Will you find someone to marry us, Sarah?" he asked.

Sarah laughed.

"I will."

Artemis sat in the apartment she shared with Rusty Scott. The morning meeting had been a brief affair with three protagonists away. It was lunchtime. If Rusty got home soon, they could spend an hour or two together before she went underground for her eight-hour shift.

Artemis glanced at the date on the newspaper she was reading. The sixteenth meant only seven days remained before Phil Hounsell arrived to work at Larcombe. She knew Phoenix and Athena would do everything possible to keep him segregated from the senior personnel. However, Artemis wasn't sure what his reaction would be if they accidentally bumped into one another. Ah well, she had seven days' grace before needing to worry about that.

The rest of the week passed with little incident. Bakar al-Hamady disappeared into a Parisian suburb until he knew it was safe to return to the UK.

Ahmed Mansouri and Omar Harrack submitted to the strict regime of the mosque. They were safe from harm, for now.

Geoffrey Fox busied himself throughout the week, looking for suitable properties on the coast and checking storage facilities for his furniture if the house sold quickly.

He spent time with Hope and Maria Elena but allowed Phoenix and his daughter space. They thought he was sensitive to their needs, but really, he wanted to avoid any conversations about Henry Case.

Hugh Fraser had called Ambrosia to inform her he would drive up to Manchester on Monday for the funeral. She had invited him to join her in her home outside Leeds that evening. Ambrosia wanted to cook a special meal for the occasion. They had much to discuss, and if Olympus could spare him, she hoped he would stay until after lunch on Tuesday.

Giles Burke set the wheels in motion, yet again, to spread misinformation around events in the North and the Midlands. People go missing all the time. The police didn't have the resources to check; that was easy to handle. In Winson Green, the house where Uddin and Rahman had died now lay empty. A cleaning crew visited the house within twelve hours. They could have arrived earlier, but they were cleaning two other properties. The ice-house team was happy that no links to Olympus existed.

Henry Case visited a Bath jewellery store on Friday morning.

He was driving to Surrey in the afternoon. Everything was sweetness and light.

Chapter Thirteen

Monday, 22nd September 2014

A few miles away from Larcombe Manor on the other side of Bath, Erica Hounsell stared out of her kitchen window. She and Phil had been married for nine years. During the time they had known one another, she always felt secure.

Erica remembered the night they first met. She had been working behind the Waggon & Horses pub bar, and he breezed in with the gang from work. They came from the police station in town, but there was something about this more senior officer. He kept finding excuses to pop to the bar for a chat.

Romance took its own sweet time as his long hours interfered with progress, but they got there in the end. Their children, Shaun and Tracey, quickly followed the wedding in 2005. The eight-year-old and six-year-old made her little family complete.

When the kids were still young, and her Mum was still alive to babysit them, Colin Bailey kidnapped Erica. The killer wanted Phil to call off the chase. Phil had been tracking him from Durham to Manchester with a young colleague, Detective Constable Zara Wheeler. Bailey wanted to use Erica to gain free passage to travel to London to murder men who had avoided getting caught by the law.

It had been a tense time, but Zara helped discover where Bailey held her, and Phil rode to her rescue. Within twenty-four hours, Bailey was back in the centre of Bath, and Phil had attempted to arrest him. Phil survived the violent struggle in the water, but Bailey disappeared.

Phil was then promoted to Detective Inspector and transferred from Bath to Portishead. Zara was then his Detective Sergeant and had followed him to the Avon & Somerset Police HQ. The pair had a one-night stand in Bristol. Somehow, the marriage survived, and they put the matter behind them. Not long after, Zara left the police and moved away from the area. Things got back on an even keel.

The stability Erica craved had returned. Nothing was ever forever. Phil was so frustrated with how the force was changing that he resigned and took an early pension before he got sacked. Erica recalled her concerns when Phil talked about going into security work.

It had seemed speculative. The money might be plentiful for a single high-profile assignment, but where would Phil get the bread and butter work? The kids were at school, and she worked in a building society. The family wouldn't starve, but the uncertainty caused her several sleepless nights.

As it turned out, Hounsell Security Services proved an attractive proposition. While Phil was at the Glastonbury Festival in 2013, he met Wayne Sangster. Wayne had the contacts and the off-the-wall ideas of people who might offer them work. So for the past twelve months, Phil hadn't stopped working. He had employed two more staff, who travelled up and down the country, providing security for stars of stage and screen.

From an office in the centre of Bath, Wayne and Phil had traced dozens of missing persons. Every week was different and as far from a dull nine-to-five job as you could imagine. But, today, everything was to change again. Her husband was to work for a charity based at Larcombe Manor.

Phil had gone into little detail on this new job, except it was an administrative role. When he told her the salary, she thought he was joking. It was far higher than what he had taken from the HSS business.

So, that was why she stared out the window, wondering what he was mixed up in; Erica had never heard of the charity. There were stories of the low percentage of donations reaching the people they were supposed to protect. It didn't sound very stable.

Phil was moving around upstairs. He'd be down for his breakfast soon. Erica prayed this new venture would work out. The two lads Erica had never met had agreed to become self-employed. There was enough personal security work for two individuals with an average height of six-foot-two and a combined weight of thirty-seven stones. Phil assured her they would manage.

Wayne had spent the evening here last night, having a few drinks with her and Phil. Since the middle of last month, when Phil accepted this new post, the two friends had discussed the best way forward. Wayne knew he could follow the others into personal security if there were a uniform.

There were no hard feelings about the possibility of the

business closing. Wayne had moved around in dozens of jobs since he left school. He had been a policeman for eight years when they met at Worthy Farm and watched the Rolling Stones. Before that, he had worn a paramedic's uniform, the RAF, a zookeeper, and a traffic warden.

The enquiries kept coming in while they decided whether to close for good last Friday or let Wayne complete the outstanding searches. It was evident there was work out there if he wanted it. Phil convinced Wayne he was competent to run the firm alone. So, they continued to accept new commissions.

The pair had established a good reputation. The lease on the office space wasn't a problem. Once they decided on a new name and got the stationery altered, Wayne would fly solo. He had passed on the good news when he arrived last evening.

"I'm thinking of calling Triple S, boss," he said.

"That stands for Sangster Security Services, I presume?" asked Phil.

"Yes, boss."

"You can stop calling me boss, Wayne," said Phil. "Triple S is a good choice. I worried you might drop the middle S now the personal security aspect has gone its separate way."

Wayne had thought about what Phil had said.

"The uniform would have been easy to get hold of, though, on eBay. But I can see what you're saying. I might change the habit of a lifetime and opt for smart, casual wear for the office and out on the road."

"Progress at last," said Phil.

"You taught me loads, Phil, and I'll never forget that. I've got other news too. I called The Wishing Well café in Kilburn on Saturday morning to talk to Bridie Carragher.

She's still serving customers that delicious Guinness cake of hers. We chatted for ages. I'm going up to London to see her next weekend."

"It's all happening, Wayne," Phil said, "striking out on your own in the business world, and who knows? The last days of being a confirmed bachelor? I'm pleased for you. Just one thing."

"What would that be, Phil?" Wayne had asked.

"Don't rush out to buy new smart, casual clothes for a while. You may need to accommodate an extra inch or two on the waistline if Bridie's spoiling you with her cakes."

Erica smiled at the memory. The two men shared an easy camaraderie she feared Phil would miss in the coming months.

"What's made you smile this morning then, love?" asked her husband as he appeared by the kitchen door.

"I was thinking of you and Wayne, poking fun at one another. You'll miss him."

"I will, but it will be okay when I know more people at Larcombe. Different, no doubt, but I'll make new friends."

The couple sat and ate breakfast together in companionable silence. The children were stirring; the quiet would soon shatter as the new school week began.

"What time will you be home tonight?" Erica asked.

"I won't be working police hours or staying out of town on surveillance. Those days are behind me. I'll be home around half-past five every weekday evening. We'll have the weekends to ourselves. The kids can get to know me again."

Phil waited until Shaun and Tracey came downstairs. He said his goodbyes and then finished dressing. Suited and booted, Phil drove across the city and made his way to Larcombe Manor. He parked his car and walked towards the front door of the main building. It was five minutes to nine.

A young man emerged from inside and blocked his path.

"Good morning, sir," he said, "we are expecting you. Hayden Vincent will collect you in two minutes. Please wait in your car and then follow him to the transport section garage. You will find a space reserved for you there. Hayden will take you to your office and issue you a restricted passkey. He will give you the other details you must be aware of in due course. For future reference, this building is off-limits to you, and from tomorrow you will proceed directly to your parking space to arrive at nine-fifteen and no earlier."

Phil returned to his car. He had imagined Annabelle Fox, the charity's CEO, would have met him on his first day. The secrecy surrounding this whole organisation was hitting home. A car swung around on the gravel behind him. It was Hayden Vincent. The agent indicated that Phil should follow, and they drove the few hundred yards to the transport section.

Phil took in his surroundings. In the distance, he saw several figures on the lawn. They walked towards the manor house. He was too far away to make out faces, but it appeared to be two men and a woman.

Two mechanics were working on a limousine. Phil saw a collection of small and large vans, a taxi, and a saloon car parked near the garage workshops. Each carried the Olympus logo on the side door. Hayden had stopped his car. Ahead of him on the building wall, Phil spotted a wooden board. It carried his new name, Orion.

Phil parked and switched off his engine. There was no

turning back. He was starting work at the heart of the Olympus Project.

Hayden Vincent led him inside the building. The rooms he passed seemed small and functional, similar to barracks. He followed Hayden inside when they stopped at the door with his name on it. He was impressed by the high-end equipment at his disposal. Everything he would ever need when searching for missing persons was at his fingertips. He never needed to leave the room. Which, of course, was the idea, not that it had dawned on him yet.

"I'll leave you to get accustomed to your surroundings, Orion," said Hayden, "the file containing the details of your first task is on the desk. After that, you can expect other files and reports to arrive now that people know you're here. You can do a half-day today if that suits you, or if you want to stay longer, please make sure you leave at five. I'll be back in fifteen minutes with that passkey."

Hayden left the room, and Phil opened the file. Fiona Grant-Nicholls sounded a refined lady. He wondered how she ended up on a missing person list. Phil switched on his brand-new computer and tried to find his way around the new system.

"Oh, Wayne, where are you when I need you?" he said.

It was slow-going. The morning dragged by. Hayden dropped the passkey in, and Phil compared the places he could access against the overall scale of the estate. Hayden hadn't been kidding when he said it was restricted. Phil looked at the clock; it was a quarter to two. He decided a half-day was appropriate for this first day. He walked out of the stable block and bumped into a familiar person.

"Zara, what are you doing here?"

"I left the police force to find a career I could love," she replied.

"I thought you left the area. How did you come to work here?"

"I met someone," she said.

"Good, I'm glad," Phil replied.

That was awkward. Phil was about to walk to his car when Zara stopped him.

"Don't run off, Phil. We needed to face this eventually. The bosses here wanted it to be much later, but there we are. I met Rusty Scott in Bristol the day the suicide bombers destroyed Pero's bridge. I was checking cars in a lane off Prince Street and would have died if Rusty hadn't stopped me from opening the boot of a car. We started seeing one another, and then he asked me to move in with him. That meant living here, and they offered me a job. I'm starting at two o'clock."

"I haven't seen many places yet. Where do you work? What are you doing?"

"I can't tell you," she smiled, "but if we bump into one another again, you should call me Artemis."

"The Huntress, that's good for an ex-copper,"

"Well, you're Orion. We're well-matched."

"We were, weren't we?" said Phil.

"That was a long time ago, Orion," said Artemis. "I've moved on since then. Things are very different now."

She waited for him to get to his car and drive towards the exit before she walked to the ice-house.

Well, you've been told, thought Phil as he turned out of the gateway to go home. This place held so many secrets. He wondered what he would uncover next.

Tyrone O'Riordan sat in his office in the Glencairn Bank. The Grid's finances were healthier than they had ever been under Hugo Hanigan's reign. The network of organised crime gangs was more robust too. Weak links had been exposed and eliminated. His mother was pleased with the results.

Tyrone had met with Frank Rooney last week in Sheffield. As he promised his mother, Rooney soon agreed to toe the line. That meeting had secured Frank's steadfast support. Any gang that might have wavered in their total backing for Colleen O'Riordan as head of the Grid would now fall in line, like kids in a playground.

There was just one problem niggling Tyrone.

He and Frank discussed the covert operators; if they existed at all. In the ten days between their first conversation and meeting in Steel City, they spoke with gang leaders across the country. Every sighting, every story about these men was collected, and Tyrone had now collated them.

There were common themes. Dark blue or black vans were always in the vicinity. They worked in pairs on most operations, but occasionally they arrived en masse. Two men stood out from the rest. Similar descriptions came from every region, so they had to be the same. They were senior to the others and prepared to operate alone.

The group were ruthless. When they carried out an attack, ninety-five per cent of their targets died on-site, or their bodies were removed and never seen again. The remaining five per cent were taken away unharmed. Where they disappeared was a mystery.

Tyrone had summed up what he read into these figures.

"This suggests that the team we're facing numbers only a thousand. That would be the absolute maximum. Their methods point to a military background; these men are ex-soldiers or marines. They cherry-pick their targets. Just run your finger down the pages; there's not a lightweight among them. They're hardened criminals, terrorists, and scum that have damaged kids or stalked young women. If you were an honest man, Frank, you would say they deserved it. It's what they do, Frank. They deliver justice for the common person where the law falls short. They're vigilantes, and it must stop. We decide within the Grid who lives and who dies. We decide who deals drugs, trafficks the women, and delivers the arms shipments. There's one thing in this summary: a weakness we might exploit."

"I'm damned if I can see it," said Frank.

"Why leave that five per cent alive? Where do they take them? They must have a home base. Somewhere they can do what they wish with their prisoners. Question them on the local gang structure and ultimately about us, Frank. Squeeze them until they break and spill what they know about the Grid. We need to find that place and put it out of business.

"Where do we start to look?" asked Frank.

"Do you have anyone in mind?" asked Tyrone.

Frank Rooney thought for a second, then realised what Tyrone was asking.

"Expendable, you mean. I do. So, we set a trap for these jokers. Get them to pick my guy up and take him back to their base for a chat."

"You've got it in one, Frank."

Tyrone called his mother.

"I know how to remove the last effective opposition to the Grid,"

"Tell me, what do you plan to do?" asked Colleen.

"We're sacrificing a pawn to get to the king."

Next in The Phoenix series

vinci-books.com/frequent-peal-of-bells

A nation under terrorist siege. A hero pushed to the brink. Justice hangs in the balance.

Amid a resurgence of Islamist terror and the rise of the Grid, a nation battles overwhelming crime waves and strained resources. In this gripping tale, The Phoenix Series explores resilience in the face of austerity, as government measures push society to its breaking point, exposing deep vulnerabilities.

Turn the page for a free preview…

A Frequent Peal of Bells: Chapter One

Monday, 29th September 2014

Henry Case left the Olympus car with the transport section, collected his bag from the boot, and walked to his quarters in the stable block. He was tired but happy. The weekend in Surrey with the Reverend Sarah Gough had flown past.

Henry couldn't believe twelve weeks had passed since his first visit. That crazy weekend in mid-July, when Sarah invited him to the annual flower show and fete, was a high summer spot for her parishioners.

Sarah had booked him into the Hurtwood Hotel on that occasion, three miles away in Walking Bottom, Peaslake. Modesty was the order of the day. Her neighbours mustn't catch a whiff of scandal in the air, she had told him.

Last Friday evening, Henry had arrived at the vicarage and parked in front of the main house. He checked his jacket pocket as he stood on the doorstep with his dozen red roses. Yes, the surprise was still there where he had put it before leaving Larcombe Manor.

"Hello, darling," cried Sarah as she threw open the door, "come inside."

Henry followed her indoors. Sarah took his bunch of flowers and went to the kitchen. She found a vase in one of the lower cupboards, arranged them to her satisfaction, and then topped up the glass container with water.

"There," she said, "now for a proper welcome."

Sarah took Henry by the hand and led him to the bottom of the stairs.

Henry stopped.

"Before we go any further, there's something I need to do," he said.

Sarah gave him a quizzical look.

"Not more revelations, surely?"

Henry smiled. His mother had always told him the truth will out, and it did two weeks ago. Sarah now knew most of his duties at Larcombe for the Olympus Project. She had come to terms with them. His concerns over whether they could ever have a lasting relationship were over. He was ready to move forward to a bright future.

"Nothing sinister, I promise," said Henry, taking the small box from his pocket.

"Will you marry me, Sarah?" He opened the box, revealing the elegant diamond solitaire he bought in Bath. Sarah's only response had been to extend her left hand so that Henry could slide the ring onto her finger.

"It's perfect, Henry," she said, "yes, I'll marry you."

"Excellent," said Henry, "now let's carry on what we had started."

The vase of red roses remained on the work surface in the kitchen for several hours as the happy couple made love upstairs. There was no question of Henry needing to drive to Walking Bottom tonight. The car could stay in the driveway.

"Oh, Henry," sighed Sarah, "that exercise has made me hungry. So let's walk up to the Royal Oak for a bite to eat and a few drinks. I'll keep flicking my hair out of my eyes until someone notices the ring. That should start the tongue's wagging."

"The sooner the locals see us together, the better," said Henry. "I expect they've wondered why I haven't been back."

They dressed and returned downstairs.

"Did you bring a bag?" asked Sarah.

"It's still in the car," Henry replied. "I waited until you accepted my proposal before moving my gear indoors. Regardless of your answer, I wasn't driving to a damn hotel."

"That would never happen, darling," said Sarah.

The couple had strolled up the street to the pub, had a meal and shared a bottle of wine. When the Royal Oak landlord called time, Sarah and Henry were threading their way through a crowded bar. Several customers spotted the new adornment their vicar had acquired. Drinking-up time ended before the well-wishers let them leave.

Henry and Sarah had returned to the vicarage arm in arm. There were no furtive glances or snatched goodnight kisses behind the greenery this time. Instead, Henry stopped to collect his bag from the car. Sarah let them into the house, and although the downstairs lights went on to appease the neighbours, the newly engaged couple had headed upstairs.

On Saturday and Sunday, Sarah had parish duties to fulfil. She disappeared on her bicycle to spend an hour or two fulfilling her commitments, and when she returned, the couple discussed their plans.

"Where shall we marry?" asked Sarah.

"I thought you wanted the service here," said Henry.

"If we were to live here as husband and wife, and I continued to work in the parishes this ministry covers, then yes, it makes sense. However, I'm not sure that's practical."

"What do you propose then?" asked Henry.

"I wasn't born here in the village, so I have no strong ties to the place. My parents lived in Hungerford, and that was where they raised me. My father died when I was in my early twenties. Since my mother's funeral three years ago, I've not returned to the place. There are happy memories there, but nothing that makes me yearn to marry in the church where I was christened and confirmed."

"Where do you wish to marry?" Henry asked.

"If Annabelle agrees, I would love it to be at Larcombe Manor. Neither of us has a large family to invite, and your friends and colleagues live there. I can ask a friend to officiate. She shares duties with me in the four parishes we cover."

"What are your plans following the wedding?" asked Henry.

"I'll call the Bishop first thing on Monday and ask him to look for a move further west. If he asks, how soon will the wedding be?"

"There's no cause for concern, is there?" asked Henry. "We haven't taken precautions this weekend."

Sarah dug him in the ribs with an elbow.

"My first job when I get back is to explore the possibilities of moving into the main house," said Henry, rubbing his side. "Rusty moved from the stable block with his good lady, and they aren't married yet. My quarters are no place for a married couple to live. Your new position may come with a vicarage, but it's not practical for me to live off-site while I work for Olympus."

"Right," said Sarah, "that's settled. We set a date as soon as I secure a new parish near Bath. If Annabelle agrees, we'll get married in that delightful church on the estate and live in one of the apartments. I know from my visits how comfortable they are. We can make a home there. If we're blessed with a child in time, it will be an idyllic setting to raise a baby. Hope thrives on it."

They visited the Royal Oak for refreshments between the wedding plans and Sarah's parish duties. Henry felt the effects of the superb food on his waistline. It had been a memorable weekend. Now, it was Monday lunchtime. Henry had missed the morning meeting and had a long list of jobs that needed his attention. As he reached the door to his quarters, all he planned to do was drop the bag and sleep.

Hugh Fraser heard Henry's door close. He checked his watch; someone had a good weekend, he thought. Hugh was leaving the estate to drive to Manchester later. Tomorrow at three fifteen, he was attending the funeral of Monty Jacks, the disabled ex-serviceman murdered at New Street station, Birmingham. Monty was the first casualty suffered by the Irregulars.

The logistics officer worked with Phoenix in the orangery over the weekend. Phoenix was keen to keep the pressure on organised crime gangs across the country. It didn't matter where you looked; even the most unlikely towns added to the statistics.

Hugh Fraser knew only too well those areas in Glasgow

where crime was rife. It was nothing new in Drumchapel and Govan. They had been in the Top 10 for decades. Even in Scotland, he had raised an eyebrow when violence or burglary became a hot topic in the smaller towns in the countryside. Phoenix and Rusty kept turning over stones in affluent areas of the South or the Midlands, and the worst low-life criminal crawled out.

Despite the authorities' claims of an improving picture, crime was no longer under control. On the contrary, it spread further than ever before and faster than a forest fire. Olympus did what it could, given its resources, but the battle would be lost unless they reversed cuts to services.

The ringing phone interrupted his thoughts. Ambrosia was calling him.

"I wanted to catch you before you left," she said. "I've just learned from Zeus that the funeral for the other agent murdered in Winson Green is on Friday."

"Finn's family came from Rugeley, in Staffordshire," said Hugh, "I had better attend."

"We'll go there together," said Ambrosia. "I told Zeus I thought a senior Olympian should be present and offered my services. When will you arrive in Leeds?"

"I'm leaving Larcombe within the hour. Olympus has booked me into a budget hotel tonight. The funeral in South Manchester tomorrow is mid-afternoon. I should be with you by seven in the evening."

"I can't wait for you to taste my food," said Ambrosia, "it will be a pleasure to cook for someone. Living alone makes it easier to eat out or get a takeaway."

Hugh thought of the lonely nights after his wife had moved out. He had the local pizza parlour, chippy, and Chinese restaurant on speed-dial on his phone. Things had moved fast with Ambrosia. She was ambitious and knew what she wanted. Who was he to complain?

"I'm sure I'll enjoy everything," he said.

Hugh heard Ambrosia's trademark giggle.

"Don't worry, I'll make sure of that," she replied.

"I must drive back to Larcombe on Wednesday morning," he said. "Unless I can persuade Phoenix, I'm owed two days' leave."

"Stay with me," begged Ambrosia, "we need to discuss future roles for the Irregulars. I'll clear it with Zeus if there's a problem. We'll make our way to Rugeley on Friday. You can head home after the service, and I'll return here. Can I convince you to spend time with me?"

"Do you have an extensive range of dishes to tempt me with?" asked Hugh.

Ambrosia laughed out loud.

"My skills in the kitchen only stretch to enough dishes to feed you tomorrow evening. After that, we'll phone for a takeaway. I only want to get out of bed for food, don't you?"

"That sounds good," he replied, "I look forward to seeing you tomorrow evening."

"Drive safe," said Ambrosia, "and sleep well tonight."

Hugh listened to her laughter before she ended the call. Then he packed a bag for four nights away from Larcombe. When he moved south from Scotland, he had known that this was a tough assignment, but someone had to do it. Hugh puffed out his cheeks, hoisted his bag on his shoulder, and left the stable block. It was time to drive to Manchester.

Athena was wondering why Henry Case hadn't been present in the meeting room this morning. She knew he planned to spend the weekend with her friend, Sarah, but had assumed he would return late on Sunday evening. It was unlike Henry to miss a meeting without warning.

Her husband was taking the others through the mission plans agreed upon for the coming week. Phoenix had disappeared for half a day on Saturday and Sunday to work on them with Hugh Fraser in the orangery. It was for a good cause, but it would be nice to spend quality time together. A week ago, Phoenix had started delegating tasks to less senior agents. Stress affects everyone in time, no matter how tough they appear.

"Will these missions cause the Grid any long-term damage, Phoenix," asked Minos. Athena forgot Henry for now and switched her attention to the matter at hand.

"I think we've used this comparison before, Minos," replied Phoenix, "it's like that Whack-A-Mole game for kids. Heads pop up all over the place, and we try to hit them. Every head we take out of the game hurts the Grid for a while; there's no doubt. How long it lasts depends on how soon they select another soldier to fill the gap."

"My concern is that we take risks every time we send agents into the field. First, they get killed, as we have on several missions in the past six months. Second, during those actions, our enemies uncover their identities. That poses a danger to everyone here at Larcombe."

"We take every precaution against both eventualities," said Athena. "Our losses are painful, but weighed against the benefits we have secured, they represent a low percentage of our assets."

"It's not our job to inflict lasting damage on the Grid," said Rusty, more animated than Athena had seen him of late.

"Exactly," agreed Phoenix, "our missions often target the vilest criminals. People we must eliminate before they can carry out any further crimes. On occasion, we encounter the soldiers, the low-level villains who operate in regions plastered across every media outlet for a few weeks. Then, we hope the nudge we give the police galvanises them into positive action. So far, that element of our strategy has yielded the smallest fruit."

"The authorities have been slow to respond in every arena," said Alastor. "One can understand the logic behind not spending money you don't have. But this extended period of austerity is punishing the wrong people. Whoever said crime doesn't pay was a fool. The Grid has increased the profits from organised crime in the last month by a percentage that is manna from heaven for any of the world's leading companies."

"I have been distracted of late, with good reason," said Athena, "and I haven't kept up to date with your reports, Alastor. I apologise. Can you bring us up to speed? It might help everyone here."

"Please don't apologise, Athena. No matter what we face at Olympus, the family must always come first. I introduced the Grid into this conversation because something concerns me with the latest figures from the Glencairn Bank. Things moved on since the Spring when we sought the identity of the elusive 'H'. The ice-house named him Ardal James Hannon, an entrepreneur who five years ago lived in Cricklewood. Everything in his background suggested he was the perfect fit for the mastermind behind the Grid's increasingly cohesive network."

"Matching locations of a string of deaths to the letter 'H' was down to Orion's work," said Rusty. "We then discovered Hannon had changed his name, didn't we?"

"By the end of April, we knew Hannon had gone to ground five years ago. When he opened the Glencairn

Bank, he had taken his mother's maiden name, Hanigan. He ditched his first name. In his new persona, Hugo Hanigan controlled the bank and out-performed the opposition on every level. Hanigan covered his tracks well. Any photographs of him from his youth were useless. There were no current photographs of him online. In the summer, we stationed an agent on Gresham Street to capture images of frequent visitors. His vigil has been intermittent for security reasons. The images he has sent through to Giles left us with eight possibilities. We deferred progress on nailing the identities of those men whenever another crisis has arisen."

"We've had people work on those images, Athena," said Artemis, "but most are likely to be seasoned criminals. They are skilled in avoiding being caught on camera. A quick dash from a car to the bank gives us little to work with."

"However, we named five of the frequent visitors," said Giles Burke, "and none of them was Hanigan or Hannon. We have three sets of photographs of men who often visit the Glencairn, but we can't trace them anywhere. They are of a similar age, white, and well-dressed. As Alastor pointed out, getting a face for Hanigan has been a lower priority in the past ten weeks. He may be among those three, or our agent could have missed him altogether. Who knows how often he visits the bank? He could work from home these days."

"Keep searching for those identities, Giles," said Athena. "Can we work back from the images of the three unidentified men to discover where they live? I know that's like finding a needle in a haystack, but it could help confirm who they are."

"If I may, Athena," said Alastor, "that's unnecessary. I've often seen those photos since the first ones arrived in early June. When I studied the latest batch from Gresham

Street, I spotted something. That's what raised my suspicions about last month's performance. One of the three men hasn't visited since before the Bank Holiday weekend. After being a frequent visitor for four months, four weeks is a long time."

"You believe the sudden improvement is due to a change of management at the bank?" asked Phoenix, "could that mean someone has replaced Hanigan? Or has he appointed a new person and given his total concentration to Grid business?"

"I checked the discarded photos in the latest batch," said Alastor, "the ice-house is focussing on the three that are still unidentified. A much younger man was snapped by our agent two weeks ago. He visited the Glencairn at the same time as one of its regulars. The image was sharp and in focus — no attempt to hide his face. I checked for him online, and in hours, I found him on social media. His name is Tyrone O'Riordan."

The room fell silent. The implication was evident to everyone sitting around the table.

"Tommy O'Riordan's son?" asked Rusty. "What is he doing at the Glencairn?"

"Tyrone and his sister Rosie lived in Marbella," said Artemis. "Tommy had a place out there. That was where the police arrested him for the murder of Michael Devlin."

"The two kids came home for the funeral," said Rusty. "Have they moved back in with their mother?"

"Not in the family home in Kilburn because they've sold that," said Alastor, "the Marbella apartment has gone too. With Tommy dead, I imagine money was tight, and Tommy's widow made cutbacks. She doesn't appear to have worked ever since she and Tommy married. I doubt she wants to start now."

"They will have done better than scrape by on his ill-gotten gains," said Phoenix. "I doubt she's living in poverty. I hope they don't blame me for getting rid of the family breadwinner?"

"We both had a hand in that," said Rusty with a grin.

"Giles, we need to learn more about young Tyrone," said Athena. "What's his history? Where does he live?"

"Will do, Athena," replied Giles, "should we add Colleen and Rosie to the list?"

"It can't do any harm," said Athena.

"I think what you have uncovered is gold dust, Alastor," said Phoenix, "well done. If we add other things into the mix, we could answer questions that have concerned me for a while. For example, who took over as leader of the Kilburn gang after we disposed of Tommy?"

"Tommy's deputy at the time of his murder trial was his brother-in-law, Sean Walsh," said Artemis, "he would have been Hanigan's first-choice. We must assume Walsh was the go-between for the gang while Tommy was in Belmarsh. With Tommy dead, Hanigan had to have let Walsh continue in the role unless he under-performed. Giles and I will check the current status."

"It may already be too late," said Phoenix. "We received intelligence that a member of the old guard, Michael Quinn, was murdered last month. It wasn't obvious whether it was an internal struggle for power in the borough, or the gang from Kilburn, next door, spreading its wings."

"So, the question I need to answer is, who succeeded Sean Walsh in Kilburn?" said Giles, "and are they looking to expand?"

"You two have got plenty to be getting on with," said Athena, "I suggest you get below to the ice-house and make a start. If you bump into Henry Case on your way, could you ask him to call into my office this afternoon?"

Artemis nodded, and she and Giles left the room. Athena looked at the others.

"I think we've found a chink in the Grid's armour, don't you?"

"Whatever role Tyrone O'Riordan plays, he's a different breed to Hanigan," said Minos. "His digital footprint is easy to track. It might be because he was thrust into a new role and hasn't learned to be more guarded in his actions."

"Or he's an arrogant sod, who thinks he's untouchable," muttered Phoenix.

"Either way, we can investigate his link to the Glencairn, discover what happened to Hugo Hanigan, and see whether the Kilburn gang's ambition has any limits."

Athena couldn't think of anything to add to Minos's comment, so she called the meeting to a close.

When they were back in the apartment, Athena was restless. Maria Elena had prepared them their lunch. She was helping Hope grapple with hers. Phoenix soon polished off his second sandwich and stopped to take a sip from his cup of coffee.

"A penny for them, darling?" he asked.

"I wanted to catch up with Henry to hear about his weekend. It's not vital, given what we learned from Alastor this morning, but all the same…."

"That's the first time since I've been here that he surprised me," said Phoenix, "he and Minos are such dry sticks. They churn out report after report. Their attention to detail is amazing."

"Yet, your in-tray is always full," chided Athena, "I have to pester you to take time to catch up with your reading."

"This was different," said Phoenix, "Alastor showed

initiative. Something bothered him in the numbers he saw from the Glencairn. Because those two delve into the minutiae daily, it registered with him. Normal people would have missed it. Or they would have dismissed it as a seasonal blip or an adjustment from earlier in the financial year."

"I've always told you not to underestimate them," said Athena.

"Fair point. As for what Alastor spotted in that photograph, I'm itching to hear what Giles and Artemis uncover regarding the O'Riordan family."

"I hope they can work fast; you'll be away after Wednesday."

Maria Elena had disappeared to the nursery with their daughter; Athena was still only picking at her salad. Phoenix rested his eyes and went through the actions planned for later in the week. It never hurt to check those plans.

When he opened his eyes, Athena was in the kitchen.

Phoenix walked to the door and watched as his wife stacked the dishwasher. Athena's heart wasn't in it; he could tell.

"Why don't you see if Henry is waiting for you?"

Athena looked at her watch.

"Where did that hour go?" she cried, flew along the corridor, and took the stairs to the administration area. Minos and Alastor were hard at work on their next batch of reports. Henry Case stood outside her door like a naughty schoolboy.

"Henry, you're alive and well. What a relief."

"Apologies for the late arrival, Athena," said Henry. "Sarah and I didn't want the weekend to finish."

"I'm only teasing you, Henry. Sarah called me yesterday on her way to church for evensong. She told me she left you snoring on the sofa in front of the television. I take it the food at the Royal Oak is as good as ever? Congratulations on your engagement. I didn't share your good news with the others this morning. You can do that yourself."

"Did Sarah mention the wedding?" asked Henry.

"No, she was too excited about the ring you gave her. I imagine you've started to make plans, though?"

"I won't put off matters," said Henry, "Sarah's calling the Bishop to ask for a transfer closer to Bath. Sarah doesn't want me to feel obliged to leave Larcombe and move nearer to her. If you agree, we want to marry in the tiny church. One of her colleagues has agreed to do the honours."

"That sounds lovely," said Athena.

"What are the chances of us living here afterwards? Not in the stable block, but in this building, the same as Rusty and Artemis."

"I'd be disappointed if you went somewhere else, Henry," said Athena. "This old Georgian manor house has eleven bedrooms and seven bathrooms. Daddy will move out in a few weeks, based on what he told me at lunchtime. Even if he stayed with us permanently, we could still find a spot for you both."

"Oh, jolly good," said Henry.

"I imagine the wedding date will depend on how soon the Church finds a new living for the soon-to-be Reverend Sarah Case?"

"Sarah has her heart set on Easter Saturday," said Henry.

"Well then, her matron of honour and the flower girl accept," said Athena. "That was another thing she mentioned during her frantic phone call last evening."

"I shall ask Giles to be my best man," said Henry, "he asked me if I would do the job when he gets married. Of course, I said I'd give it some thought, not realising I would be engaged only weeks later."

Henry trotted back to the stable block to call Sarah with the good news. He hoped she would receive positive news soon on her next parish. October was upon them. April seemed a long way off. If the last year had taught him anything, it was that things could change before you know it.

A Frequent Peal of Bells: Chapter Two

Tuesday, 30th September 2014

"This makes a change, Mum. You are visiting me."

Tyrone O'Riordan welcomed his mother into his penthouse apartment with a peck on her cheek.

Colleen didn't hold with this foreign malarkey. She had been more used to getting a slap from Tommy. A kiss meant he wanted something else. She couldn't see anything wrong with shaking hands if it was business. People were too friendly by half these days. They didn't know how to keep their distance.

"I suppose you mean when you're here?" Colleen replied.

She sensed Tyrone's annoyance at finding she had paid a visit to the apartment while he was in East Anglia. The wall safe contained plenty of information the apartment's previous owner had gathered on his enemies and those who might have thought were his friends.

Hugo Hanigan's body was now somewhere on Hackney

Marshes among tonnes of the capital's waste. It was only natural the head of the network of organised crime gangs in the UK wanted access to that information. It could prove invaluable. Tyrone would have to get over it.

Tyrone shrugged. He knew better than to argue with his mother.

"Can I get you a drink?" he asked.

"It's not even eleven o'clock. OK, I'll have a gin and tonic with a twist of lime," Colleen replied, "easy on the gin. We've got matters to discuss."

"What did you want to discuss?" Tyrone asked.

"I don't want you to take me through your ideas on uncovering this so-called secret organisation you and Frank Rooney have dreamed up, that's for sure. Where you got that notion from beats me. I'm more interested in the Grid's major robberies in the lead-up to Christmas."

"When we pull those off, it will bring a whole new rival to Black Friday, believe me," said Tyrone.

"We'll see," said Colleen. "Who's running the show, and how much do we stand to make?"

"The team will be three Albanians who came to the UK six years ago. They claimed to be Kosovans fleeing the troubles but were seasoned criminals. They've majored in importing cocaine in the past, but there's big competition in that market, so they added to their skill set."

"Where do you go to do that? Night school, I suppose, or the Open University? Can you trust them?" asked Colleen.

"They understand the punishment if they try to cheat us," replied Tyrone. "As for the amounts involved, we have high hopes of collecting over one hundred million."

Colleen took a large sip of her drink and swallowed. A hundred million pounds? That would make the headlines. It could be just the push the Grid needed to prove its vice-like grip on the nation.

It would further emphasise the lunacy of cutting police numbers. If the Albanians got full credit for planning and executing the robberies, it would fuel the argument against open borders. The public would be outraged. The brazen disregard for law and order could topple governments. Serve them right.

"Did you want to go into the details?" Tyrone asked.

"Sorry," said Colleen, "no, not today; I'm having my hair done in an hour. Do you have a file on your computer you can send me?"

"I won't risk sending anything important in an email attachment," said Tyrone. "I'll drop a memory stick over to your place in a day or two. Don't worry. I'll show you how to use it."

"You're a good boy, Tyrone. We're going places, aren't we?"

"Onwards and upwards, Mum."

At Larcombe Manor, the ice-house team had worked their magic. Giles passed files around the table for the others to read.

"Tyrone O'Riordan, thirty-one-year-old son of Tommy and Colleen. His father insisted he stay in education until he had enough qualifications to make an honest living. Tommy had been keen for his children to stay on the straight and narrow. He's a qualified accountant and has an MBA. He lived in his father's place in Marbella rent-free. For the past decade, Tyrone has lived a high life. Fast cars, women, and late-night cocktail parties four or five nights a week. He has dabbled in drugs, but it's never become an issue. He picked up a handful of parking and speeding fines, but the Spanish police never linked him with anything more sinister. Members of crime families who knew, or worked for his father, have retired to Marbella over the years. Tommy O'Riordan kept his kids away from those people on holiday, but Tyrone chose to spend time in their company. He never got involved in criminal activity, but he likely gained the knowledge."

"So, his financial expertise marks him as the new head of the Glencairn Bank," said Athena.

"That's a fair assumption," said Giles, "as for Rosie O'Riordan, she's twenty-nine. Tommy used to call her his princess. She was a Daddy's girl. Rosie moved to Marbella, lived there on the cheap and got herself a sports car as soon as she passed her driving test at eighteen. At college in London, she had completed a hair and beauty course. Rosie partied with the same crowd as Tyrone and spent every euro she earned in Marbella's salons having a good time. She moved from salon to salon but was never out of work. Plenty of men have been prepared to spend their money on her because little Rosie is a beauty, as you can tell from her photos. There's no sign she's involved with anything criminal."

"Apart from the length of that skirt," said Minos.

"You're showing your age," said Rusty.

"If you've got tanned legs, you want to show them off," said Artemis.

"We red-headed Scotsmen keep our delicate skin covered," said Rusty. "The only tan I've worn was from my father on my backside."

"We can discount Rosie O'Riordan," said Athena, eager to make progress. "What do we have on Colleen O'Riordan, Giles?"

"Colleen will be fifty in a few weeks. She married Tommy at eighteen. Tyrone arrived ten months later. The gap between Tyrone and Rosie was eighteen months. Most accounts of her life with Tommy are anecdotal. He was a villain and treated her the same as most villains have treated their women over the decades. She stayed home, looked after the kids, kept the house tidy, cooked his meals, and kept her mouth shut. She's as hard as nails but has never had even a fine for dropping litter. Since Tommy got jailed for Devlin's murder, she has been active. As we discussed yesterday, this was a natural reaction to the drying up of the money supply."

"Did she begin that process before Tommy escaped from Belmarsh?" asked Phoenix.

"Yes," replied Giles, "the Marbella apartment was already on the market, and the cars the kids leased returned. The sale of the house in Kilburn brought in a million pounds, give or take. Oh, and she sent a Mercedes and an SUV to auction at the end of May."

"I told you Colleen O'Riordan wasn't skint," muttered Phoenix, "but if she needed cash to pay for Tommy's escape bid, it makes sense. He didn't enjoy his freedom for long. There would still be enough left for her to survive, especially as she forced her kids to stand on their own two feet."

"Rosie continues to live in Marbella?" asked Minos.

"Afraid so, Minos," said Rusty, "you're not likely to bump into her on one of your nights on the town."

The former High Court judge gave a thin smile.

"I wonder where the mother and son live?" he said.

"Colleen lives in an apartment on a property overlooking the City and the financial district. I expect she can see the Glencairn Bank. Tyrone doesn't live with her. Colleen ensured the kids couldn't run home by buying a one-bedroomed place. We haven't found the exact spot where Tyrone is living, but the way he approached the bank on foot suggests he's close."

"Hang on," said Alastor, "that makes no sense. He may be a financial genius, but there was no evidence of saving money in the past decade. Properties in that part of London are fetching exorbitant prices. You can't find evidence linking him to the purchase of a flat. Is he renting a place paid for by the Glencairn?"

"We never traced Hanigan after he left Cricklewood," said Artemis, "but he must have owned property near the City. If we found details of high-priced apartments sold around the time of the sale of that house in the suburbs, we might find where Tyrone now lives."

"You're not suggesting they're living together?" asked Athena.

"No, Hanigan hasn't been seen for weeks. I'm suggesting he's dead."

"Killed by Tyrone? That's a leap from speeding fines," said Phoenix.

"Who can say what he learned from those Marbella villains?" asked Giles. "Despite Tommy wanting his kids to stay away from a life of crime, perhaps it's a case of like father, like son."

"How does Colleen fit into this?" asked Athena.

"Her brother, Sean Walsh died in the Dominican Republic," said Giles. "His funeral was in Kilburn in the middle of last month. The local police report reported it as a professional hit."

"What was he doing in South America? Was he on holiday?" asked Alastor.

"An extended holiday?" asked Giles. "Or it could be related to his brother's escape. If he was behind it, supported by Colleen's cash, they might have told him to make himself scarce until the heat died."

"Who wanted Walsh dead?" asked Henry Case.

"Hanigan," said Phoenix, "the O'Riordan family didn't order a hit. If Walsh had gotten jittery, his family would have persuaded him to disappear for a while. But Hanigan wanted to ensure the prison escape and its aftermath didn't link to the Grid. Because we stopped Tommy from reaching Harwich, the blame for his death may have been aimed at Hanigan. Tyrone or one of the Kilburn gang killed Hanigan in retaliation for Tommy's and his brother-in-law's killings."

"So, who's head of the Kilburn gang, and who succeeded Hanigan at the head of the Grid?" asked Rusty.

"There aren't too many candidates for the first," said Artemis. She counted names off on her fingers: -

"Colleen, Tyrone, and whoever acted as second-in-command to Sean Walsh. It's hard to imagine them considering anyone from outside the families from the start."

Phoenix looked at his wife. It wasn't unheard of for a woman to control an unruly mob. Athena did it every day.

"Tyrone's the money man for the Grid, and we can discount him for the local leadership. We don't have a name for Walsh's deputy, which tells me he was a nonentity. No, Colleen O'Riordan is my bet for taking control of the borough. Giles said she was hard as nails. She would have learned the business from Tommy in thirty years."

"Are we overlooking someone senior from the other gangs in the network that may have replaced Hanigan?" asked Minos.

"If Colleen ordered the hit on Hanigan, she's unlikely to let a bloke from another gang waltz in and take the top spot," said Phoenix. "She would get the deed done and then bring the others into line with a show of force."

"Michael Terence Quinn, of course," said Artemis, "the jigsaw pieces fit together nicely."

"I doubt Quinn was alone," said Rusty, "if we dig, we'll uncover more bodies. Colleen O'Riordan has convinced the Grid to accept her as a leader by showing what happens if they disagree. Tyrone's work at the Glencairn is another way of showing the Grid members that they're better off with the O'Riordan family at the helm."

"What's next for the Grid?" asked Henry Case.

"We don't have the firepower to annihilate them, which is what they deserve," said Phoenix. "We'll continue hitting them as often as possible and avoid exposure. As for the Glencairn, if there's a way to reduce that improving trend in performance, we should explore it."

"Understood," said Henry, "but what do you think *they* will do next?"

"They've got fingers in so many pies, I don't know what they might do," said Phoenix. "I'd try something spectacular — the crime of the century. Hanigan was an arrogant swine and dreamed of controlling everything criminal from Land's End to John O'Groats. You know what they say about power corrupting. Colleen O'Riordan could plan something to bring the country to its knees."

Long after his mother left for the hairdressers, Tyrone was hard at work. He ignored Colleen's suggestion that a hidden hand in many recent Grid setbacks was far from genuine. Instead, everything he heard of the Malik story convinced him he was on the right track.

Tyrone studied a map of the UK on his computer.

Hugo Hanigan had kept a file that highlighted every gang headquarters. Few corners of the country remained where a number didn't appear; each number linked to that gang's leader, its strength, and whether it represented a general duties outfit or a group of specialists.

Tyrone made a few adjustments. Some gangs were parochial; their reach extended to the boundaries of a borough and no further. The next-door neighbours wouldn't appreciate them meddling in their affairs. Other gangs controlled large areas that crossed county barriers, even if much of it was countryside.

Two hours later, Tyrone could pinpoint the Grid's blind spots. Hugo had done him the favour of noting the few pockets of resistance. Those gangs that refused to join the network. Tyrone grasped the nettle. They must be put out of business if they don't join us.

Tyrone needed every inch of the UK covered. Any specialist outfit was exempt, but hundreds of street criminals would suffice. He could switch them from committing the petty crime to hunting for clues about this organisation. That meant minimal losses compared to the gains of removing the threat.

They would watch for the transport linked to the attacks. Tyrone was willing to pay a significant bonus for photographs of either of the two men most often seen during these attacks. If this organisation wanted to remain secret, they had to stay home. Wherever that home might be, their days of interfering in Grid business must end.

Tyrone took one last look at the amended map. Time for action. He called the heads of the gangs that surrounded these rogue enclaves. One by one, they received the same message: -

"Remove the top tier. Tell the others to fall in line or suffer the same fate."

He sent eight messages. They referenced eight areas that, when added, gave the Grid total control. They acquired extra foot soldiers to add to the band of watchers. Tyrone was content with his morning's work. Now, he must visit the Glencairn Bank. Tyrone expected more good news on the financial front to greet him when he arrived. Within an hour, he could stroll up Gresham Street to a French restaurant he loved. All work and no play never did anyone any good.

Tyrone returned to his penthouse at four in the afternoon. He phoned Frank Rooney.

"You might hear of activity in a few trouble-spots over the next day or two, Frank," he said, "don't worry; it won't affect you."

"Pleased to hear it," said Frank. He breathed a sigh of relief. His run-in with Colleen O'Riordan must have slipped her son's mind. He got on better with the son and hoped they could build a stable relationship. It seemed possible.

"I'm keen to build on the successes I expect before the week's out, Frank," Tyrone continued. "I'm implementing a country-wide search for these busybodies that keep hampering our activities. What I need from our gang leaders is eyes and ears on the street. Photographs too, if it's possible. Pick people you can afford to lose for a period, but make sure you can rely on them. I'll send the details to everyone this evening."

"Always glad to help," said Frank.

"I called you directly because we need to firm up our plan for this Trojan Horse."

"What's that when it's at home?" asked Frank.

He wasn't the sharpest knife in the box.

"It's from Greek myth, Frank. The story doesn't matter. You need to know that it represents a person we get inside this organisation. He will help us undermine and destroy it from the inside."

"Ah, the expendable scrote I thought of when you asked last week. Got it, we get our man picked up for questioning, and if this gang take him back to their headquarters, we've got them."

"Only if they take him back, Frank. Then, we need him to be useful enough for them to keep him alive. Otherwise, they'll interrogate him for information on us, and we'll become the target. What guarantee do we have they won't kill him? We need a strategy that works to our advantage, whichever way they play it."

"Tricky," said Frank, totally lost.

Tyrone expected nothing useful to come from the other end of the line.

"Leave the thinking to me, Frank. Make sure you have the right guy available when I call him."

"Got it, boss," said Frank.

Tyrone worked on getting their man on the inside and sending them details of the secret base's location. Whether that man came out alive afterwards wasn't relevant.

Wednesday, 1st October 2014

Phoenix and Rusty were on the road early, their destination North London. Day One of their missions against gangs of youths in the city had begun.

"We may miss an update on the O'Riordan's this morning," said Rusty as he eased into the flow of traffic on the M4.

"We can't help that," said Phoenix, searching through the glove-box for his CDs.

"Those changes at the top of the Grid came as a shock, didn't they?" asked Rusty.

"I remember Athena telling me it was vital to know your enemy. We had distractions this last month, but it's unacceptable to fall one or two steps behind, whether behind the Grid, the terrorists, or any opposition we face. The whole point of the ice-house is to keep us right on the money with intelligence."

"I'll have a word with Artemis," said Rusty, "tell her to pull her finger out."

"I don't blame Artemis or Giles. The system was state-of-the-art when Erebus had it installed. Things have moved so fast in that world. Your kit can be out-of-date within two years. We may need to consider forking out for an upgrade. Perhaps that's the best way to approach the matter with Artemis?"

"Try to blind her with the promise of something shiny and new? Rather than tell her, she's coming up short with the piece of kit she uses now? If that's your plan, I'll leave you to tell her."

Phoenix pretended he hadn't heard. He wondered what state the safe house was n they were staying at tonight. They were used to the place in Chiswick. It was easy to access from the M4, and generally, it was one of the better safe houses. But, on the other hand, the properties Olympus used in the north of the city were unfamiliar to him.

"We turn off at the Hogarth roundabout," said Rusty. "We should be in St John's Wood a half-hour later."

"What class of an area is it?" asked Phoenix.

"I'm not sure you'll be interested, but the safe house is a two-minute walk from Lord's cricket ground. The boundaries of St. John's Wood are the Regent's Canal to the south, Maida Vale to the west, Boundary Road to the north and Primrose Hill Park to the east. Little Venice and London Zoo are on our doorstep. It's a posh neighbourhood. If you own a property in NW8, you live in the fifth most expensive postcode in London. The rents for residents are the highest average in London."

"That's good to know," said Phoenix, "we should enjoy it while we can, though. If we need that computer upgrade, I suggest selling this place. We'll stick out around here."

"We're staying there for a reason. It's a hot-spot for this spate of attacks by kids on scooters."

"How did these things become such a menace?" asked Phoenix, "I can remember kids at school on mopeds and scooters. A few progressed to proper motorbikes, but they booked in for driving lessons as soon as the weather turned cold."

"Minos and Alastor analysed reports from last year of the sharp increase in offences committed in the capital. Minos reckoned the first six months of this year had seen a further steep rise in reported incidents. Our task is to nip this problem in the bud."

"Yeah, I read their analysis," said Phoenix, "well, I skimmed through it."

Rusty smiled. They had passed Reading. Another hour and they would arrive at the safe house. It wasn't difficult to understand the attraction for the feral teenagers of today. Easy enough to steal a scooter, and the second-hand market in the new iPhone was strong.

They stole a bike, covered their heads with helmets or balaclavas and rode away. The driver cruised the leafy streets around the affluent boroughs, and the pillion passenger grabbed handbags and phones. Easy pickings. The national pastime in the UK has become walking with a phone in your hand, not concentrating on your surroundings. Even when crossing the road.

When the lads moved into an urban environment, they added delivery drivers to their shopping lists. Vans and motorcycles stopped every few hundred yards in the city for at least sixteen hours a day. Mobiles were still a target, but the van drivers carried cash, too, so the older boys stopped and mugged them.

It was small-scale at present, but as Minos stressed, the police should do more to stop its spread. The public was as much to blame. They needed to be more aware of their surroundings. Rusty wondered why the scooter manufacturers and the phone companies didn't toughen up their security.

Rusty remembered the last sentence in the report. Calling on his years of experience in the High Court, Minos had warned that crime could shift up a gear. What starts as a rash of petty crimes escalates to a stage where serious offences are more common. Minos highlighted an occasional acid attack among the more severe incidents.

While Phoenix rested beside him, not offering to start a conversation or make him suffer a musical interlude, the traffic continued to build. They crawled through the streets from Chiswick to their destination, arriving at the safe house at eleven fifteen.

"This looks terrific," said Phoenix, "it's a shame it's only for one night."

The two friends moved their gear inside. The five-bedroomed detached house was several steps up the ladder from Chiswick; they found little or no food, as usual. So their first visit had to be to a supermarket. Parking looked like a nightmare in the district, so they elected to walk.

As they left the store with their provisions, Phoenix nudged his mate.

"Over there," he said, "where those scooters and bikes are in the staff section park."

Rusty spotted two lads, fourteen or fifteen years old. They were furtive in their movements, looking to see if anyone nearby was watching them. Then one lad darted to a scooter in the rack. He grabbed the handlebars and twisted them hard, breaking the steering lock. Rusty watched as the pair then wheeled the scooter away.

"They didn't bother to check for a tracker," he said. "I guess they'll whip out the ignition barrel, cross the wires, and be mobile in five minutes."

"Let's get these bags back to the house," said Phoenix. "Have a bite to eat, and then look for these little villains."

In the distance, they could hear the buzzing sound of a scooter revving its engine. Those kids were in business.

"What can they expect to earn from these ride-by robberies?" asked Phoenix.

"Two hundred and fifty quid for five minutes of work," replied Rusty.

Phoenix shook his head in disbelief. Minos had convinced Athena this caper was worthy of their time. He wasn't sure when it first surfaced. Olympus wouldn't take any of these kids out of the game permanently, and Henry didn't want them in the ice-house crying for their mothers. A short, sharp shock was what Athena had ordered.

If these muggings equated to three grand an hour, then it was well worth him giving these scumbags the shock of their young lives. All they had to do now was catch a few in the act.

The two agents left the safe house before five in the afternoon. They carried the gear they planned to use inside their zipped jackets.

Phoenix was the bait. He strolled along the pavement with an iPhone in his right hand. In his ears, earplugs suggested he listened to his beloved Judas Priest. He was in constant contact with Rusty, who followed him, at a distance, in the van.

Two scooters buzzed past the van like angry hornets. The leading bike slowed as he passed Phoenix. The second mounted the pavement and crawled up behind him.

"He's five yards behind you, Phoenix. Three, two, one....go," said Rusty.

As the pillion passenger made his move, Phoenix removed his left hand from his jacket. He batted away the grabbing hand with his right arm and used the stun gun on the rider. The young lad tried to accelerate away from danger, but three seconds was plenty to cause loss of muscle control and loss of balance and disorientation. The bike was on its side, and both boys lay on the floor.

Rusty had already pulled in front of them. He stopped the van, opened the doors and bundled the bike and the two lads into the back. Phoenix jumped inside with them; he covered his face and threw hoods over their heads, securing their hands behind their backs. Rusty drove back to the safe house. Less than ninety seconds had passed since the initial grab for the phone and the van leaving the scene.

At the safe house, Phoenix and Rusty dragged the boys indoors. Rusty took off the driver's helmet. He looked seventeen, maybe eighteen and had almost recovered. The stun gun Phoenix had used delivered a lower voltage than a standard Taser, and the buzz lasted only two seconds.

Henry Case reckoned the likely recovery period at ten minutes maximum.

When he removed his pillion passenger's helmet, Phoenix was shocked to find the boy looked about twelve.

"Time for you to listen, boys," said Phoenix, "you won't get a second chance."

"You ain't the police," said the older boy, "they don't care."

"Why do you do it?" asked Rusty.

"It's easy money. How else am I going to earn that much? We stick to our patch because we know the streets. If we go up West, we can hit rich tourists with better quality phones."

"Do you realise the harm you cause your victims?" asked Phoenix.

The older boy laughed.

"Are you for real? People can get a better phone tomorrow on their insurance. That's why the police don't bother with it. There are no victims here. They ain't going to chase us."

"What do you mean?" asked Rusty

"They can't follow if we aren't wearing a helmet. Health and safety stuff, so if we pick up a tail, my brother takes his off, and we're home free."

Phoenix took photos of both boys and the helmets they wore.

"What's that for?" asked the younger boy, whose swagger at the outset had disappeared. His bottom lip quivered.

"I told you when we arrived, this was your last chance. You're right. We're not the police, but we know how to find you, and you'll never identify us. One more slip and I promise you the punishment will be severe. Worse than what the courts could give you. Think yourselves lucky this time. We're taking you back when it gets dark."

Rusty drove the van back to Chalk Farm and the road where the youths had tried to snatch the phone at seven-thirty. Phoenix left them standing on the pavement.

"What about the scooter?" shouted the older youth, "how are we supposed to get home?"

"We'll drop it off somewhere safe, ring the police and say we found an abandoned scooter. The police will return it to its rightful owner, don't worry."

Later, Rusty pulled away from a supermarket car park, where they dumped the bike and headed back to spend the night in the safe house.

"Phoenix," he said, "can we take off the stupid Pinky and Perky masks now? It's getting hot under here."

A Frequent Peal of Bells: Chapter Three

Thursday, 2nd October 2014

There was no warning a series of sudden deaths would dominate today's news headlines. Athena sat alone in the apartment at Larcombe Manor. Her husband was at the safe house in St John's Wood; he completed half of his mission yesterday. He and Rusty were returning later today. After delivering more shocks to the moped gangs that threatened the city.

Should she cancel it? These killings were a clear sign the Grid had toughened its stance against its opposition. News reports came in from around the country. Athena prepared for the morning meeting as usual. Her senior agents would help decide the best course of action. Minos and Alastor were wise and experienced. Henry Case, Giles Burke and Artemis were younger but equally adept at guiding her on the right path.

She called Maria Elena and asked her to look after

Hope earlier than usual. She wanted to watch the news updates on the large screen in the meeting room.

As the eight o'clock news summary began, Athena sat with a mug of coffee, listening to the latest from local reporters in each area. On the outskirts of Newcastle, three men had been shot dead in a bar last night. The men were known criminals involved in drug dealing, extortion, and loan sharking. A Detective Chief Inspector from Northumbria Police stood outside the pub and told the reporter it bore the hallmarks of a feud between rival gangs over disrespect. When pressed by the reporter, the DCI claimed gun crime was not out of control in the city. The public at large wasn't in any danger. Athena didn't think the reporter looked convinced. Anyone can get caught in the crossfire when someone enters a crowded bar, and both sides start shooting.

Before she had time to reflect on that attack, the next reporter appeared. The interior of the building looked to be Canning Place. It must be an Assistant Chief Constable from Merseyside. There must have been more trouble here to warrant the higher-ranked officer.

"How can you reassure the public the streets of the city are safe? There were five shootings between eight and one last night. Two men died as they answered their front door. One was riddled with bullets in his car when he stopped at traffic lights. A fourth man died in a drive-by shooting outside a pub. He stood with several others in the smoking bay. Three bystanders got hit but didn't sustain serious injury. The final man sat in a private booth in a strip club, enjoying a lap dance. The door burst open, and two masked men entered. One grabbed the girl and threw her to the floor, as the other opened fire with a machine pistol."

Athena closed her eyes as she listened to the ACC's response.

"A long-running investigation has monitored disputes between organised crime gangs on Merseyside. We have increased foot patrols. These shootings were on specific targets. I don't accept that the threat to the wider community has increased."

Athena wondered if these senior officers ever ran out of platitudes. The men that died were hardened criminals and senior people in organised crime gangs. The method used by the Grid was pre-meditated. Luck had governed that more deaths did not occur.

Liverpool and Newcastle now had several streets in gangland areas on lockdown. Armed patrols stood ready to strike if the violence escalated. Athena knew it was over. The focus would soon switch to another city, another region. The Grid had eliminated its opposition in the full glare of the media spotlight. They didn't fear the police, and they didn't consider the public. They wanted every gang leader to join their network.

It was now nine o'clock, and the meeting room was filling. Athena continued to watch.

"Have you heard from Phoenix?" asked Minos.

"We talked last night; everything went as planned."

Cardiff, Bristol, and Nottingham followed as the morning bulletins continued. The BBC studios at MediaCityUK saw a procession of experts who attempted to explain, calm, and excuse what had happened in front of the country's eyes.

The death toll stood at eighteen so far.

"What can we do?" asked Henry Case.

"We wait," said Athena, "this will be over soon. We can't strike until the media focus has moved to the next outrage, natural disaster, or sporting fiasco. Our time will come."

"How will the authorities react?" asked Alastor.

"The bulletins have ended so that they will wheel the experts into the studio after the weather report. Listen to what they say and make up your mind."

An interviewer asked in the TV studio about the availability of guns across the country. Experts explained that weapons came into the UK from Eastern Europe. Free borders meant just that. You lost the right to object to what entered. Opposition politicians pointed to years of severe budget cuts that hampered operations aimed at managing inter-gang disputes.

Athena and the others had agreed to set aside the planned agenda and watched and listened.

As the Grid cleared the three remaining areas of resistance, interviewers asked why these criminals thought it acceptable to attack people in daylight. In Tottenham, a husband and wife had left Tesco with a loaded trolley at one o'clock in the afternoon. The couple had reached their car, opened the boot and unloaded shopping bags.

A car pulled up behind them with its registration plates covered. A gunman forced the husband to his knees and shot him in the back of the head in front of his wife. The supermarket's CCTV caught every second of the action. They didn't air the actual execution —scenes of the police clearing the car park aired instead. They covered the body on the ground with a sheet. A reporter at the scene said the trolley attendant had told him he could still hear the wife's screams of terror.

"We'll be here for ages," said Athena, "we need to send out for lunch. Alastor, can you make the arrangements, please?"

"I'm not sure I'm ready for food," said Artemis. She wasn't alone.

Alastor left the room. Stewards carried the refreshments into the room twenty minutes later; there was no rush towards the table where they had left it.

"Do you believe we've heard the last of it now?" asked Giles.

"Hard to tell," said Athena, "unless you can tell me the exact number of gangs still operating outside the Grid?"

"Less than ten," said Artemis, "we mapped the locations of organised crime centres while I worked with the force. We knew the scale of their operations, the numbers directly involved, and the additional low-level criminals that had loose links with the main gang structure. But, monitoring it was one thing, having the capability to impact it altogether another matter."

"Gangs in the major cities are amorphous," Giles added. "They can split without bloodshed due to many reasons. The different factions then merge with a neighbouring outfit that's a better fit, whether it's because of its culture or its ambition."

The senior agents waited to see whether this marked a lull in proceedings or whether the carnage had ended.

"I'll call Phoenix," said Athena. "He and Rusty are due on the streets later this afternoon. They should be resting now. No doubt, they're watching this unfold. I want to add their thoughts to what we've discussed. They return home later tonight. We need to prepare for another long day drawing up our battle plans."

Athena made the call.

"Tell me your view, Phoenix," she asked, without her usual friendly preamble. "You're on speakerphone in the meeting room."

"Our list of opponents has reduced," he replied, "we understand the top-level command of the Grid far better now. Total control will mean a unification not only of personnel. Every member of the network will do as instructed in the future. They saw the alternative in graphic detail. That message was for the total Grid membership as much as the authorities and the British public. In a way, it makes our job easier. We are less likely to face the loose cannons that existed when it was a free-for-all. Life's about balance. This unification also means the Grid has improved its chances of identifying and countering our activities."

"I agree," said Athena, "so I advise caution. We must increase our level of security and delay any action against the Grid until we can ensure our anonymity."

"Are you suggesting we return to Larcombe at once?" asked Phoenix.

"The youths we are targeting aren't associated directly with the Grid's network," said Rusty, "they're street-level punks who could gravitate to more serious crimes in time. If we pull out now, there's a risk this moped gang menace will spread. I know we can make a difference through what we're doing. The risk of Olympus being seen as involved is low, and Phoenix and I can take extra precautions in light of what's been happening elsewhere. The spotlight is firmly on those killings. A few punishments in North West London will struggle to get two lines in a footnote in the media."

"We must be positive," said Athena, "go ahead with the mission, take care, and come home safe."

"If the authorities stamped out this threat from the outset, they wouldn't have the list of problems they face today," said Henry. "I agree with Rusty. The risk is low. The potential benefits are high."

After the conversation with the two men in St John's

Wood ended, the team turned their attention back to the TV screen.

In the middle of the afternoon, Big Phil Sykes, a notorious criminal who never took a backward step in his life, stood on the cliff tops near Dawlish in Devon. He controlled large tracts of the South West with operations in four counties. The man facing him carried a sawn-off double-barrelled shotgun. Eye-witnesses a hundred yards away reported seeing the man continue to advance towards Sykes.

There were no shots fired. Sykes stepped back at last and lost his footing.

A seventh gang had lost its figurehead. The death toll rose to twenty.

As news of this latest killing was received, a Chief Constable sat in the hot seat. He called for communities blighted by gun crime to support the police. The interviewer interrupted his well-crafted prepared statement and switched the focus of her questions.

"How many more deaths are we going to witness today, Chief Constable?" she asked. "When are the police going to restore law and order in the country?"

"I can assure the public that my colleagues and I are doing our utmost to keep the public safe...."

"You realise many people are drawing comparisons between today's atrocities and those that plagued Chicago in the 1920s?"

A promising career in public relations crashed and burned as the unfortunate representative of what had once been a force with teeth struggled to find the correct answer:

"These inter-gang feuds have been with us in the UK since the 1920s. They're nothing new. It is just a readjustment of our organised crime power base. The public is not in danger."

The silence in the studio echoed the silence in the meeting room at Larcombe.

"Wait for it," said Minos, "he's left the door wide open. Here come the coach and horses."

The female interviewer couldn't believe her luck — an opportunity to be part of something meaningful on live TV.

"The police have failed to tackle organised crime for one hundred years. It's now established a power base that covers the entire country. Their activities threaten the economic fabric of this country. They reach into the deepest and most remote corners of our everyday life. Organised crime costs the economy between fifty and sixty billion pounds every year. How can you possibly maintain the public are not in danger? These killings may or may not be confined to criminals, but surely the British public deserves action against organised crime, not acceptance?"

"We have succeeded in combating organised crime on many occasions, young lady...."

"Oh, quit now," said Henry, "you're deep enough in it. Stop digging, you fool."

"Our viewers would be excused for thinking you've lost the battle given today's events. Let's join Sam for a summary of the news."

The focus switched to another newscaster on the other side of the studio. Sadly, for the Chief Constable, his microphone still broadcasts his comments. As the nation awaited the next catastrophe to hit the headlines, the senior police officer provided his own.

"You stitched me up there, didn't you? The sisterhood will be over the moon."

At Larcombe Manor, despite the seriousness of the situation, that remark brought a smile to several faces around the table.

"The BBC may have stumbled onto a winner," said Minos. "This could bring daytime TV viewers back in their millions."

"They're moving another expert in to take his place," said Giles.

"What a shame. I enjoyed watching that policeman squirm," said Artemis.

**Grab your copy...
vinci-books.com/frequent-peal-of-bells**

About the Author

Ted Tayler is the international best-selling indie author of the Freeman Files and Phoenix series. Ted lives in the English West country, where his stories are based. He was born in 1945 and has been married to Lynne since 1971. They have three children and four grandchildren.

His thought-provoking mysteries appeal to readers of Sally Rigby, Joy Ellis, Pauline Rowson, and Faith Martin. His action-packed thrillers are a must for fans of Mark Dawson and J C Ryan.

Gus Freeman's cold case investigations are carried out with reasoned deduction rather than bursts of frantic action. In each of the 24 books, unsolved murders are accompanied by romance, humour, and country life. The core message in the 12 Phoenix novels is that criminals should pay for their crimes. Unfortunately, the current system fails to deliver the correct punishment, so Phoenix helps redress the balance.

Acknowledgments

The love and support of my family; without them, this would have been impossible.

The love and support of my family meant the world to me.

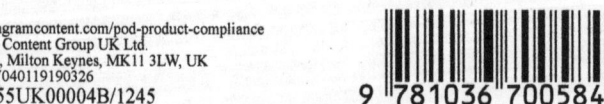